# The Scarred Spinster's C

## A Clean Regency Romance Novel

## Martha Barwood

Copyright © 2022 by Martha Barwood
All Rights Reserved.
This book may not be reproduced or transmitted in any form without the written permission of the publisher. In no way is it legal to reproduce, duplicate, or transmit any part of this document in either electronic means or in printed format. Recording of this publication is strictly prohibited and any storage of this document is not allowed unless with written permission from the publisher.

*Jacob Kingsley*
*Cassandra Matthews*

## Table of Contents

Prologue..................................................................................4
Chapter One............................................................................7
Chapter Two ..........................................................................11
Chapter Three........................................................................16
Chapter Four..........................................................................23
Chapter Five...........................................................................28
Chapter Six.............................................................................32
Chapter Seven.......................................................................37
Chapter Eight ........................................................................43
Chapter Nine.........................................................................48
Chapter Ten ..........................................................................55
Chapter Eleven.....................................................................60
Chapter Twelve ....................................................................69
Chapter Thirteen..................................................................74
Chapter Fourteen ................................................................81
Chapter Fifteen ....................................................................87
Chapter Sixteen ...................................................................92
Chapter Seventeen .............................................................99
Chapter Eighteen ...............................................................106
Chapter Nineteen ..............................................................112
Chapter Twenty ..................................................................118
Chapter Twenty-One .........................................................123
Chapter Twenty-Two .........................................................129
Chapter Twenty-Three.......................................................136
Chapter Twenty-Four.........................................................142
Chapter Twenty-Five..........................................................149
Chapter Twenty-Six............................................................157
Chapter Twenty-Seven .....................................................164
Chapter Twenty-Eight .......................................................170
Chapter Twenty-Nine........................................................176

| | |
|---|---|
| Chapter Thirty | 184 |
| Chapter Thirty-One | 191 |
| Chapter Thirty-Two | 197 |
| Chapter Thirty-Three | 208 |
| Chapter Thirty-Four | 213 |
| Epilogue | 218 |
| Extended Epilogue | 224 |

# Prologue

*London Countryside, 1803*

Her heart was racing. She couldn't tell when last she'd been this excited, her skinny limbs trembling both from her exuberance and the unforgiving cold. The time was drifting toward winter, when Cassandra would be forced to bundle up in countless layers, sit before the fireplace in the drawing room, and pretend she was reading. She hated this time of year, preferring the summertime when she was free to roam outdoors as much as she wanted. Before long, she wouldn't get another chance to do this until the snow melted away.

That spurred her legs on, even though she was already beginning to regret not bringing a coat. She'd remembered her riding gloves in her haste, not bothering to take a candle. She knew the hallways as well as she knew herself. It would be no issue finding her way downstairs and out the back door in the dead of night.

Cassandra couldn't keep the smile off her face as she raced down the staircase, her steps light enough to keep her silent. She jumped down the last couple ones and didn't bother lingering to find out if her heavy thud had woken anyone. She was already racing out the back door.

Frigid wind hit her square in the face. It brought tears to Cassandra's eyes, but she kept going even as she shivered. Cassandra's steps slowed as she drew closer to the stable and once she was inside, she took a moment to savor the warmth inside.

"Bindie?" she called, the air cold enough for her breath to be visible.

A neigh sounded deeper within the stables. Cassandra grinned. Even though it had only been a few weeks, she'd already developed quite the bond with four-legged animal.

She made her way to Bindie's stall within seconds. The pony on the other end lifted her brown head at Cassandra's approach, her hair shimmering under the moonlight shining through the high square window behind her. Even though Bindie was smaller than the other horses, she was still taller than Cassandra. That had been daunting to Cassandra at first, but now nothing about this pony frightened her.

"Did you miss me?" she whispered to the steed and the pony snorted in response. Taking that as an affirmative, Cassandra grinned as she quickly slipped into Bindie's stall and mounted her.

"Let's go." Cassandra eased her forward, carefully. She knew she shouldn't be doing this. Her mother always warned her never to go riding alone. But Cassandra was ten-and-three now. Surely the fact that her parents had gifted her this pony for her birthday meant they thought she was a proficient enough rider?

Cassandra shook off the feeling of uncertainty that came over her as she led Bindie out the stables. Once they were out in the open, Cassandra let the pony fly. She knew how to handle her, knew how to rein her in and let her loose. She savored the wind blowing through her hair, though it stung in its coldness. Within seconds, she left behind the trepidation, forgetting why she'd hesitated in the first place.

Before she knew it, they'd raced past the invisible line her riding instructor always cautioned her not to pass. The land became too uneven, she would warn. You are not ready to handle such terrain.

"Bindie, slow down," Cassandra yelled over the roar of the wind in her ears.

Bindie did not such thing. She continued, delving into the copse of cedar trees that surrounded the small pond Cassandra liked to frequent with her governess.

"Stop, Bindie!" she screamed as branches flew too close to her face.

Suddenly, Bindie listened, skidding to halt right in before a massive root jutting out of the earth. The next moment, Cassandra felt herself become as light as air.

And when gravity took control, the ground rose to meet her.

# Chapter One

*Springtime, London, 1811*

*Perhaps I should go for a walk.*

The thought had crossed her mind three times in the past hour and Cassandra was no closer to mustering the courage. Instead, she remained seated in the corner of the ballroom, watching as guests wandered by, enjoying the ball. She tried not to sulk, wishing she could be anywhere but there.

With a sigh, she lifted her eyes to the chandeliers above, brilliant with dozens of candles. Her mother had certainly outdone herself with tonight's decorations, she thought, taking in the silky drapes running down the walls like water. It matched the linen that covered the refreshments table and nearly every seat in the room. With the orchestra playing a gentle tune at the back of the ballroom, it almost felt as if Cassandra had been transported to the palace itself.

It should have been as magical an evening as it looked, but a few hours had already passed since the commencement of tonight's ball and all Cassandra wanted to do was return to her chamber and sleep. Her darling sister, Elizabeth, had dragged her around Bond Street all afternoon and she hadn't gotten a chance to rest before she had to get ready for tonight's ball. And yes, this was supposed to be her debut ball, so did it really matter that she was here when no one else seemed to care?

"Careful, Cassandra," she whispered to herself. "You're pitying yourself again."

But on a night like this, Cassandra couldn't help herself. Without thinking, she reached under the blue veil she'd donned to match her silver-blue gown, fingers brushing against the left side of her jaw. As soon as she did, she was brought back to that night eight years ago, that weightless feeling before she'd crashed to the ground.

Cassandra quickly withdrew her hand. The scar that now laid there, a reminder of that night, seemed to burn.

"I think I passed by this current location three times and this is my first time noticing you here."

Cassandra smiled, looking up at the gentleman who came to her side. She rose, accepting the glass of punch he held out to her. "That is because I have become a master of disguise."

"A master is right. I thought you were a statue. I almost screamed in surprise when you moved."

Cassandra giggled behind her hand. The Viscount of Bancroft, Lord Simon Bancroft, laughed alongside her, tucking his hands into the pockets of his breeches. Simon always knew the right thing to say to cheer her up. Cassandra wouldn't be surprised if he'd approached her because he knew she was wallowing.

"Thank you for the punch," she said. "Somehow you knew that I was dying of thirst."

"And was either too lazy or too uncomfortable to make your way to the refreshments table."

"I will not say which."

Simon tilted his head back to laugh. "And I'm not surprised. You're quite welcome, Cassie."

"How fares your night, Simon?" Cassandra asked before taking a sip of the punch.

"Your mother has outdone herself yet again. It'll be hard for anyone else to top this ball, which is quite a feat considering the Season has only just begun."

Cassandra eyed him. He was handsome with sandy hair cut Brutus-style and a broad build that made him appear far more athletic than he was. Both Cassandra and her parents had once entertained the thought of being courted by him until she'd actually gotten to know him and realized they would be much better as friends. And in the years they'd known each other, Cassandra quickly came to realize that Simon Bancroft was well aware of how handsome he was—and was not afraid to take advantage of it.

"How many ladies have you made swoon since the evening has begun?" she asked.

"Swoon?"

"You know what I mean," she pressed, smiling. "I'm sure you've already made a handful of them give over their hearts to you already."

"Cassandra Jessica Matthews, are you saying that I am a rake?"

"That is exactly what I'm saying." When she caught his eyes, she saw amusement shining in within the green. "So out with it. You know it has always intrigued me to see how easily you make ladies fall for you."

"And yet it has never worked on you, has it?"

"And it never will," she stated confidently.

Simon sighed dramatically, which only made her laugh again. It was partly the truth. Cassandra had quickly realized that she had no romantic interest in him and he had none in her. But she also knew where his heart truly lied.

As if by design, her eyes came to rest on a dancing couple in the center of the ballroom. Cassandra drank in her sister's graceful figure, how elegant she appeared with every step she made to the waltz. Her dance partner paled in comparison and had a red face as if he knew it, as if he was well aware that he stood in the presence of goddess-like beauty. Tonight's ball was for her—Lady Elizabeth Matthews.

And she'd certainly made the best of it. While Cassandra had spent her time sitting in the corner and counting the seconds until it was over, Elizabeth had not had a single moment to rest. The moment the dancing commenced, Elizabeth's time had been occupied by one handsome gentleman after another, all wanting to dance with her. The sight had filled Cassandra with pride—and just a bit of longing.

Glancing at Simon, she saw the same longing in his eyes.

They were for different reasons, she knew. For her, she longed to debut, to have gentleman after gentleman vie for her dance. Cassandra had tried to remind herself that that would never happen. The scar her veil kept hidden would never allow it. But, as she watched her sister's brilliant smile, she wished for a second that things had been different.

And for Simon, Cassandra knew he longed to be the one holding Elizabeth in his arms.

"Have you asked Elizabeth to dance yet?" Cassandra blurted out before she could stop herself.

Simon frowned at her. Had she not been staring at him, she might have missed the way his cheeks colored. "Why do you ask?"

"Oh, come now, Simon. Wouldn't it be odd that one of my dearest friends and a friend to the family did not dance with the lady of honour?"

Simon swallowed hard, eyes returning to where the dancers swept by. "I'm sure her dancing card is full."

"And I'm sure she will make space for you if you asked."

He was considering it, Cassandra could tell. She fell silent, waiting for him to come to his own conclusion.

Just as the set came to an end, he spoke again, "I suppose it would not hurt. Just to keep up appearances, of course."

"Of course," Cassandra drawled. But he was already walking away, eyes set on Elizabeth.

Cassandra polished off the rest of her punch and rested the empty glass on the table nearby before reclaiming her seat. She was watching as her dear friend approached her sister just as she'd returned to her mother's side. He bowed, said something, and sadly kept his head bowed. Which meant he did not see the joy that lit Elizabeth's face at the request.

Cassandra sighed, watching as they made their way to the center of the room in time for the next set. They looked lovely together. Cassandra hoped that one day Elizabeth would come to see Simon as a potential match.

And she secretly prayed that one day, she too could entertain the idea of love.

# Chapter Two

A gentle breeze drifted through the open bay windows Cassandra sat next to and she let out a sigh of relief. The morning had been uncommonly hot for the springtime and the afternoon promised to be even worse. She shifted uncomfortably, longing to wipe at the sweat coating the back of her neck and wishing she had chosen to pin her hair up before coming down for tea.

"I'm telling you, Viola. Both you and Elizabeth are the talk of the *ton*! Everyone has your ball on the tips of their tongues."

Cassandra pinched off a piece of cake and slowly lifted it to her lips as she studied her aunt. Lady Mildred Jones, wife to the Earl of Hanebridge, looked nearly identical to her sister but shared none of her personality. She'd been smart enough to put her hair up, though Cassandra couldn't help but wince at how tightly she'd pulled her blond hair into her chignon. She was dressed a little more conservatively as well, with a high neckline and long sleeves. How she was not bothered by the heat, Cassandra didn't know.

"I agree, aunt," Phoebe spoke up with a nod. She looked more like her father than her mother, Mildred. She sipped her tea and Cassandra held back her shudder. She had no intentions of touching the stuff when she was seconds away from overheating. "You did throw a wonderful debut ball for Lizzie last night. I enjoyed myself so much that I hardly wanted to leave."

"Oh, we know, Phoebe," Elizabeth spoke up with a smile. "You were the last person to depart, after all."

Phoebe didn't seem bothered by it, continuing to sip her tea. "You can blame yourselves for making my night so enjoyable."

The ladies laughed at that, except Cassandra. She was hardly paying attention, her mind drifting from the unbearable heat to how badly she wanted to take a nap. The ball had not ended until after dawn and she'd barely gotten enough sleep last night. When she'd come down for breakfast to see her mother and Elizabeth looking as fresh as ever, Cassandra could hardly believe her eyes.

Lady Viola Matthews, the Countess of Wiswall, touched Elizabeth on her shoulder. Both Cassandra and Elizabeth had adopted her strawberry-blond curls, though Cassandra's had a tendency to frizz while Elizabeth's always remained perfect. Viola had lovely deep brown eyes though, which she had passed on to her younger daughter. Cassandra had taken her father's sky-blue eyes.

"I hardly had anything to do with it," Viola said, pride stark in her voice. "Elizabeth was lovely as always. I watched her all night and she did not take a single moment to rest from dancing. I was half afraid that she would fall down!"

"Oh, Mother, you know I've prepared extensively for that night," Elizabeth told her. "I wanted to be prepared. Just ask Cassie, I spent hours dancing in both our rooms so that when I finally debuted, I would not be tired."

The three ladies looked at Cassandra and so she nodded, even though she did not wish to be a part of the conversation. She wanted to *sleep*. "I can confirm," she mumbled, biting into her cake simply to give herself something to do.

Elizabeth beamed. "But did you see Lord Vassell? He was so tall, I thought I might break my neck just looking up at him."

"Of course, I took note of him," Phoebe said, batting aside a lock of dark hair that had fallen against her cheek. Her eyes glittered with interest. "And I also noticed Lord Gregory, the second son of the Marquess of Fairway. Wasn't he as kind as he was handsome?"

"He certainly was," Elizabeth agreed. "Though I wonder if he is a bit old."

"The older the better," Mildred said. "They have a world of wisdom."

"Mother!" Phoebe gasped and Viola laughed.

"She's right, though," Viola agreed. "But I don't think too much attention should be placed on one gentleman. It's important to get to know each person who shows interest in you, so that you make the right decision."

"The right decision for me will be any gentleman who has wealth and status," Phoebe stated. "I am already on my second Season. I have no time to waste."

Cassandra looked out the window, staring at nothing. She tried and failed to cast aside the discomfort rising in her at the conversation. This wasn't something she could partake in. Debuts, courting, marriage...all a part of a life that Cassandra could never have.

Try as she might, she could not stop that pinch of longing that seized her chest. She curled her hand into a fist under the table to stop herself from touching her scar. In her home, she did not bother to wear the veil. Her family did not care. But outside of these walls, she had to hide the thing that kept her from finding love, from having a family of her own.

"Well, not to worry, ladies," Mildred said, drawing Cassandra's attention away from her wandering thoughts. "The masquerade ball I will be hosting in a few days will help us narrow down the perfect bachelors for you two."

"Who will be in attendance?" Elizabeth asked excitedly.

"Have you invited Lord Bane?" Phoebe questioned. "I hear he is quite wealthy and he isn't too bad to look at."

"Of course, I have," Mildred stated proudly. "And he has already confirmed that he will be in attendance. You'll have to move quickly though, Phoebe. Don't think you are the only lady who has her eyes set on him."

"You don't have to tell me twice, Mother," Phoebe said determinedly and then Cassandra turned her attention back to the window, letting her mind wander once more so that she did not have to long for the things she would never have.

***

She had to endure another hour of tea and talk of eligible bachelors before Cassandra was able to retire to the library. The moment she was in the large room, she drew in a deep breath, casting aside the uneasy emotions that had been plaguing her ever since the start of the Season. It would only get worse, she knew. With every ball, party, or soiree, Cassandra knew that the hole in her heart would grow larger.

But for now, she supposed she could immerse herself in a book and forget the world around her.

She wandered over to the Shakespearean section, running her fingers along the spines of each publication. For the past few months, Cassandra searched for her favorite novel, Romeo and Juliet, and could not find it. She'd gotten into the habit of bringing it everywhere with her and must have misplaced it somewhere. She came here often hoping that it had been found and returned to its rightful place.

Since the spot was still sadly empty, Cassandra opted to read her second favorite, A Midsummer Night's Dream. She took the book with her to her usual spot on the chaise lounge by the window, propped her legs to the side, and began to read, savoring the gentle breeze that brushed against her neck. As soon as Mildred and Phoebe had left, Cassandra had gone straight to her chambers to pin her hair up before coming to the library.

She'd gotten though a few pages when the door opened and Elizabeth swept in.

"Oh, Cassie!" Cassandra watched as her sister hurried over and dramatically threw herself into the armchair nearby. "I feel so overwhelmed."

Cassandra slowly closed the book, noting the last page she'd read, then gave her dear sister her full attention. "What's the matter?"

Elizabeth held out the scandal sheets in her hand. "Here," she said. "Read it for yourself."

Cassandra had just barely reached out to take the scandal sheets before Elizabeth pulled it back. Cassandra held back her smile. Elizabeth had always been a bundle of energy. Though they were two years apart, Cassandra sometimes wondered when Elizabeth would shed the childlike enthusiasm that usually had her bouncing from one place to the other. Not that she minded much. Cassandra remembered a time when she'd been just like that, when she would much prefer chasing cats around the backyard to sitting in silence reading. That was before the incident, before her life had changed forever.

"It says here," Elizabeth began to read, springing to her feet. Cassandra followed her with her eyes as her sister paced back and forth. "'The Countess of Wiswall's hosted one of the first balls of the Season, and has truly set the tone for all the rest. With her beautiful daughter debuting as the Season's 'Diamond', Lady Elizabeth Matthew's coming out was a major success!'"

"I don't understand," Cassandra said, straightening. "I see no problem with what was said. You've been dubbed the Season's 'Diamond', which I think is quite accurate. The ton has finally said something right, for once."

"But that's just it!" Elizabeth blew out a frustrated breath as she collapsed in the chair once more. Somehow, not a single strand of hair fell out of place. "It is far too much pressure."

"This is good news, Lizzie," Cassandra told her with a warm smile. "There is nothing to be afraid of, I assure you."

"How can you be so sure?" Elizabeth pouted. "With so many eyes watching me, what if I were to do something scandalous and embarrassing?"

"In all your ten-and-seven years, have you ever done anything scandalous or embarrassing?"

Elizabeth made a show of thinking about it. "No, I don't think I have."

"Then there is your answer. Certainly nothing to worry about." Cassandra propped her feet up once more, opening her book. "And now that you know that, leave me be so that I may read."

Cassandra was not at all surprised when Elizabeth threw herself onto the chaise lounge next to her, wrapping her arms around Cassandra's neck. "Oh, Cassie, you always knew exactly what to say."

"Yes, yes, I am the wise big sister. What else is new?"

Elizabeth giggled at that, which brought a smile to Cassandra's face. Through all the longing that panged her heart, she was truly happy for Elizabeth. She wanted the best for her sister, wanted her to find and marry for love—even if that fate was never destined for her.

# Chapter Three

"There is something on your mind. I know it."

Her Grace, Angela Kingsley, the Dowager Duchess of Edingdale looked up from her steaming cup of tea, looking surprised. "What do you mean, dear?"

Jacob wasn't fooled by the act, but he supposed it would not hurt to entertain it. He studied his grandmother for a moment, noting the way the sunlight made her grey hair appear white and deepened the lines in her face. Despite her age, she adorned every inch of her body with pearls, rings glinting at her fingers.

"You have been glancing at the door every few seconds," Jacob told her as he crossed his arms. "Not to mention the fact that you have not said anything but 'Oh, yes' despite the topic of conversation, which makes me think you weren't really listening."

"There are so many times I can hear you talk about your favourite novel, Jacob," his grandmother drawled.

Jacob held back his chuckle, fixing her with an intense stare. "Tell me what you're thinking about."

"What makes you think you are right?"'

"Because I am right."

"Quite cocky, you are."

Jacob only shrugged, sipped his tea, and waited. They had tea like this nearly every afternoon since he came to Bath a year ago. He'd been residing with his grandparents while overseeing business matters on his father's behalf and Jacob had never felt more at peace. He much preferred Bath to London, much preferred his grandparent's company to that of the *ton*.

But from the way Angela set her cup down, Jacob had a weird feeling that something was wrong.

"Your father sent a letter," Angela explained. She reached behind her and picked up a sealed letter Jacob had failed to notice before. "And I have a feeling I know what it contains."

"Have you finally discovered your prophetic gifts, grandmother?" Jacob tried to joke but Angela only shook her head. She handed him the letter.

"Open it," she urged. "Tell me what it says."

Jacob felt a tremor of anxiousness as he broke the Edingdale seal. Had his father sent word of someone's death? Has his mother fallen ill? Had *he* fallen ill and was sending this letter to inform Jacob of his duties as the heir to the dukedom? Every possibility had his heart beating a little faster.

Jacob quickly scanned the letter, then frowned at his grandmother. "Father is simply requesting that I return to London."

Angela sipped her tea as she closed her eyes, nodding slowly. "Just as I suspected."

"Goodness, you are rather dramatic."

His grandmother waved a dismissive hand at him. "Call me dramatic all you want but it doesn't change the fact that I knew what was coming. And so I prepared this for you."

Again, she reached behind her, this time picking up a small grey box. She put it on the table and slid it toward Jacob.

Jacob frowned at it, not picking it up just yet. "And this is?"

"Why don't you open it and see?"

Unnerved by his grandmother's tone, Jacob gingerly picked up the box and opened it. Sitting in the center was a bright red ruby, entombed within the folds of a golden ring. Jacob sighed.

"The ring has been in our family for years," Angela said. "And I hope that when you return to London, you will have some use for it. The London Season has begun, after all."

Jacob resisted the urge to sigh. Instead, he closed the box and gave his grandmother a grateful smile. "Thank you. Perhaps I shall find use for it."

Angela scowled. "I hope so. It would be nice to meet my great-grandchildren."

"And with that," Jacob said on a laugh, rising and slipping the box into his pocket, "that is my cue to leave."

"You should listen to me, Jacob," Angela called out to him as he retreated. "Your grandmother knows best."

"I am well aware," he said in return, just as he left the drawing room. Jacob's smile lingered all the way to his study. The truth was, he didn't want to rush into marriage. While it wasn't something he hated the thought of - like many other bachelors his age, Jacob was really hoping to find one thing. He wanted something rare, a love match much like the one his grandparents shared. A marriage without that would be no marriage at all.

*** 

Edingdale Manor was shrouded behind layers of shrubbery, many of which lined a long driveway that led up to the manor's front entrance. It was located in Mayfair, a sizeable plot of land that rivalled many countryside manors. Trellis crept up the side of the white and red brick walls, bending around the balconies located on the second and third floors. Growing up, it had been Jacob's little slice of heaven and, returning after being away for so long, a comforting warmth spread throughout Jacob's body.

And it brought a smile to his face when he noticed his mother standing on the porch, waving at his approach.

Jacob waited until his carriage came to a full stop before he alighted, loose stones crunching under his boots. Behind him came another carriage bearing his trunks, even though he wasn't certain how long he would be staying in London. His father hadn't specified in the letter.

"Oh, my darling son!" Her Grace, Maria Kingsley, the Duchess of Edingdale, threw herself down the steps into the driveway, her loose morning gown billowing out behind her. She wrapped her arms around Jacob, smelling exactly the same as he'd last remembered. Like clovers.

"Mother, did you miss me?" Jacob asked, his tone lightly amused.

"You know I did." She pulled away and seized his hand instead, eyes scanning his face as if searching for anything she didn't remember. "I've written to you nearly every day and you've never cared to respond to me as often as I do. The true question , Jacob, is if you missed me."

"Perhaps I could have gone another—"

"Oh, don't you dare!" She slapped him lightly on the arm as he laughed.

Jacob pulled Maria into his arms once more. Even though it had only been a year, she'd changed since the last time he saw her. There were a few more grey hairs threading through the brown, though it was done in a perfect chignon as it always was. She seemed a little fuller as well, the lines around her mouth deepened just a tad.

"I'm sorry if I was not as attentive as I should have been, Mother," he told her, squeezing her tightly. "I promise that I shan't neglect you while I'm in London."

"Oh, don't worry about me. I have a life of my own, you know. It is time for you to get your own."

Jacob sucked in a breath. "Harsh."

Maria laughed. She pulled away slightly, keeping her arm around his waist as she began to steer him towards the door. Footmen were already streaming in and out, carrying his luggage up to his old chambers. Jacob had left Edingdale Manor when he was five-and-twenty, opting to live in his bachelor pad in Park Lane. But his father had mentioned in his letter that his mother was insisting that he stayed here.

"You must be tired after the long the ride," she said once they were in the foyer. "Go upstairs and rest, my dear. I'll wake you when it is time for dinner."

Considering that it was nearing late afternoon, Jacob surmised that dinner will be ready in a couple of hours. At the mention of nap, the exhaustion of the ride settled squarely behind his eyes. Still, he studied the foyer, noting that his mother had added a few more paintings to opposite walls. Other than that, it was the exact same dark wood, wide burgundy rug on top, with a few end tables housing small statues that cost a fortune.

"Where is Father?" Jacob asked. He should at least greet him first.

"He's away right now. An important meeting, he says. You'll hear about it later."

That took Jacob by surprise and, judging by the way Maria bit her lip, she realized her slip up. His father never involved his mother in talk about the business. So if she was aware of the details then that would mean...

"Don't worry about it," Maria said quickly. She pushed him towards the grand staircase on the other end of the foyer. "Go and rest. We can talk more later."

"Mother, are you hiding something from me?'

"Now what could I possibly be hiding? Perhaps what I shall have prepared for dinner tonight? If you wish to know then it is your favourite—roasted pork."

Jacob frowned at her, but Maria kept pushing him to the stairs. She was rambling, a clear indication that she truly was hiding something. But he supposed if it was important, he would learn about it soon enough. So he let her guide him away, conceding as he left her at the base of the stairs and continued by himself. By the time he'd made it to his room, Jacob felt so tired that he didn't bother to take off his coat. He collapsed onto his bed and was asleep in seconds.

His valet came to wake him two hours later and assisted him through the gruelling process of changing his clothes for dinner. By the time he made it down to the dining room, Jacob felt a bit of the grogginess drift away, leaving him capable of issuing a proper greeting to his parents. His Grace, Henry Kingsley, the Duke of Edingdale's eyes crinkled into a half smile as he greeted Jacob and dinnertime passed in easy comfort, mostly with talk of his time in Bath.

Jacob had almost completely forgotten about what his mother had said until he was sitting in the parlor with his father—Maria having retired to bed early—and Henry said, "Son, there is something important we should talk about."

Jacob twirled his glass of whiskey, observing his father closely. Though he'd adopted his mother's light brown hair, Jacob's strong jaw, sharp nose, and hazel-green eyes were wholly from his father. Henry Kingsley had certainly been handsome in his younger years, but life had taken a toll on him. On bad days, he walked with a cane, his shoulders hunched and his eyes drawn. On better days—like today—he appeared ten years younger, eyes focused.

"Does it have anything to do with what Mother mentioned?" Jacob asked, sipping his whiskey and holding back the wince when it burned down his throat. He'd never developed a taste for it. He didn't know why he'd said yes when his father offered in the first place.

"What did she say?" Henry asked.

"Only that you were in a meeting when I arrived and that I would know all about it when you came back."

"Goodness, will she never learn how to keep her tongue," Henry said with a sigh, not unkindly. "But yes, that is what I want to talk about. Do you know the Earl of Wiswall?"

"The title rings a bell."

"We go to the same gentlemen's club," he said. "And he told me that his youngest daughter, Lady Elizabeth, debuted recently. She is on the marriage mart."

Jacob didn't like where this was going. "That is good for her," he said nonchalantly, downing the rest of his drink. He rose and made his way over to the sideboard to pour himself another. He had a feeling he was going to need it.

Henry watched him steadily. "I think you know where I'm going with this, Jacob. It is high time you settled down. You are nine-and-twenty years old, after all. You cannot remain a bachelor forever."

"Perhaps not forever, but I'm sure a few more years won't hurt." Jacob's throat felt thick. Could it be that invisible noose slowly wrapping itself around his neck? The thought of marriage frightened him.

No, not the thought of marriage. The thought of being married to someone he didn't love, of being forced to share a life—and a family—with a lady he hardly knew. That was what scared him.

"How long?" Henry questioned. "Two? Five? Ten? Have you even given it a single thought?"

"Is this the reason why you asked me to come to London?"

"Yes. The London Season has begun and I thought it would be far better for you to court Lady Elizabeth during this time, rather than have the two of you rush into a marriage. I'm sure you would prefer it that way.'

"How considerate of you, Father." Jacob sighed, regretting his slightly sarcastic tone. He pinched the bridge of his nose, putting aside his second glass of whiskey, untouched. "Nothing is set in stone yet, right? At least give me some time to consider the matter."

"How much time?" the duke pressed but Jacob was already making his way to the door. If he stayed here any longer, the conversation would stretch on until his father had succeeded in wearing him down.

"As long as I need to," Jacob called over his shoulder as he left the parlor, not giving his father a chance to respond.

# Chapter Four

Cassandra didn't think she'd ever seen this many gentlemen enter the drawing room of Wiswall Manor before. And they were all coming to see her beautiful sister, who seemed both excited and exasperated at the attention.

At first, they came one by one, starting right at the fashionable calling hour. Dukes, marquesses, viscounts, and barons alike all came bearing gifts, compliments pouring off their tongues the moment they spotted Elizabeth. After a while, Elizabeth told the butler to send them all in as they came, miraculously entertaining multiple men at once as they all vied to be in her top spot. Cassandra observed it all from her quiet spot in the corner of the drawing room, acting as a chaperone though she might as well have been invisible. None of the gentlemen paid her any mind, which didn't bother Cassandra half as much as she thought it would. Elizabeth deserved the attention, looking absolutely darling in her cornflower blue gown that clung gently to her curves, her curls pinned to the top of her head.

Only one gentleman remained—a baron whose name Cassandra could not remember. He was a handsome man, though a little too eager. Cassandra studied him under the cover of her green veil—to match her green morning gown—and wondered if his palms were sweating under his gloves.

"I'm afraid I do not know much about riding, my lord," Elizabeth was saying. She still looked as perfect as she did hours ago. "Perhaps you would teach me one day?"

"I would love to, Lady Elizabeth!" the baron all but yelled. Realizing he was getting overexcited, he visibly shrank into the plush couch opposite Elizabeth. Cassandra giggled under her breath.

Elizabeth only gave him a graceful smile. "Thank you. I'm already looking forward to it. I can tell that you will be a kind and attentive teacher."

"You honour me, my lady. Shall we arrange for our next meeting from now then? We could go riding in Hyde Park. Or perhaps Regents Park is more to your liking?"

"I shall write to you, my lord, and let you know," Elizabeth told him with a charming smile.

The baron didn't know whether to smile or not. Cassandra understood his confusion. Elizabeth hadn't given him anything solid to hold on to, but had spoken so nicely and with such a welcoming smile that it would be hard to read into it.

Elizabeth let out a pretty yawn. "Oh, forgive me, my lord. I am dreadfully tired. It has been a long morning, as you can imagine."

Cassandra tried not to laugh again as the baron colored. He'd arrived when two other gentlemen were leaving. Elizabeth had just kindly reminded him that he had competition.

"Ah, I should take my leave then, my lady," he said as he rose. "I apologise if I overstayed my welcome."

"Oh, don't worry about that, Lord Gregory." *Ah, Lord Gregory James*, Cassandra remembered, *that is his name*. "Please, Mr. Hanson will walk you out. Thank you so much for coming to see me today. I really enjoyed your company."

Lord Gregory flushed profusely. As if he'd overheard his name from the other side of the door, Hanson—their butler—appeared to escort Lord Gregory out the door. The poor baron wasn't given a chance to say anything else before he was ushered out, leaving the sisters alone.

Elizabeth collapsed against the chaise lounge. "Oh, thank God," she breathed. "I thought that would never end."

Cassandra came closer, lifting her veil as she did. "What do you mean? There is a kind viscount waiting for you outside."

Elizabeth's eyes widened as she straightened suddenly. "Are you serious?"

Cassandra giggled. "No, I jest. But it was worth seeing the fear in your eyes."

"You're quite horrible, you know."

"Yes, I am aware," Cassandra said simply, sitting by her sister's side. "But you love me all the same."

Elizabeth did not respond, choosing to rest her head on Cassandra's shoulder instead. Cassandra's heart warmed. Seeing how popular her sister had become in such a short time gave her hope that Elizabeth would one day make a love match. It was the only thing Cassandra wanted for her.

"How does it feel," Cassandra began, her tone teasing, "to have so many gentlemen vying for your attention?"

Elizabeth lifted her head, facing Cassandra as she prepared to answer. Before she could though, Hanson reentered the drawing room, announcing, "The Viscount of Bancroft has arrived, my ladies."

Before either sister could do or say anything in response, Simon swept through the door bearing two full bouquets—one of white lilies and the other of pink peonies.

"Ah, my two favourite ladies in the world," Simon said by way of greeting. "I could not come to see either of you with empty hands."

Cassandra grinned at her friend, accepting the bouquet of peonies he held out to her. It was her favorite flower, as the lily was Elizabeth's. But when she looked at her sister, she didn't miss the slight annoyance that crossed over her face as she studied Simon.

*How curious*, Cassandra thought. She watched as Elizabeth accepted the flowers, wiping away her irritation before Simon could see.

"Thank you, Simon," Cassandra said since clearly Elizabeth had no intentions of saying anything. "And of course, that means you wish for some tea to be prepared for you, doesn't it?"

"And that, dear Cassandra, is why you are my dearest friend." Simon settled into the couch opposite Elizabeth, spreading his arms along the spine. He looked quite at home, as if he'd lived here all his life. Considering how often he would come by, Cassandra supposed he had to consider this manor his second home.

Simon grinned at Elizabeth as he propped one leg perpendicular to the other. "How has your morning been going, Elizabeth?"

"You ask as if you do not know," Elizabeth said, her tone a bit stiff. "I am sure you questioned Hanson all about it before you came in. Or perhaps you did so with Lord Gregory as he left."

"You break my heart, Elizabeth. Why do you think I would do such a thing?"

"Because that is how you are," she said simply.

*And because you love her*, Cassandra added silently. She busied herself with preparing tea off to the side before bringing it closer, leaving it on a waiter for them to access.

"I take it your morning was rather busy then," Simon said. Cassandra didn't miss how strained his smile became. "Well, I'm happy to say that I came here for a reason."

"That's a first," Cassandra murmured, sipping her tea.

Simon rolled his eyes at her but continued, "I have procured a rented box for the performance of a famous Shakespearean play at Covent Garden Theater. A week away from today."

Cassandra perked up at the mention of Shakespeare. "Which play?"

Simon shrugged. "I did not get that far, I fear. I merely thought it would be a lovely evening out with my two favourite ladies. So, what do you say?"

Cassandra watched hope fill his eyes as he stared at Elizabeth, waiting for her response. That hope banked when Elizabeth said, "I will be busy that evening."

"Ah." If he'd hoped to hide his disappointment—at least from Cassandra, who knew him so well—he failed. And if Elizabeth noticed, she gave no indication. "And what of you, Cassandra? Don't tell me you're also busy?"

"As it happens, I am free that evening," Cassandra told him. "Though I suppose that comes as no surprise to anyone. I would love to attend the theatre with you."

The smile returned to Simon's face, though not as bright as before. "Then it is a date. I'm already looking forward to hearing you explain every scene to me."

Cassandra gave him a broad smile. "I shall prepare my notes."

Simon laughed—and Elizabeth said nothing. So Cassandra made sure to fill any silence that came up, not wanting the weird tension between her friend and her sister to become palpable. She managed to keep the discomfort at bay until Simon finished his tea and bid them good afternoon before leaving.

# Chapter Five

"Why did you tell him that you would be busy?" Cassandra asked the moment Simon was out the door. "I do not recall you making any commitments to any of the gentlemen earlier."

Elizabeth shrugged, her posture indicating dismissal. "I would much rather spend the evening alone at home than be in Simon's company."

Cassandra frowned at that. This wasn't the Elizabeth she knew. Elizabeth would have welcomed Simon's company, would have jumped at the chance to spend time with him. So much so that Cassandra hardly understood why neither of them saw that they shared in their feelings for each other.

Yet Elizabeth spoke coldly, her eyes focused out the window though she was clearly staring at nothing. Cassandra studied her for a second, considering the approach she should take.

"It has been some time since I've seen you act this childish," Cassandra said at long last.

Elizabeth's eyes cut to her, a scowl marring her perfect brows. "And how, exactly, is it childish if I do not want to share in his company?"

"Because you seemed perfectly content with doing that during your debut ball. If something happened, if he did something to upset you, then being cold to him is not going to help the situation. It only makes you appear, as I said, childish."

"Cassandra, you don't know what you're talking about."

She was angry, Cassandra noted. Between the chill in her voice and the fact that she'd called her by her full name, Elizabeth had sunken into a rare upset mood. But Cassandra remained calm, unflustered by her sister's tone.

"Tell me the real reason why you lied to him," Cassandra pressed.

"I did tell you the real reason."

"Then I was right. You are being childish." Cassandra sipped her tea as Elizabeth fixed her with a glare. "Simon is a good gentleman, you know. It would not hurt for you to give him a chance."

Elizabeth's cheeks went red. It was the first time Cassandra had ever hinted at the fact that she knew Elizabeth's true feelings for him. "If he's so wonderful, Cassandra, then why don't you court him? Ah, that's right. You would if you could, wouldn't you?"

Those words flayed Cassandra, though she kept her composure. Slowly, she rested her cup down, watching as Elizabeth shot to her feet and stormed out the room, slamming the door shut behind her. Only when her sister was gone did Cassandra let the hurt feelings show, tears pricking her eyes. She wiped at them, annoyed, but they were quickly replaced.

The door opened. Cassandra lowered her head, tears dropping into her lap.

"Cassie?" It was her mother. In a second, Viola was by her side, hand on her shoulder. "What's the matter? Why did I just see Elizabeth storming through the hallway?"

"Apparently, I upset her enough for her to remind me that I am unlovable." At least, that was what Cassandra had heard, hidden between Elizabeth's words.

Viola enveloped her in her arms, resting Cassandra's head against her heart like she would do when she was a child and had gotten hurt. "I don't know what she said exactly but I'm sure she did not mean it in the way you are taking it."

Cassandra only heaved a heavy sigh and willed her tears away. She'd told herself that she'd stop crying about her scar, about the pain that it brought though it had long since healed. It was now a part of her and if it meant she would never be loved, then so be it. It would hurt for a while, but she'd learned long ago how strong she could be.

But hearing such words from Elizabeth, who would often tell Cassandra how beautiful she was despite the scar, cut deeper than anything she'd ever felt.

"Come now, stop the crying," Viola urged. She pulled away, smiling gently at Cassandra. "If you cry too much, you might cause your eyes to become swollen. We can't have that happening before the masquerade ball this evening, now can we?"

"Oh right," Cassandra mumbled. "I nearly forgot about that."

"It is time to get ready for it, actually. Go ahead. I'm sure when you're done, you two will forget all about what was said and will become the best of friends again."

Cassandra nodded, though the lingering pain made that hard to believe. Squeezing her mother's hand in gratitude, Cassandra rose and left the drawing room.

Sally, her lady's maid, was already waiting for her in her bedchamber. The young girl, twenty at most, stood at attention when Cassandra walked in, hands clasped behind her.

"I've prepared your costume, milady," she said eagerly.

Cassandra nodded, barely managing to give her a warm smile. She instantly made her way to the center of the room and waited for Sally to assist her in undressing. Sally did so shyly, her confidence mounting slowly as the silence stretched on. Cassandra's mind wandered to Elizabeth's last words, barely going through the motions.

"Sally, may I ask you a question?" Cassandra asked suddenly, making her lady's maid jump.

"Y-yes, of course, milady," Sally mumbled. Her fingers began to shake.

"Relax, Sally," Cassandra said as gently as she could. "It is nothing regarding your work. You are wonderful, as always."

Sally visibly relaxed at that. When Cassandra was down to her chemise, Sally moved to the costume laid out on the bed. Cassandra ignored it for now.

"We have only known each other for a year now, haven't we?" Cassandra asked.

"Yes, that's right, milady," Sally responded, sounding a little more confident now.

"And would you say that I have a dreadful personality?"

Sally eyes went wide. "Of course not, milady! I would never!"

Cassandra laughed. Hearing her question aloud, she realized how insecure she sounded. "I suppose it would be unfair to ask you that."

"But I do not lie, Lady Cassandra," Sally pressed. "You are the best mistress I've ever had the pleasure of working for. You are so well-read, so elegant, and you've always treated me kindly."

"You speak of the bare minimum, Sally."

"And yet it is what makes you such an exceptional person."

Cassandra's chest warmed at that. "Thank you, Sally. I apologise if my question caught you off guard. I've been doing a bit of thinking and...well, I suppose I doubted myself for a second."

A smile flitted across Sally's face but whatever courage that had spurred her on before was gone. Her cheeks went red and Cassandra decided to keep the silence as Sally helped her into her costume. It was a simple gown with golden damask fabric, favouring the fashion of the Elizabethan years. Cassandra was grateful that the skirt was not nearly as large as the ones during that time, however, and that the matching mask would cover nearly all of her face, save for her eyes and a sliver of her forehead.

After a moment of getting dressed, Sally whispered, "Are you excited for tonight's ball, milady?"

Cassandra had to think of a response. After a moment, she could only sigh as she said, "I do not know what I am anymore, Sally."

# Chapter Six

It would have been a lovely morning in Bath. Perhaps he would have started his day with a brisk walk through the small forest behind his grandparent's manor. Or maybe a horse ride would have tempted him more. Jacob was certain he would have spent the morning outdoors no matter what he ended up doing, enjoying the fresh breeze and the warm sun on his face.

His body might be in London, but his heart was certainly still in Bath. And his mind...so far away that Jacob was hardly aware of anything going on around him.

Still, he reached for his cup of coffee, taking a sip without realizing it. His eyes bore into the dark wood of the table before him though he saw nothing. He tapped his finger on his arm rest, his father's words echoing in his head. Jacob hadn't been able to stop thinking about it and the imaginary noose his father had put around his neck seemed to tighten a little more.

"Perhaps I should simply throw myself onto the floor and scream until my throat grows hoarse."

Jacob blinked, pulled sluggishly from his thoughts. He'd hardly registered what his mother had said, had only heard 'scream'. "Pardon?" he asked after clearing his throat. "Who is screaming?"

Maria rolled her eyes and set down her cup of tea with a loud clink. The irritation on her face was enough to bring Jacob fully to the present. Ah, right. He had accepted his mother's invitation to have tea in the drawing room, though he couldn't remember how much time had passed. From the moment he sat down and served himself a hot cup of coffee, Jacob's mind had wandered off.

"I think I have been talking for the past twenty minutes without a single response from you," his mother complained. "Do you wish you were elsewhere? Doing anything other than spending time with your mother?"

Jacob tried to ignore the pang of guilt at how close her words came to the truth. He did wish he was in Bath, but not because of her. He'd missed his mother, of course. But now that he knew coming to London meant his father would pressure him into marriage, all Jacob wanted to do was tuck his tail and return to the blissful countryside.

"I'm sure it wasn't that long," he protested.

Maria shook her head. "How would you know when you were so dazed for so long? Come now, out with it. What has gotten you so distant?"

Jacob considered brushing off the question, but his mother's determined look stilled his tongue for a second. Then he sighed. "I think you can guess, Mother. It is the only reason I was asked to return to London, after all."

"Ah, so this is about what your father told you." Maria shifted in her seat, the irritation on her face melting away to contemplation as she gazed out the window. Jacob studied her face, sensing that she was looking for the right thing to say. A part of him hoped that she would tell him that she didn't agree with what his father had said, even though his hope was fringed by what he knew was the truth. Maria, like nearly every other mother in the ton, wanted to see her son married. Wanted to begin her life as the doting grandmother.

"Is the thought truly that troubling?" Maria asked at long last and Jacob's hope deflated.

"It is not that I do not want to be married, Mother," Jacob tried to explain without sighing. "I do plan to, in the future. But I would much rather it be done when I am good and ready, when I have found a lady who know I will be happy with."

"But perhaps Lady Elizabeth is that lady," she pressed, though her eyes were sympathetic. "Not all arranged marriages are bad, you know. That was how your father and I came to know each other and came to care for each other over the years."

"I would much rather not leave it up to chance. She could be a lovely lady who I will certainly fall in love with. Or she may harbour a terrible personality that makes living with her quite horrid. It is even more likely that we live in contentment with each other, but not in love."

"And you are not willing to find out the hard way." She spoke it like a question, rather than a statement but Jacob nodded as he tried not to sigh again. To distract himself from his agitation, he sipped his coffee again and grimaced when he realized how cold it had gotten.

"That last thing I want is to marry in the hopes that it eventually becomes a love match. The ton is full of unhappy marriages created through these kind of arrangements. I have no wish to join them."

"I think perhaps you are not being open-minded about the situation," Maria said softly.

Jacob knew she wouldn't understand. At least, not fully, even if she was trying to. "It is simply how I feel, Mother," he said. And left it at that.

Maria looked like she was about to push a little further but thought better of it. Instead, she said, "I believe it is time we prepared for the masquerade ball, my dear. We wouldn't want to be late."

Jacob nodded, though the thought only served to worsen his mood. Once upon a time, he'd enjoyed the events of the Season, when he knew he would be free of the pressures to marry for a while. So many gentlemen in London did not even entertain the thought until they'd passed their thirtieth year. Jacob, at twenty-and-nine, thought he might have had a few more years of bachelorhood to enjoy.

Now though, the thought of leaving the manor this evening weighed on him, even as he nodded and left the drawing room behind his mother. As he made his way to his bedchamber, he thought of what would be expected of him at this masquerade ball. If Lady Elizabeth was in attendance, would this be their official meeting? Would they be forced to share a dance while they engaged in strained conversation?

Would he allow it or would he fight his father tooth and nail about this matter? Jacob was yet to decide, his heart pulled in opposite directions. His duty and what he truly wanted.

I should at least try to enjoy this evening, he thought as he entered his room to see his valet waiting on him. Jacob gave him a nod in greeting. I won't let this ruin my enjoyment of masquerade balls.

His clothing consisted of a simple, fitting domino costume paired with a black mask covering his eyes. He was finished within an hour, making his way downstairs to meet his parents. They were already in the carriage, his mother and father dressed in matching Egyptian inspired outfits.

The sight made a bit of Jacob's hope return. He observed his parents as the carriage began its journey to the Earl of Hanebridge's townhouse. What his mother had said was true—that over the years, his parents had grown closer together. Even now, as they sat in comfortable silence, Jacob could only admire how handsome they appeared next to each other.

But when Henry cleared his throat, Jacob braced himself for what was to come.

"The Earl of Wiswall has invited us to have dinner with him and his family tomorrow evening," the duke stated to the carriage, though his eyes bore into Jacob. "I trust you will be in attendance?"

"Have I been given a choice?"

"The dinner will give you a chance to meet Lady Elizabeth," his father went on. "Perhaps then you will not be so against this."

Perhaps. "I would much rather spend the evening at my club. I have not been since returning to London."

"Jacob," Henry growled in a warning tone.

Jacob only looked out the window. He knew it would take more defiance on his part to get out of dinner. And he couldn't deny that he was a little curious.

"I'm sure you will like her a lot, Jacob," Maria interrupted. "I have been reading the scandal sheets and they have dubbed her this Season's diamond!"

"That means little to me."

"She is a beauty and is rumoured to have a wonderful personality," Henry added. "Many gentlemen will be vying for her hand in marriage."

"Ah, so do you suppose making it a competition will increase my interest in this arrangement at all?"

"I am hoping that it will at least help you to understand how valuable this could be for us."

Jacob didn't bother to respond to that, staring blankly out the window instead. Those words only made it more certain to him that nothing good could come from this. This would be no marriage, he deduced, but a business transaction. And that was the last thing he wanted.

## Chapter Seven

As the years had stretched on and Cassandra had slowly turned into the lady she was now, she began to understand a few things about herself. Firstly, she was no coward, and that daring behavior she'd exuded as a child had scarred her so terribly—inside and out—that it was a wonder she hadn't shut herself entirely.

Secondly, Cassandra did not know how to hold a grudge. While she tended to speak her mind, a blunt tongue she'd often been scolded for, it also led to many arguments over the years. With Simon, with Elizabeth—though rare—and even with her parents. Cassandra had learned how to admit when she was in the wrong, though it oftentimes didn't help prevent her from speaking her mind a next time.

But as she made her way down to the grand foyer, Cassandra felt a tremor of trepidation. The brief conversation with Elizabeth, and her sister's scathing words, had bothered her the entire time she was preparing for the ball. Cassandra knew the others were waiting for her, that she was the last of them to be ready. And she still did not know what to say to her sister when they saw each other again.

Perhaps an apology would be a good start, Cassandra thought, putting a hand to her chest as she descended the staircase.

But what was she apologising for? Pushing Elizabeth to tell the truth? To open up about her feelings for Simon? Cassandra couldn't help but feel as if she had been right in pressing her, though she supposed she'd taken it a step too far by calling her childish. No one would take kindly to such accusations.

She faltered in her steps when she took note of her mother and Elizabeth waiting for her in the foyer. Her darling sister looked as breathtaking as ever, her masquerade costume resembling that of the queen's, with elaborate bows, a large tulle skirt, and sleeves that clung to her upper arm then flared down to her wrists. The soft blue color complimented her fair complexion, her strawberry-blond hair pinned to the top of her head with tendrils framing her face. As Cassandra neared, she noticed the pink tinge on Elizabeth's face, her eyes shifting all over the room.

"Cassie..." Elizabeth started, then bit her lip, eyes falling to the floor.

Cassandra raised her chin, pushing aside the shame that rose in her as she remembered what she'd said to her sister. "I'm sorry, Elizabeth," she told her, her voice strong. "I realise now how uncouth my words had been, not sparing your feelings much. I thought I was only being honest, but I did take it a step too far. For that I am sorry."

Elizabeth's eyes filled with tears in an instant. She bit her lip, trembling from the force the sob she was clearly holding back. "Oh, Cassie, why do you have to be so—"

She broke off as her sob went free. Cassandra's heart sank. "Have I offended you further?" she asked breathlessly, half-afraid though she couldn't fathom how.

"No!" Elizabeth cried. "No, of course not. You're just so...mature! Here I was trying to figure out how to apologise to you for being so dreadful and here you are apologising to me when you have no reason to do so."

Relief flood Cassandra, her shoulders sagging from the force of it. A soft smile found its way to her lips. Of course, Elizabeth was only being a tad overdramatic.

"I was not kind with my words," Cassandra said, reaching out to take Elizabeth's gloved hand. "And I pressured you about something that you clearly were not ready to talk about. Isn't that reason enough to say that I am sorry? Besides, I am your older sister. I should be more mature."

Elizabeth blurted out a giggle despite her tears. Without warning, she wrapped her arms around Cassandra so tightly that it knocked the wind out Cassandra's lungs. "I'm the one who should be saying sorry," Elizabeth said. "For what I said and how I left things when I stormed out. I shouldn't have mentioned..."

"Apology accepted, Lizzie." Cassandra stroked the back of her head carefully, making sure she did not ruin Elizabeth's curls. The trepidation she'd been victim of just seconds before dissolved into nothing. Now that she was on good terms with her sister again, all felt right in the world once more.

Before Cassandra could pull away, Viola approached to wrap her arms around them as well, filling the air with the scent of her lavender perfume. "Oh, it truly warms my heart to see my girls getting along," she crooned. "I knew you two would work things out."

"You two are stifling me," Cassandra drawled.

Neither Elizabeth or Viola budged. "That's too bad," Elizabeth said. "Because I am enjoying this quite a lot and have no intentions of moving."

"Well, my dear, I fear I come bearing bad news then." Elizabeth and Viola slackened their hold enough for Cassandra to look over her shoulder at her father's voice. He approached from the side hallway, likely coming from his study where he spent all his time. There was a rare small smile on his otherwise grim expression. He stopped next to the three of them and continued, "The carriage is waiting for us outside, so it's time for this to come to an end."

"Oh, you have always been such a bore," Viola sighed, though her voice was lined with amusement. The side of his eyes crinkled as the smile deepened slightly.

Cassandra grinned at her father as she gave him a nod of gratitude. He winked. Growing up, the Earl of Wiswall, Lord Gilbert Matthews, had been a dour and serious man who had frightened Cassandra to no end. Yet she'd idolized him and found that, as she grew older, he had an odd sense of humor that only Cassandra seemed to understand. Ever since she came to that realization, their bond had deepened to something Cassandra couldn't explain.

She knew her father hated to see her like this, scarred and fated to live as an outcast. To have the younger of his two daughters debuting before the older, simply because she stood more of a chance at a decent marriage. Cassandra understood the pain that came with that as a father, the shame he must feel when he faced the other gentlemen with daughters to marry off. Once upon a time, it had bothered Cassandra. Now, she accepted the disappointment.

"Shall we?" Gilbert asked her as he offered her his arm. Elizabeth was already sidling to Viola's side, arms interlocked.

Cassandra gave him a curtsy, smiling under her mask as she took his arm. Arm in arm, they made their way outdoors to the waiting carriage. The Earl of Hanebridge's townhouse was perhaps a twenty-minute carriage ride away from the manor. Cassandra settled into the cushions of her seat, content to let her mind wander as she stared out the window.

"The Duke of Edingdale and his family will be joining us for dinner tomorrow evening," Gilbert announced suddenly. His face had returned to that serious expression, his brows knitted.

"The Duke of Edingdale?" Elizabeth echoed. "Have we met him before?"

"I do not believe you have. He has not taken part in any events of the Season since it's commencement. I am not even certain you will see him this evening. However, that is not important." Cassandra took note of how her father's gaze bore into Elizabeth. "What truly matters is that he has a son."

"Oh, does he?" Elizabeth said, her tone curious. Cassandra returned her eyes to the window. She had a feeling this conversation was not meant for her.

"He is a very eligible bachelor. He has returned to London for the Season and will be in attendance for tomorrow's dinner."

"I'm sure he is a lovely person," Viola interjected. "Elizabeth, perhaps you could play the pianoforte after dinner?"

"That would be nice. It has been a while since I've played, though."

Cassandra's lips twitched. She couldn't tell if Elizabeth was playing along with them or if she truly had not picked up on how obvious it was that they wanted her to impress the marquess.

Whichever one it was, Cassandra didn't get the chance to find out. The conversation lulled into a comfortable silence all the way to the townhouse and only then did Elizabeth speak again, her voice filled with excitement.

"Oh, I cannot wait to get inside and see how everyone is dressed," she gushed as a footman opened the door for them. He offered her his hand and helped her out of the carriage, assisting Cassandra next.

Cassandra waited until they were making their way into the townhouse to respond. "Do you think you will recognise anyone?"

"I hope so, though I do not have much faith in myself. I have not known many people well enough, save for you and...Simon."

Cassandra fell quiet, letting the awkward mention of Simon fade as they neared the ballroom. Elizabeth's palpable excitement bolstered her own and by the time they arrived, Cassandra could hardly contain it either. Without thinking, she touched her mask, as if to ensure it was secure on her face. No one would cast confused looks her way with this on. Everyone would be shielding their faces, would be making a game of trying to figure out who was who.

For once, Cassandra felt like she could actually fit in.

*** 

Perhaps it was not all bad. Jacob thought he could actually enjoy himself at this ball if he would only allow himself to relax. But every time a lady so much as looked in his direction, he tensed. He hoped the scowl under his mask was visible enough to ward them off.

Jacob took a sip of his wine, his eyes snagging on Lady Hanesbridge as she flitted around the ballroom. She'd taken it upon herself to introduce him not only to her daughter—who had boldly told him that she would save a spot on her dance card for him—but nearly every other lady in attendance. His own parents had abandoned him, his father playing cards in one of the card rooms while his mother chatted with her friends in one corner of the ballroom. Only when the dancing had begun did he manage to slip away from the countess' grasp.

He slunk further into the corner, hoping she wouldn't see him. Her daughter—Lady Phoebe, he believed was her name—was already occupied, dancing with someone else. Thank God.

Jacob polished off the rest of his wine and made a reach for another. At that moment, he caught sight of his mother staring at him, a disapproving look in her eyes. Jacob made himself a glass and raised it at her, which made her shake her head.

*No dancing for me tonight*, Mother he thought with a wry smile. *Not when I am basically betrothed to another lady.*

The thought only worsened his mood.

Resisting the urge to sigh, he finished his wine. He certainly would not be enjoying himself tonight, but at least he could numb his overwhelming thoughts a bit.

A flash of gold caught his eye. Jacob leaned against the wall, half shrouded behind a tall potted plant. It was a lady, he realized. And when she turned, he straightened.

He could only see her from the side, but that was enough. Her gown was unlike any other, simple yet detailed, clinging to her gentle curves. And her gold mask nearly covered her entire face, which Jacob found odd. Every other lady made sure most of their features were on display, opting to cover only their eyes or nothing at all. But as Jacob studied this lady, he could not make out a single distinct detail save for the thick head of strawberry-blond curls that tumbled down her back.

And then she faced him fully—and their eyes met.

The world seemed to still. Jacob held his breath and he could have sworn she held hers, unmoving. From the distance, he could not make out the color of her eyes, could only tell that she was focused solely on him. As if he was the only person in this crowded ballroom who mattered.

The seconds stretched on endlessly and Jacob could not will himself to step away. Instead, he pushed off the wall, his legs moving without thought. He was going to approach her, he realized belatedly, though he hadn't a clue what he planned on saying.

But before he could make another move, someone stepped before her and the tantalising connection severed instantly.

## Chapter Eight

A tall figure stepped in Cassandra's path and it felt as if she had been doused with cold water. Even so, the heat of her cheeks burned her face under her mask, her heart racing as the effect of that stranger's long stare lingered. Even as she lifted her eyes to the gentleman before her, the host of butterflies in her stomach did not decrease, her throat a tad dry.

"Good evening, my lady," the gentleman before her said.

Cassandra licked her lips and tried to ignore the urge to step around this gentleman and find the mysterious stranger. Something had shifted in those few moments they'd gazed at each other. Cassandra was determined to understand why.

But she stomped the need down and dipped into a curtsy as the gentleman bowed. "Good evening, sir," she greeted. "How fares your night?"

"I am enjoying myself even more now that I have seen your lovely..." He trailed off as if searching for the right words. "Presence," he ended with at last.

Cassandra frowned, finally taking a good look at him. There was something about this gentleman that struck her as familiar. Perhaps it was his voice? Or the broad cut of his shoulders? Cassandra didn't know many gentlemen personally so it shouldn't be too difficult to figure out.

Unsure of what to do with the awkward compliment, Cassandra only inclined her head in a slight nod, saying, "Thank you, sir. May I ask your name?"

"Now where is the fun in that?" She could see the smile in his eyes, under his white mask. "It is a masquerade ball, after all."

"I see. It sounds as if you wish for me to guess, then."

"That sounds far more like it." He extended his hand, leaning slightly towards her. "And while you are doing so, why don't we share this first dance? I promise I will try just as fervently to discover your true identity as well."

Cassandra tilted her head to the side. She couldn't help glancing over his shoulder when she did, but the mysterious gentleman had disappeared. She turned her eyes back to the man before her. "I have a feeling I am at a disadvantage here," she said and he chuckled. "But I accept. Shall we?"

She placed her hand in his, still studying him as he led her into the center of the ballroom. She simply couldn't put her finger on why this man seemed so familiar. Was it the head of dark hair, a tad unrulier than the other men in attendance? Or perhaps the cadence of his voice?

A lively jog started up, forcing them to stand apart at first. Cassandra held his gaze as much as he did hers, his mirth deepening.

"Have you given up?" he asked as they began to dance, twirling around each other. Their hands came together, then apart. Cassandra whirled away, her feet moving on their own accord as her mind lingered on the puzzle before her.

When she faced him again, she said, "You will have to give me a little more time. All this movement makes me dizzy, you see. It makes it a little hard to think."

"It sounds as if you're stalling for more time."

"Am I so transparent?" she asked innocently and he tilted his head back and laughed.

"Cassie, have you gotten even more droll since the last time we saw each other?"

His voice was suddenly different. Cassandra faltered in her steps, her lips parting in a silent gasp. "Ethan?"

Now those humor-filled eyes made more sense. Her mischievous older brother had returned.

They continued dancing without missing a beat. Ethan said, "Surprised?"

"Of course I am!" she gaped. "Why didn't you let us know that you'd returned to England?"

"Because I was looking forward to seeing this reaction. I'd almost forgotten how focused you get when you're trying to figure something out."

"You are absolutely horrid," she told him, feigning annoyance. "When did you arrive then?"

"Two days ago?"

"Two days ago?" Cassandra nearly shouted. Had it not been for the loud music, perhaps the entire ballroom might have heard. "And you wait until now to show up?"

"I needed to rest after that long voyage," he explained.

"Two days seems like a bit much to me," Cassandra grumbled and Ethan laughed again.

"Oh, don't be upset now, Cassie. Others might think I have snubbed you in some way."

"I wouldn't mind if they did at all. It is the least you deserve." But the smile was evident in her voice. She couldn't truly be mad at him. In fact, Cassandra didn't think there was ever a time she'd gotten upset with her brother. He was five years her senior, yet had a much quicker start on life than she did. Dubbed a genius, he had left Cambridge at the tender age of ten-and-six to travel. Now and again, he would return home only to leave once more. The last time he'd been back, Ethan had stayed for only a month.

She wondered if he had come back now to take part in the Season. His dear sister had debuted, after all, and would likely be married by the end of it. Whatever the reason was, Cassandra fully intended on taking advantage of his return, savoring these moments with him before he was gone again.

"How did you know it was me?" she asked him.

"I saw when you exited the carriage," he explained. "Also, both you and Elizabeth stand out, I hope you know."

"Oh? In what way?"

"Your gown is far more unique than anything I've seen at any masquerade ball I've ever attended. I simply knew that you were the one wearing it, my dear sister who always has her nose in history books."

"I've retired those years ago," Cassandra told him, though she couldn't resist the smile that stretched across her face. "I mostly read Shakespeare novels these days."

"I'm not surprised to hear that. Nothing could truly hold your attention for very long. As for Lizzie, that grand dress and small mask leaves very little to mystery."

Cassandra's eyes fell on Elizabeth, who she'd last seen standing on the other end of the dance floor smiling brightly at her dance partner. She didn't fail to notice that Elizabeth was the object of nearly everyone's attention nearby.

"I believe she will be dancing all night," Cassandra mused aloud. "I hope she has worn proper shoes."

"And what of you? Have you taken the same preparations?"

"I have, though I doubt it will do me any good."

"I beg to differ, Cassie. Clearly you have not noticed how many gentlemen stare at me with envy since this dance set began."

She made sure he saw when she rolled her eyes. "You lie too easily."

"And you too readily doubt yourself."

She opened her mouth to argue but then Ethan stepped away from her just as the song drifted to an end. With a broad grin, he swept into a bow, eyes twinkling as if he knew he was giving her no chance to respond. Cassandra couldn't help breaking into a smile herself, sinking into a curtsy.

"Now, if you will excuse me," Ethan said. "I think I will try my hand at beating Father in a game of whist.'

"I wish you all the luck," Cassandra called after him. She watched him go for a moment before she turned and made her way back to her corner of the room. As soon as she faced the ballroom once more, Cassandra tried—and failed—to find the mysterious gentleman from earlier. Despite the height of him, it seemed as if he had simply upped and disappeared. Disappointment stung her.

"Oh, heavens."

Cassandra frowned at her mother's approach. Viola was fanning herself, eyes drooping. "Mother? Is everything all right?"

"No, it is not," Viola said wearily. "I feel quite dizzy all of a sudden."

"It might just be the heat." Cassandra took her mother gently by the arm, guiding her towards the nearest door. Her voice remained calm, even as her disappointment was quickly replaced with worry. "Let's go to the parlour."

"And miss out on such enjoyment?" her mother asked, even as she allowed herself to be led.

Cassandra waved a dismissive hand over her shoulder. "We'll only be long enough for you to regain your bearings. I'm sure we'll miss nothing."

But as they slipped through the door, Cassandra couldn't help throwing one more glance over her shoulder, hoping to catch another glimpse of the mysterious stranger.

# Chapter Nine

Hours stretched on in an endless sea of nothing. Jacob couldn't remember how he'd passed the time, what had consumed him while it did. All he knew was that it was well past midnight, his feet were hurting, and he was praying that the masquerade ball would soon be coming to an end.

Lady Hanesbridge had found him again, though she had only cared to talk about her own daughter rather than introduce him to any other. Not that he had listened much. And she clearly hadn't cared to hear anything other than her own voice as she droned on and on about the prodigy that Lady Phoebe was. The very same Lady Phoebe was currently batting her eyelashes at him even while she was dancing the waltz with another man.

Jacob nearly heaved a great sigh. At least one good thing had come out of his father's attempt to marry him off to Lady Elizabeth of Wiswall. His parents were not trying to force lady upon lady on him, each content to enjoy the ball in their own way. No, rather than his own parents, it was the mothers of these young ladies that forced their daughters upon him and Jacob hardly had the strength to turn them down.

Which was why he now found himself wincing with every step he took as he held the petite Lady Annabelle in his arms.

"What do you think of my dress, my lord?" she asked him, peering up at him with round, blue eyes. She hadn't cared to wear a mask, opting to carry hers with a stick instead. Jacob had found that interesting until he realized she'd likely only wanted to put her full beauty on display.

"It is lovely," he responded blandly.

"Isn't it?" Clearly his lacklustre response did not bother her. "It was made from the finest fabric imported from India, you know? Not many can afford such a thing but my father is quite wealthy and gives me whatever I ask for. He often tells me that a lady with beauty like mine should never want for a thing."

"Is that so."

"Oh, yes. I have perfect blond hair, deep blue eyes, a petite frame..."

Jacob stopped listening. The dance set had only just begun, yet it felt like hours had passed in slow agony. He couldn't wait for them to part ways, so that he could turn his back to her and never involve himself with Lady Annabelle and her family again. If she was this irritating, then imagine the people who had raised her?

That wasn't to say she wasn't beautiful. Jacob was willing to believe that she was one of the most beautiful ladies in attendance—though he supposed the ones who wore full face masks stood a chance at proving him wrong. But Lady Annabelle had quickly proven that she was far too conceited to think about anything other than herself. She hadn't made a single attempt to get to know him, had only asked him questions that would coax a compliment out of him. And he didn't know how many times he could hear her say how wealthy her father was.

"What do you think, my lord?" she asked, pulling Jacob back to the conversation.

Be polite, he told himself. "I am not sure." Simply because he hadn't been listening and wasn't certain what she was referring to.

Lady Annabelle scowled. "But you said just a few minutes ago that I was lovely."

Ah, he supposed he could have guessed what the topic had been. She wasn't very imaginative. "Then why bother to ask again?" he couldn't help but question her.

She blinked in surprise. "Pardon?"

Jacob shook his head just as the song ended. It wasn't worth it, he told himself. "It is nothing, my lady," he said as he stepped away from her, relief flooding him. "Please enjoy the rest of your night."

"Lord Charling—"

Jacob turned and walked away, not wanting to listen to another word. He quickly found his way to the refreshments table and got himself another glass of wine, though he yearned for something stronger after that dance. As he finished his wine, his relief deepened when Lady Hanesbridge announced that the last dance for the evening would be commencing shortly. Which meant the ball was nearly over, thank God.

Idly, his eyes roved across the ballroom once more and it took him a moment to realize that he was yet again searching for the lady in the gold mask. How she had captured his attention for so long, he hadn't a clue. But he hadn't given up on trying to find her again, looking for her in every corner of the room. At some point, he deduced that she must have left the ball entirely yet he continuously caught himself looking whenever he was not occupied.

The disappointment that washed over him when he could not spot her felt muted this time. He supposed it was silly of him to be disappointed at all. She was a stranger, after all. A stranger who had caught his attention for longer than any other stranger in attendance.

But just as he turned to set his empty wine glass down, he caught sight of her. Jacob's heart leaped as he watched her emerge from a side door, hand on her mask as if ensure it was properly fixed on her face. His heart began to race once more and he didn't stop, wouldn't allow her out of his sight. He didn't want her to disappear again.

There was only one dance left and he had every intention of sharing it with the lady in gold.

\*\*\*

Cassandra didn't know what to do with herself. She caught sight of him as soon as he moved, a tall figure breaking away from the refreshments table. The way he walked snagged her attention, with a commanding stride that had others giving him way without thought. He didn't take his eyes off her as he approached and with every step that brought him closer, Cassandra's heart sped up a little more.

"My lady."

His voice was deep, sensual. The sound washed over her and had gooseflesh rising on her arm. Cassandra didn't know how she managed to curtsy, how she even knew how to speak as she said, "Sir."

"Please." He held out a gloved hand and captured her eyes once more. Hazel, she realized. And intense. "May I have this final dance?"

Cassandra lost her voice, not knowing how to tell him that she would want nothing more at that moment. Perhaps it was the mask she wore, covering her horrible scar, but Cassandra felt an unnatural bout of confidence as she nodded and took his hand. He had come to her, had sought *her* out. And he hadn't a clue what she truly looked like underneath.

Wordlessly, they made their way to the center of the room. Cassandra didn't know where Elizabeth was, nor Ethan and her parents. She didn't care. Right now, only she and this gentleman existed.

"I have been trying to find you all night."

His words had her heart stilling in her chest. She gazed up at him to see him already looking down at her. He came closer, pulling her into his arms and Cassandra thought she might melt entirely.

She nearly asked him why. But another response rushed to her tongue, though she hadn't a clue where it came from. "I am here now, my lord."

"Thank God. I thought the night might end before I saw you again."

Oh, dear! What was happening? She couldn't believe what she was hearing, couldn't handle it in the slightest. If there wasn't any music, they would have heard the heavy beat of her heart.

They spoke to each other as if they were long lost lovers, torn apart while desperately seeking each other out again. But this man was a stranger to her, she knew. The cut of his shoulders, how he dominated her presence with his towering height, the intensity of his eyes...it was unlike anything she'd ever known before. In the back of her mind, a sensible thought rang out, reminding her that she shouldn't fall prey to the endearing words of this strange gentleman. But before she could think twice, Cassandra was slipping under the lure of his gaze, something she'd never felt before trembling between them.

"I do not understand this, my lord," she whispered, tearing her eyes away from his and praying that would be enough to cool her overheating body.

"What do you not understand, my lady?"

"You. This." She didn't have to say more than that, she knew. Certainly he felt it too.

He drew in a shaky breath. "Neither do I. But on a night like tonight, I do not wish to turn away from it. My heart will not will it."

"Then what will you do?" she breathed, hardly hearing herself.

He leaned closer to her, his breath brushing her ear as he said, "Anything you wish."

A soft smile spread across her face. "Then, I'm sure you will not mind a bit of questioning then?"

"What line of questioning are you proposing?" he asked, curiosity and intrigue filling his voice. "If it has anything to do with my identity then I shan't indulge you."

"And why not?"

"The mystery makes this far more exciting, don't you think?"

Cassandra's heart skipped a beat at that. She couldn't deny the truth of it. Twirling in the arms of this mysterious stranger, with a voice as deep as sin and such strong arms, Cassandra was in a fairytale that she did not want to be free from.

"Very well then," she conceded, biting her lip on a smile. Her jaws were fast beginning to hurt. "I shall make my questions a little more...simple."

"Somehow, my lady, you strike me as anyone but simple." He didn't look away from her for a second, as if he was afraid she might disappear in a puff of smoke if he dared to.

"I have heard those words before."

"And has anyone else told you how lovely you are tonight?"

"I have not had the pleasure."

"Fools, the lot of them. Anyone with eyes can tell how delicately you shine among all these ladies. The moment I laid eyes on you, I could not tear my gaze away."

Cassandra managed a small laugh, even though her heart was doing somersaults in her chest. "How poetic, my lord. You may even rival Lord Byron himself."

"I find my words resemble Shakespearean script far more," he mused, his voice rumbling with amusement.

"Are you fond of his work?" Cassandra asked him, unable to mask the excitement in her voice.

"I most certainly am. Though I suppose I spend most of my free days exploring the past."

That infernal smile grew wider as Cassandra chuckled. "What a confounded way of saying you enjoy history."

"Well, I suppose there is no need to hide that I am trying to impress you with my eloquence."

"There's no need, my lord," Cassandra laughed. "Your dancing is more than enough."

"Is it? Then perhaps you will enjoy this then." With a cunning grin, he whipped her around with a little more force than what was necessary and they caught the confused eyes of the nearby dancers. Cassandra didn't care if they seemed a little odd though. She was in her own little world, on cloud nine.

"My lady," he whispered to her and those two words were filled with such sudden pain. Before Cassandra could question it, the music slowed as it neared its end and she suddenly understood.

"I do not wish to leave," she said honestly. This evening, she wore her heart on her sleeve and prayed she did not embarrass herself.

"Neither do I," he said, pulling her close to him. Again, the world around her faded to nothing. Cassandra knew she should be stepping away from him, saying her respectful goodbyes and preparing to leave. But she could not bring herself to and, from the way he gripped her hand tightly, his hand resting gently on the small of her back, she didn't think he liked that idea either.

But any longer and they would begin to draw the attention of others. Remembering that, she pulled away as quickly as she could, her heart hammering in her chest. He did not move, eyes filled with longing.

Cassandra stepped further away, her heart racing. She did not want to watch him walk away, afraid of what it would do to her. And as the song was quickly replaced by the hum of excited chatter, Cassandra's mind stilled with only one realization.

On this magical night, she'd fallen a little in love.

## Chapter Ten

Blue eyes. Right now, they were as dark as a stormy sea, and just as intense. But Jacob wondered what they would be like when they were alight with laughter, catching the glint of the sun. His curiosity grew as he studied her, openly. Not caring about what others might think. The dancing had come to an end, but he knew he had a little more time before the ball itself was finished and it was time to leave. He had every intention of taking full advantage of it.

"I suppose I should..." she started, eyes shifting away as she took yet another step away from him.

Jacob jerked forward, stopping himself just in time to keep from grabbing her arm and keeping her there. He didn't want to frighten her. God knows he'd already scared himself with his intense emotions and all the things he'd said so far.

"Wait," he called instead and she froze. Around them, guests milled about, finding their friends to say their goodbyes. Jacob could not see anything but her. "We have time still. Stay with me."

"I should find my family..." she said tentatively.

"And miss out on our riveting conversation about Shakespeare and history?" he tried to joke.

Jacob's heart soared when he saw a smile light her eyes. With most of her face covered, he could only try to read her emotions through her eyes, which were far more expressive than he'd ever seen before.

She tilted her head to the side and asked, "What kind of history interests you?"

"Ancient?"

She huffed a laugh, the sound music to his ears. "Are you asking me? It is not a test, my lord."

"Ah, forgive me," he said. Jacob laughed, even though he couldn't fathom how nervous she made him. She couldn't see half his face and he couldn't see any of hers, and it should have made this far easier. Yet he felt like a ten-and-five, stumbling over his words in front of a pretty lady.

"Then let me go first," she went on with that glint in her eye. "I have quite the passion for Egyptian history. Perhaps that is why I chose to wear gold this evening.

"Quite fitting, my lady. They did believe their gods and goddesses bore golden skin after all."

Jacob didn't know how but he could tell she was blushing. At least, that was what he told himself.

Yet she didn't look away, her eyes boring into his unflinchingly. It was quite unlike any other lady he'd met tonight. No demure looks under her eyelashes, or nervous glances. She was bold, unyielding. It stirred something in him, drawing him deeper into this small world where only the two of them existed.

"You are quite the flatterer considering you do not know how I look, my lord," she observed after a long moment.

Jacob was mildly aware that their time together was drawing to a close but he didn't dare to acknowledge it. "I do not need to."

"That doesn't sound like decision-making to me."

"The heart hardly acts the same way as the mind," he told her, resisting the urge to come closer still. "And, for some reason, I do not want to listen to what my mind says."

"Then what is your heart telling you, my lord?" she whispered as if she was afraid to know the answer.

The words rushed to his lips, as insane as he knew they were. "That this is fate. That I have been offered one of the greatest opportunities known to man and I do not intend to squander it."

Her eyes went wide. This time, she did look away. "Perhaps you have been reading too much Shakespeare…"

Jacob couldn't help but grin. He knew he sounded insane. He was well aware that the feelings coursing through him did not make sense, since she was still a stranger to him. Perhaps it was the wine but he did not care.

Just then, Lady Hanesbridge's voice rang out, silencing the rush of chatter around them. "Ladies and gentlemen! We have finally come to the end of tonight's masquerade ball and I would like to thank you all for attending. If I might say so this is certainly how the London Season should begin!"

She turned away from him, facing Lady Hanesbridge's voice. He did not bother to look at the host. He took the time to appreciate her from the side, to admire her. She glanced at him then back at the countess, the movement so quick that he'd almost missed it. Jacob smirked.

"And now time for the part of the ball you have all been waiting for," Lady Hanesbridge continued, her words cutting clear throughout the ballroom. "Ladies and gentlemen, please remove your masks!"

One by one, the guests removed their masks. Gasps and laughter echoed throughout the ballroom as the talking started up again, everyone greeting each other with renewed vigor.

Jacob's heart raced. Slowly, she looked back at him. He said nothing as he removed his black mask, watching as her eyes roved over his face, drinking him in.

Slowly, he swept into a bow, though he didn't dare to dip low enough that he couldn't see her anymore. A part of him was afraid that she might disappear, that this had all been a dream and she'd only been a figment of his imagination.

"It is a pleasure to meet you, my lady," he said, lifting a grin to her. "My name is Lord Jacob Kingsley, the Marquess of Charlington."

Without saying a word, she dipped into a curtsy. Jacob straightened, hope slowly spreading through his chest. "Will you show me who you are?"

She shook her head and it felt as if she'd just punched him in the chest, the disappointment sharp.

Jacob tried not to let it show on his face but he was sure she could hear it in his voice when he asked, "Why?"

"I would much prefer to keep it a secret," she said to him.

"But—"

"The dance was lovely, my lord. And our conversation even lovelier." She was leaving. Jacob couldn't let that happen, not yet.

He started forward. "Will I see you again?" he asked hastily, though he feared her answer. That nagging voice in the back of his head told her that he was bound to be hurt by this. But Jacob clung to the hope in her eyes, the longing.

"Find me." It was plea, her eyes intense.

"I will find you," he told her, even as she began to retreat. It was all he could do to keep from going after her. "I promise."

She gave him the barest of smiles before she turned and disappeared among the other guests. Jacob didn't move at first. Her presence lingered with him, the weight of their interaction resting on his heart.

"Jacob!" His mother appeared by his side, fresh-faced and breathless. Jacob could tell she'd spent the last few minutes flitting about the ballroom as she bade her goodbyes to her many friends. "Did you see her?"

"Who?" Jacob asked, barely present. He was searching the crowd now for a glimpse of gold, even though he knew she was truly gone.

"Lady Elizabeth! She took off her mask just now and as soon as she did, a swarm of gentlemen flocked to her side. I thought you would have been among them, if only to see how she looked."

"I was not, Mother."

Maria let out a breath of frustration. "You can at least try, you know? And what are you staring at?"

Jacob blinked, tearing his eyes away from the direction the mysterious lady had left in. "I was looking for her," he lied. "Lady Elizabeth."

"Oh, she is long gone," Maria said with a sigh, waving her fan. "She left with her family just a short while ago. You've missed your chance."

"There is always tomorrow," he murmured.

Maria smiled broadly at that. "Yes, you're right. There is." And, seeming satisfied by that memory, she linked her arm with his and steered him towards the exit. "But enough about that, my dear. How was your night? Did you have fun?"

"It was…unlike anything I have ever experienced before." That, at least, was the truth.

"Oh, was it? I quite enjoyed myself as well but I would not say unlike anything I've experienced before. But perhaps it is because you have not taken part in the London Season in some time…"

Jacob began to tune her out as she continued droning on. As they made their way to the carriages, his father quietly falling in step behind them, Jacob continued looking for the lady, for a glimpse of gold. But it was like she had well and truly disappeared.

This could not be the end for them. It was mad, he knew, but it felt as if she'd taken a piece of his heart as she left. And he wouldn't be whole again until he found her.

# Chapter Eleven

Cassandra hardly slept.

The end of her night began with excitement, with her heart still racing with the thrill of meeting that enthralling gentleman. The Marquess of Charlington, the gentleman who had stolen a piece of her heart in just one night. As she'd laid in bed that night, she thought of their conversation, the things he'd said to her. How easily he had made her heart race and had set her skin on fire. Her jaw had continued to hurt as she tossed and turned with that sappy smile on her face, longing to sleep but wanting to turn back the hands of time as well.

But when she remembered how he'd asked to see her without her mask, the excitement dimmed. And Cassandra was thrown back into reality.

Now, she lay awake, staring up at the ceiling as exhaustion dogged her eyes. It could not be. It was simply impossible. The moment he'd asked that question, she'd remembered who she truly was. Not the beautiful goddess he'd expressed that she was, but the scarred lady whom no man could love. It was easy for him to say those words when he did not know what she looked like. But she knew the truth. And she cursed herself for giving in to those fantasies.

*The Marquess of Charlington will never be mine*, she thought, resisting the urge to let out a deep sigh. *No man ever will.*

She was fated to live alone, had changed the course of her life with one foolish decision. If only she had listened when her mother told her never to go riding alone. If only she had been patient enough to wait until the morning, rather than sneaking out of the manor late at night. Maybe then she would have had the confidence to remove her mask, unscarred as she would have been.

*But then, I would not be here, would I?*

Though she often told herself not to indulge in such depressing thoughts, she couldn't stop it this time around. She imagined what life would have been like had she not had that accident. Perhaps she would have been married by now, with a family of her own. Or at least, she would have been free to enjoy this Season as she searched for a husband to call hers. Elizabeth would have to wait another year for her debut, but Cassandra was sure she would not have minded. The firstborn was to be married first, after all.

But she would never be married. She would never have that life. She thought she had long since come to terms with it, but as the Marquess of Charlington's face flashed in her mind once more, the pain sank its fangs deeper.

"Milady?" Sally's voice sounded on the other side of the door. Cassandra didn't move as she listened to the door opening, noting Sally's head poking inside in her peripheral vision. "Are you awake?"

"Unfortunately," Cassandra called. Slowly, she sat up, running her fingers through her blond curls. They snagged at the end as she let out a frustrated sigh. "You may come."

Sally shuffled closer, looking uncertain. "Did you not sleep, milady?"

"Perhaps for an hour or so. When the sun had already risen."

"Then would you like to—"

"Later," Cassandra cut in, not giving her a chance to voice the suggestion. If she dared to spend a second longer in bed, she was bound to drive herself mad. She dragged herself to her feet, letting out a long breath.

"You do not look well, Lady Cassandra," Sally said, coming a little closer. Cassandra turned to look at her, noting the genuine concern on her face.

That was the only reason why she plastered a smile on her face. "I am well, Sally. Only tired. I shall nap later."

"Won't Lady Elizabeth have callers this afternoon?" Sally questioned innocently.

Cassandra fought against the stab of jealousy as she nodded. She knew Sally meant no harm with the question. "Maybe. But Mother can chaperone her if I am not up to it."

"Ah, I see." An uncomfortable silence settled around them before Sally rushed towards the armoire. "Is there anything special you'd like to wea—"

"No." Sally flinched and Cassandra silently reprimanded herself for being so curt. "Anything is fine, Sally. I trust your judgment."

Sally bit her lip as she nodded and began to rummage through the array of morning dresses in Cassandra's wardrobe. Cassandra wandered over to the window, staring out into the garden as her mind drifted back to last night.

As if she sensed the direction of her thoughts, Sally asked, "How was the masquerade ball, milady?"

"It was fine."

"Only fine?" Sally pressed, her voice tinged with excitement. "I have heard many great things about masquerade balls. I've always wanted to attend one, you know. It must be so romantic."

"In what way?" Cassandra asked, facing her.

Sally brought forth a primrose-colored morning gown, her cheeks flushed as she said, "The mystery of not knowing your dance partners, milady. I always imagine how enchanting it must be to dance in the arms of a tall, wonderful gentleman and have such lovely conversation without knowing what the other looks like. And the grand reveal at the end! Oh, it is like something out of a fairy-tale!"

Cassandra studied her, beginning to undress. "Tell me, Sally. Do you believe in love at first sight?"

"I most certainly do, milady," Sally said with the most passion Cassandra had ever heard her speak with.

"Even when you have not truly seen the other person?"

"What do you mean?"

Cassandra bit her lip. She trusted Sally enough to know that she would not tell anyone else what Cassandra revealed to her, but she was afraid to speak the words aloud. They sounded senseless, even though she could not deny what she was feeling.

"I mean, do you think a gentleman could fall in love with you even though you have not shown them your face? Even though they have revealed theirs to you?"

Sally gasped. "Is that what happened last night, milady? Have you fallen in love?"

"No! Of course not!" Cassandra felt her cheeks grow hot and she quickly turned away, trying to avoid Sally's eyes. "I am only asking. Nothing more than that."

"Oh...well, it would be quite uncommon. But I do believe it possible."

Cassandra straightened, looking back at her lady's maid and forgetting her previous discomfort. "Truly?"

Sally nodded. Her eyes betrayed the belief in her words and Cassandra couldn't tell if her admission made her feel better or worse. "I see. Thank you."

She left it at that and, thankfully, Sally didn't press the issue. Cassandra had spent half the night convincing herself that what she'd felt had been the effects of two glasses of wine and the allure of the masquerade. Nothing more, nothing less. The things they'd said to each other, the way she'd felt in his arms...it had all been an illusion that she'd created. And now that it was the next day, surely it meant she could see a little clearer now.

But all that crowded her mind was Lord Charlington's hazel green eyes, shifting between brown and emerald with every drift of the light. She thought of his strong jaw, the full lips that had been curved in a slight, hopeful smile, the way his light brown hair had curled a little over his temples. He was the most handsome man she'd ever laid eyes on and she almost wondered if she'd simply imagined him.

*Enough! I should stop thinking about this or else I will drive myself mad.*

Cassandra got dressed in silence. Sally did her hair simply, in a small chignon that left a few tendrils framing her face. By the time she was finished, Cassandra had successfully convinced herself that everything that happened last night should be left in the past. She managed to hold on to that belief as she made her way down to the drawing room where her parents and Elizabeth were already gathered for breakfast.

"Cassie!" Elizabeth called excitedly, waving her over to sit in the chair next to her. "Come sit! We were just talking about Aunt Mildred's ball."

Cassandra nearly sighed through her teeth. *And I was just trying to forget it.*

Without a word, she sank into the chair next to her sister and reached for a piece of toast, intending to immerse herself entirely in her meal even though she had no appetite.

"How did you like it, Cassandra?" Viola asked, sipping her tea. Next to her, Gilbert was quiet, a cup of steaming coffee before him and *The Times* in his hands. "I, for one, thoroughly enjoyed myself."

"It was fine," Cassandra mumbled.

"Only fine? That was what you said last night but I thought it was only because you were tired. Did you truly not enjoy yourself?"

"If I hadn't, Mother, I would have said so." Cassandra bit her lip, realizing her words were a bit harsh. She always got like this when she did not sleep much the night before. "But I did meet a few interesting people. It was a pity though, that Simon could not be there."

"Ah, yes, he told me he would be otherwise occupied," Viola said. If she was bothered by Cassandra's curt response before, she did not make it show. "I'm sure you would have loved his company."

"He always makes the room a little brighter when he walks in," Cassandra agreed.

"Oh, enough about Simon," Elizabeth cut in. "The night was perfectly wonderful without him."

"Yes, no doubt you will have a number of suitors this afternoon, Elizabeth," their father said without looking away from the newspaper. "Prepare yourself."

"I will, Father," Elizabeth responded. "Though I am unsure of how much preparation is really needed."

"I agree," Viola added. Cassandra stayed silent, content to let the conversation mill around her. "Elizabeth has grown quite adept at handling her suitors. Though, I will admit I am a bit nervous about this evening's dinner."

"As am I," Elizabeth admitted with an anxious smile. "I've heard rumours that the Duke of Edingdale's son is quite handsome."

"As if you have not met many handsome men already," Cassandra could not help but interject.

"Yes, but he has been the talk of all of London, Cassie," Elizabeth expressed, her voice growing high. "Nearly everyone was talking about him last night as well. And all the ladies I met with last night hope to snare him as a husband."

"That isn't anything you need to concern yourself about, my dear," Viola said as she reached across to lay a hand on top of Elizabeth's. "You are the Season's Diamond, after all. He would be lucky to have you."

Elizabeth bit her lip. Cassandra watched as her sister forced a smile onto her face before it faded. Unable to resist the curiosity nagging at her, she asked, "Do you even know the name of this handsome and sought-after gentleman?"

Elizabeth shook her head. "I do not know his name, but I was told his title. He is the Marquess of Charlington."

The world spun, the chair disappearing from beneath her. Cassandra felt as if those words had driven two stakes through her heart and it took all her strength to keep from showing her reaction. She steadied her breathing, focusing on eating, not hearing what her mother said in response. But it felt as if her soul had left her body, painfully drifting away from where she sat.

"Cassie?" Elizabeth laid a hand on her arm, drawing her out of her reverie. "Are you all right?"

"I'm fine," Cassandra whispered, even though she felt anything but. Her sister had just casually mentioned the name of the man she'd felt a connection with last night. The same man their father had made quite clear he wished Elizabeth to be married to.

*If only the earth could open up and swallow me right now.*

The thought of seeing him again—of him seeing her—was enough to make her palms sweat. Despite what she'd said, Elizabeth's frown deepened, clearly not believing that she was fine.

"Believe me," Cassandra said, plastering a smile on her face and then deciding against it when she couldn't manage anything better than a grimace. "I just feel a bit dizzy, that's all. I could not sleep last night."

"Is something bothering you?" Elizabeth asked, worriedly.

"Nothing important," Cassandra lied. How could she explain to her that she'd spent half the night daydreaming about the marquess only to face the cruel reality that they would never be together? It was one thing to let her own insecurity get the best of her, but to hear it from someone else? It felt like her heart was being ripped out of her chest.

Elizabeth stared at her with a frown on her face, clearly not believing what she was saying. Before she could get the chance to question her further, Cassandra stood. "I think I might go for a wa—"

"Good day, my wonderful family!" a voice boomed as the door swung open and Ethan strolled into the drawing room.

Cassandra was thankfully saved from having to explain herself as her sister leaped from her chair, throwing her arms around Ethan with an ear-piercing squeal. Viola was next, a broad grin on her face as she joined in on the hug. Only their father remained seated, but his eyes were filled with pleasure as he turned and regarded his son.

"Have you returned home without sending us a single word?" Gilbert questioned.

"You should blame Cassie," Ethan said with a mischievous grin. "She knew I was here from last night and failed to tell you all."

As all eyes fell on Cassandra, she shrugged. "It was not my secret to tell. He surprised me too by showing up at last night's ball. I thought he would have informed you all as well."

"Oh, Ethan, you've always preferred Cassie more, haven't you?" Elizabeth whined, slapping him lightly on the arm.

Ethan let out a hearty laugh. "Of course not. I only knew she would keep my secret, which meant I would get the chance to show up like this and surprise all of you again."

"Why don't you tell them how long you've been in London, Ethan?" Cassandra said as she sank into her seat once more with a slight breath of relief. Ethan's appearance helped to distract her from her thoughts and she fully intended on taking advantage of it.

Ethan rubbed the back of his head sheepishly. "Three nights ago."

"Three nights?" Viola gasped. "Oh my, do you hate us?"

They all laughed at that, save for Cassandra though she managed to fake a smile.

"You know how he is, Viola," Gilbert said. "I don't think he's ever going to outgrow his need to play pranks."

Ethan heartily agreed and pulled a chair up to sit between Cassandra and Viola. Cassandra resumed her eating as the rest of breakfast was filled with questions about Ethan's trip and what he intended on doing in London while he stayed.

By the time Cassandra began to relax, her brother rose once more saying, "I'm afraid I must take my leave."

Elizabeth pouted. "So soon?"

"Yes, and not just from here but London overall. I have an urgent business matter that I must leave for tomorrow."

"When will you be back?" Cassandra asked. Despite all her internal torment, she did not want to see her brother go so soon.

"I'm not sure." He planted a kiss on all their cheeks, except for Gilbert to whom he only offered a hearty handshake. "But I shall be back before you know it."

"Let me walk you to your carriage," Cassandra offered, quickly getting to her feet. Before anyone could say anything else, she linked her arm through her brother's and they left the drawing room together.

"Something is bothering you," Ethan said once they reached the foyer. He stopped her, making her look at him.

She didn't bother to hold back the truth. "Yes, you're right. But I won't allow it to bother me for long, I promise."

Ethan searched her face, as if looking for a sign that what she said was true. Then he nodded, clearly satisfied. Cassandra knew he wouldn't pry but would be willing to listen when she was ready to talk.

"I trust that you will," Ethan told her, then he pressed a kiss on her forehead. "Take care of them."

"I always do."

Ethan grinned and walked away, slipping through the door. Cassandra didn't bother to follow him all the way to the carriage. As soon as he was out of sight, she turned and made her way up the grand staircase behind her, intending to go straight to the library. She would bury her nose in a book—anything other than Shakespeare or history—and pray that by the time dinner time rolled around, she was prepared to meet the duke and his family.

She wouldn't allow herself to act so foolishly when they arrived. Cassandra would make sure to meet the duke and his family with grace.

And the son who had stolen her heart and had unknowingly broken it at the same time.

# Chapter Twelve

Jacob shifted uncomfortably in his chair, crossing one leg over the other. He reached absently for his cup of coffee and, after taking a sip, realized that he'd let yet another go cold before he had the chance to enjoy it. With a sigh, he set it on the table before him and tried to concentrate on *The Times* in his hands.

In Bath, he would often read the newspaper in his office in the early hours of the day, before he'd even had the chance to have breakfast. In London, he spent his days at Brown's Gentleman Club to do the same. And though he had fallen into the same practice now that he had returned, Jacob quickly realized that he would not be able to fully indulge in his morning routine today.

All because of the lady in gold.

He let out a frustrated groan, folding the newspaper and slapping it down on the table. A full hour had been wasted trying to concentrate on what he had been reading and failing. The words constantly floated off the page, drifting before his vision until they merged into the captivating blue eyes of the lady who had captured his heart last night. The mere memory of her had his heart thudding in his chest, his stomach filled with bashing butterflies when he remembered the way she had smiled at him.

The ball had been a success, all because of her. All because of those too few minutes he'd spent in her company. Jacob recalled how flustered he'd become when she fixed her direct gaze on him, as if she could see straight through to his soul. It had taken all his strength to keep from stumbling over his words as he tried to keep her engaged, to learn as much about her as possible. Though he didn't know how well he'd managed that. All he'd done was shower her with compliments, regaling at the beauty he'd felt shining in her eyes, and the night had ended without knowing enough about her.

Why had she refused to reveal her true identity?

That was what confounded him the most. Jacob could not understand it. He thought of the flash of fear that had shone in her eyes right before she'd turned and disappeared among the sea of guests. With the way he felt now, Jacob wondered if she had taken a piece of him with her when she'd fled. And he still could not understand why she'd done it.

*Perhaps there is a secret she did not wish to reveal*, he mused, once again reaching for the coffee and scowling when the cold liquid coated his tongue. He quickly forgot his disgust as he thought of the reasons why she did not want to reveal who she was. She hadn't even told him her name.

He was probably better off forgetting about her, he thought. It was only one night and a too-brief dance. It didn't matter that he'd laid awake that night thinking about her, pouring over every second of their interaction. The way she'd felt in his arms, how she'd smiled at him, the amusement in her voice. The glint in her eyes and the way she'd spoken to him as if she'd known and loved him forever.

That was why he couldn't get her out of his head, Jacob realized with a sigh. She hadn't just captured his interest. It felt as if she'd snared his heart as well.

"I cannot tell when last I've come in here to see you scowling in your corner as if you have the world on your shoulders."

Jacob raised his brows at the familiar voice as a figure sank into the chair across from him. A smile stretched across his face as he took in the person before him. "And I can't say I missed hearing you comment on the way I do things."

"How can I not?" Simon Bancroft grinned, crossing his arms as he leaned back in his chair. "You're an interesting specimen to observe."

"You need to find a hobby."

"I have many and this just happens to be one of them." Simon paused as a server came over to bring two cups of coffee, taking away Jacob's cold one. Jacob gave Simon a nod of gratitude, knowing that he was responsible for it. Simon was one of the few people who truly knew Jacob, though they had not been in touch for a few years now. Ever since Simon lost his father and assumed the title of Viscount of Bancroft, his responsibilities had left little time to spare for friends, which Jacob completely understood. He had his own load to bear and he hadn't even inherited the dukedom yet.

"When did you come back to London?" Simon asked

"It hasn't been more than a few days, I believe."

"You believe?" Simon questioned, raising a brow.

Jacob shrugged as he sipped the coffee, letting the warmth spread throughout his body. "I've lost track of time since being here. I forgot just how intense the London Season can be."

"Ah, especially for the young and the marriageable."

Jacob tried not to wince at the reminder. He had been trying to forget about his father's wishes and Lady Elizabeth, especially since they would be dining with Lord Wiswall and his family this evening. Simon grinned as if he knew exactly what Jacob was thinking.

"Don't remind me," Jacob groaned. "To be honest I wish I could go back to Bath."

"Is it time for you to settle down already?" Simon probed.

"According to my father. He also seems to think that he is more adept at finding a wife for me than I would be for myself."

"Perhaps he sees something that you do not," Simon said with a shrug but Jacob scoffed.

"He isn't thinking about me. He is only thinking about the dukedom." Jacob heard the bitterness in his tone and took another gulp of his coffee, as if that would chase it away. "But enough about me. How have you been, Lord Bancroft?"

Simon smiled ruefully at the title. "As stressful as you can no doubt imagine, Lord Charlington. Sometimes, I wish I could go back to the days when the only thing I had to worry about was whether I would be waking with a megrim after a night of drinking."

"Ah, your father must be so proud to see the new leaf you have turned over."

Simon rolled his eyes, amusement dancing within them at Jacob's droll tone. "I could have easily succumbed to the lure of whiskey given all the stress this position causes me. And Adeline does not make it any better."

Jacob chuckled. "And how is your sister?"

"Infuriating as always."

"I take it she is not married yet?"

"My lovely sister was committed to enjoying her first Season as much as she could, courting as many men as possible and enjoying every event that took place. And now that she is in her second Season, I thought she would be more dedicated to finding the right match. But, yet again, it seems as if she only wants to have fun."

"I wonder where she gets that from."

Simon sighed, finishing the rest of his coffee and setting it down with a *thunk*. "Men play by different rules and she knows that. Another year and she will lose her chance to get married." A glint appeared in his eyes. "Perhaps you wouldn't mind…"

Jacob was quick to shut down the pending suggestion. "I adore your sister, Simon, but I do not think we would be a good fit as a married couple. We would clash far too often."

"Excuses, excuses," Simon complained. But he didn't press the issue any further. Jacob recalled meeting Simon when they had studied together in Eton. Simon had gushed about his younger sister and had spent half a term trying to convince Jacob that they should meet, and later court. Jacob marveled at the fact that, after all these years, Simon was still trying to play matchmaker.

"So," Simon continued. "Why were you glaring at the table as if the entire world was on your shoulders?"

Jacob contemplated revealing his thoughts to Simon. But what would he say? That he had caught sight of a lady in gold at last night's ball, and the mere thought of her had followed him all throughout the night? That he'd finally been given the chance to dance with her and it felt as if everything was right in the world, as if everything in his life had been building for this moment? That it felt as if he'd given her a piece of his heart and she'd stolen it away into the night without so much as a word?

It would sound ridiculous. Even Simon, who had always been the friend up for all manner of shenanigans, would not understand it.

So he shook his head saying, "I'm afraid I will have to meet the lady my father wishes for me to marry soon and I am not looking forward to it."

"Do you know if she is pretty at least?"

Jacob shrugged. "I hear that she is one of the most beautiful ladies in London."

"Then I do not know why you are complaining." Simon grinned, getting to his feet. He clapped a heavy hand on Jacob's shoulder. "You don't know how lucky you are, my friend, to find one of the few lovely ladies this town possesses."

*You have no idea*, Jacob thought, thinking about the lady in gold.

Simon fished a watch from his pocket and scowled at the time. "I have to go now. A meeting," he explained.

"I should take my leave too," Jacob said as he stood. But he had no plans, nothing to occupy his time while he waited for the dreaded dinner with Lord Wiswall and his family.

The memory of those piercing blue eyes danced around his mind and Jacob was suddenly hit with the urge to indulge, to torture himself once more with the thought of last night.

They said their goodbyes, leaving the club. Jacob stood and watched as Simon climbed into his carriage, not turning to his own until it was well on its way. He got in after informing the coachman that he wished to go for a long ride through Hyde Park. He could enjoy the fresh air and idly observe others. And let his mind wander.

And the moment they set off, those blue eyes found him again. This time, they did not let him out of their grasp.

## Chapter Thirteen

Cassandra kept her eyes fixed on the pages of her novel—a sordid tale about a young king—and tried her hardest to focus on the words. But no matter how hard she tried, they danced in her vision, her mind wandering to the very things she was trying her hardest to forget. She'd been sitting here for the past few minutes willing herself to focus, but no matter what she did, the only thing Cassandra could think about were those perfect hazel eyes.

With a groan of frustration, she shut the book and threw it atop her vanity table, watching it slide across the surface. Sally's hands stilled in her hair. A moment later, her lady's maid asked, "Are you all right, milady?"

Cassandra heaved a great sigh. "The truth is Sally, I am not. But I'm afraid that if I try to explain why I am feeling like this, you will find me insane."

"I would never, milady!" Abandoning the task of styling her hair, Sally came to stand in front of Cassandra, her brows pinched together in worry. "What is the matter? Are you feeling unwell?"

"My body is fine. It is my heart that is the matter."

Now that frown morphed into confusion. "What do you mean?"

Cassandra parted her lips, ready to explain. But something held her back: a mixture of fear and embarrassment. She couldn't tell Sally what she was really feeling. No one would understand. Surely, Cassandra didn't even understand it herself. From the moment she found out who would be joining them for dinner, the only thing she could think about was how unlucky she must be. Not only would she be forced to watch the marquess flirt with her sister—because which man wouldn't?—but she had to pretend that she felt nothing for him. That last night had not filled her with painful hope and made her feel things Cassandra had never felt before.

*At least he will not know that it was me. I can carry that secret to the end. All I need to do is ensure that I do not make a fool of myself.*

Suddenly, Cassandra remembered that Sally was watching her, waiting for a response. She shifted her eyes to the book she'd thrown down. "It's..." Cassandra snatched it up, waving it quickly so that Sally couldn't focus on the title. Though she doubted her lady's maid would have read it. "This book. It is so infuriating that I cannot read it anymore."

"The book?" Sally asked bemusedly, looking at the book as if she couldn't figure out what it was.

"Yes, the main character, he—" Cassandra broke off dramatically, shaking her head as if she couldn't finish the thought. "I cannot even say it or it's just going to upset me further."

"Oh." Slowly, Sally drifted back behind her and Cassandra let out a silent breath of relief. "Is that why you have been staying in your room all day?"

*No, I only wanted solitude to lament my foolish emotions and mentally prepare for the evening ahead of me. Though I doubt it did me any good.*

"Yes," Cassandra lied just as Sally resumed styling her hair. She felt a pinch of guilt for being so deceptive. But what other choice did she have? She needed more time to come to terms with how foolish she'd been, to have fallen under the spell of the marquess.

"I see." The small silence that followed betrayed Sally's lingering confusion.

Before Cassandra could say anything to fill the quiet, there was a knock on her door. Sally's movements grew a little more urgent as Cassandra called, "Come."

She'd expected Elizabeth to slip in. They would often get ready together whenever they had dinner with guests to look forward to. But it was Viola who entered her room, already dressed.

"Mother?" Cassandra frowned. "To what do I owe the pleasure?"

"I only came to see my beautiful daughter," Viola said, drifting towards hers.

"Elizabeth's room is down the hallway," Cassandra said, her tone slightly amused. But judging by the slight scowl pinching her mother's brows, Viola did not find her joke funny.

"Both my daughters are beautiful," Viola pressed. "But it is you I wanted to see. I wanted to make sure that you were all right."

"I am quite fine, Mother. Thank you."

Still, Viola came closer. Cassandra eyed her, sensing that there was another reason for her mother's visit. She didn't ask about it, waiting instead.

Finally, Viola asked, "Do you intend on wearing your veil this evening?"

Cassandra frowned at her. "Of course I am. If I don't, the Duke of Edingdale and his family will see my scar."

"Perhaps that is not a bad thing."

"Not a bad thing?" Cassandra echoed, her tone incredulous. "Mother, you and I both know I can never show my face like this."

Viola began to wander back and forth, a clear indication that she was uncomfortable. Cassandra was having a hard time keeping her eyes on her, seeing that Sally was still curling her hair.

"Your father and I have been talking," Viola told her. "And we believe that it may be seen as odd and rather rude if you were to wear your veil during dinner. Perhaps you can wear it before and after, but not while we dine."

"Mother!"

"It was not a suggestion, my dear," Viola continued, her tone soft yet unyielding at the same time.

Cassandra bit on the inside of her mouth, resisting the urge to argue. The thought of revealing her scarred face to strangers made her stomach twist with fear. It didn't matter that most of the scar stretched under her chin and only touched the edge of her left cheek. The imperfection had been enough to slice a dozen more wounds into her self-esteem.

She shoved down the unease and nodded. She'd promised herself that she would keep her composure tonight, starting with this. "Very well."

Viola paused to look at her in surprise. "Good," she said slowly. "I'm happy that we can all agree. The guests will be here shortly so I hope that you will be done soon."

That only made Sally move faster. Cassandra gave her a small nod, staring unblinkingly into the mirror of the vanity table. She listened to her mother's departure, her mind whirling.

Lord Charlington was going to see her face. The only thing that made Cassandra feel better was that he wouldn't know that she was the lady in gold. She hoped.

***

Sally had outdone herself. The back of Cassandra's hair fell down her back in tight ringlets, the rest pinned to the top of her head. A spread of pearls had been woven into the hold, which matched the cream-colored dinner gown Cassandra had chosen to wear. The cupped sleeves and the low neckline kept the dress fashionable, and would have kept her from standing out had it not been for the cream veil covering her face. Eyes were always drawn to her when she wore one, but they could never see what was underneath. And that was what mattered.

Her heart raced as she made her way to the parlor where her family waited. She knew that the Duke and Duchess of Edingdale hadn't arrived as yet, which gave her enough time to prepare for them. Or, more accurately, the Marquess of Charlington. Try as she might, Cassandra could not come to terms with the fact that she would have to reveal her scarred face to such a handsome man.

"Ah, she has finally arrived!"

Cassandra felt a rush of relief when she entered the parlor to see her parents sitting with Simon and Adeline. The latter sat to the right of her brother, a small smile on her lips. She was the spitting image of her brother, with sandy hair she'd opted to wear in a chignon and dancing green eyes. They would often join Cassandra and her family for dinner, so Cassandra wasn't entirely surprised to see them there. They would certainly make this dinner a little easier to handle.

"Were you all waiting for me?" Cassandra asked as she came closer. Because she was among people she trusted, she lifted her veil.

"Of course we were," Simon said with a grin. "And now we only need to wait for your sister. Who is late, as usual."

"The dinner has not even begun as yet," Adeline argued, rolling her eyes good-naturedly.

"But this is mingling time and she is late," Simon pressed. He gave Cassandra a grin and patted the chair next to him. "I reserved this seat for you."

"Oh, how nice of you," Cassandra drawled as she returned his grin. "Don't mind the fact that this is my house."

Gilbert grunted at that and the others laughed, including Viola though she hadn't let her eyes off Cassandra since she'd walked in. Cassandra wondered if her mother was looking for kinks in the armor she always wore. Cassandra ignored her, not wanting to face her quiet question.

Just as she sank into the sofa next to Simon, Elizabeth strolled in—and stopped short when her eyes landed on Simon.

Silence descended on the room as the two of them stared at each other while everyone else watched them.

"Hello," Elizabeth breathed at last.

Simon tipped his head into a small nod, his throat bobbing. "Elizabeth...you look lovely."

A blush stained Elizabeth's cheeks and her eyes fell to the floor. "Thank you. You look handsome yourself." And then she hurried away, sitting next to Viola.

Cassandra exchanged a look with Adeline. Simon's sister was as privy to Simon's infatuation with Elizabeth as Cassandra was. But unlike Cassandra, Adeline had no qualms with pressing him about it. Not that she would do so around others, of course. And certainly not when Elizabeth was nearby.

To diffuse the tension hanging in the air, Adeline turned to Elizabeth and asked, "So, Elizabeth, how have you been enjoying the Season so far?"

"It is wonderful, of course," Elizabeth gushed. "I am having such a grand time. And I've already made so many friends!"

"Potential suitors, you mean," Adeline probed and Simon shifted uncomfortably.

"Well, if I do not court them, certainly they would be content to remain as friends."

Adeline laughed, shaking her head. "You would be surprised just how wrong you are, Elizabeth. There was a kind gentleman I entertained for a while but when he asked to court me, I told him no. He was not so kind anymore."

"Are you referring to the same gentleman who sent flowers nearly every hour after your rejection and would wander outside our gate hoping to glimpse you?" Simon asked.

Adeline shrugged, but her eyes were filled with wicked amusement. "Perhaps."

"Oh, dear, I did hear that you were the diamond of the last Season," Viola cut in. "I am actually surprised that you are not already married. Why is that so?"

"I am not ready," Adeline said at the same time Simon said, "She wishes to drive me insane."

There was a beat of silence before everyone laughed. What was left of that uncomfortable tension following Elizabeth's entrance dissipated altogether.

"For some reason, Adeline," Cassandra spoke up, "I am more inclined to believe Simon."

"Well, I cannot say that he is entirely wrong," Adeline admitted.

"Please, Adeline," Simon cut in. "Tell them all about Lord Harding, who wrote you an entire publication of his horrible poems to express his love for you."

Adeline laughed, shaking her head. Yet she indulged her brother and told tale after tale of the many gentlemen who'd longed for her hand and had failed. Time passed with ease and by the time the butler came to announce the arrival of the duke and his family, Cassandra had almost completely forgotten what was ahead of her.

Almost.

Now it was all she could think about. The conversation drifted to nothing as they all awaited the arrival of the guests. Cassandra was half-afraid that they could all hear the pound of her heart, her eyes fixed on the door.

The butler entered once more, sweeping a hand towards the room as he indicated to whomever was behind him to go by. The duke appeared first, a tall gentleman that still looked rather handsome despite his age. A step behind him was the Duchess of Edingdale, a small smile on her face as we all rose to greet them. Cassandra's eyes went over her shoulder, her breath stuck in her throat as she waited.

And then he appeared, his jaw tight and his shoulders rigid. Yet it was him. The gentleman from last night. Their eyes met. And for a moment, Cassandra was certain he knew who she was.

## Chapter Fourteen

"Good evening, my lord and ladies," Henry greeted with a sharp bow. "Thank you for having us. I hope we did not make you wait too long?"

"Certainly not, Your Grace." The Earl of Wiswall rose, sticking out a hand and seizing Henry's. Jacob studied the earl. He was a head shorter than both him and his father, but stood with his shoulders back and his chin jutted out.

The Countess of Wiswall rose, draping herself on her husband's side as she gave Henry and Maria polite smiles and a small curtsy. "It is a pleasure, Your Graces. I trust the ride here was enjoyable?"

"Short but pleasurable," Jacob's mother responded kindly, wearing a smile of her own. Jacob kept to the back of them, having no wish to join in to the tight pleasantries. He wished he was anywhere but here—preferably with the lady who had weighed on his mind all day in his arms.

His parents continued to exchange polite conversation with the Earl and Countess of Wiswall until there was nothing left to be said and the other persons in the room had to be acknowledged. Only then did Jacob step forward, unable to force a smile onto his face but managing to keep his voice polite as he said, "It is a pleasure to meet you both, Lord and Lady Wiswall."

He bowed and when he lifted his head to look at them, husband and wife stood staring at him with broad smiles.

The earl spoke first, gesturing behind him. As soon as he did, two ladies came forward, heads bowed to the floor as they sank into deep curtsies at the same time. "Please meet my daughters," the earl began. "Lady Cassandra and Lady Elizabeth."

Lady Elizabeth lifted her head, a bright smile on her face. She was indeed as beautiful as everyone had said, her strawberry-blond hair curled delicately around her face. Her blue eyes shone with intrigue as she held out her hand expectantly. "It is a pleasure, my lord," she breathed, her voice musical.

Jacob moved only because he had to, only because he knew others were watching him and were silently placing their expectations. He grasped her hand, placing a kiss on the back of it. "The pleasure is mine, my lady," he murmured and left it at that. What else was there to say to her?

Lady Elizabeth was indeed beautiful but the sight of her did not chase away the image of the lady in gold. Pushing his disappointment aside, turning to greet the other sister, Lady Cassandra. The affable acknowledgement died on his tongue the moment he met the stormy blue of her eyes. They were slightly darker than her sisters, shining intensely beneath the thin layer of fabric that covered her face. She did not say anything as she stared at him, nor did she extend her hand. The seconds seemed to stretch on forever as they stared at each other, something nagging at the back of his mind. She seemed so familiar yet as he studied her, Jacob couldn't fathom from where.

"My lady," he managed to say after a long moment, remembering his manners. He bowed and held out his hand, expecting her to place her hand in his.

She did so only after a moment, as if she hadn't wanted to. "My lord," she murmured, her voice so soft that he nearly didn't hear her.

Jacob pressed a kiss on the back of her hand, unable to stop himself from glancing back up at her. Beneath the cream-colored layer of the veil she wore, he could have sworn he saw a blush staining her cheeks.

He didn't realize that he was still holding her hand until she jerked it out of his grasp. Jacob straightened, clearing his throat. He suddenly remembered what his father had said in the carriage on the way here, that the Earl of Wiswall had one daughter as beautiful as an angel and one that was horribly scarred. He found himself staring at her again but he could not see the scar his father had spoken of under the veil.

"Well, this is quite the coincidence, isn't it?" came a familiar voice.

Jacob pulled his eyes away from Lady Cassandra, a grin tugging at his lips as he watched Simon approach from behind.

"Are you following me?" Jacob asked, narrowing his eyes playfully.

Simon rolled his. "You wish. I happen to be quite close to the Earl and Countess of Wisall and I am treated like a son by this family."

"Now who is the one wishing?" said Adeline as she came to her brother's side. She offered Jacob a warm smile. "Hello, Lord Charlington. It has been a while."

"It certainly has been, Lady Adeline," Jacob agreed. "And you look as beautiful as the last time I saw you."

Adeline didn't blush at the compliment. She only gave him a small nod of thanks. Clearly that was something she was used to hearing.

"Do you already know each other?" Lord Wiswall questioned.

"We met during our studies in Eton," Simon explained. "And I suppose though we did not keep in touch after my father died, poor Lord Charlington has always been a little obsessed with me."

"No one will believe that for a second," Jacob stated confidently and grinned as Adeline nodded at his side.

"Then this night should be even more delightful!" Lady Wiswall said excitedly. "Come now, we should all make our way to the dining room."

She ushered everyone out. Jacob opted to stay back so that he could walk by Simon's side, mostly because he did not want to be shackled to Lady Elizabeth. She walked ahead with her sister, who slowly took her veil off as they neared the dining room. Jacob stared at Lady Cassandra from behind but he wasn't able to glimpse her face—nor the scar—before she passed the veil on to the butler and slipped into the dining room.

The moment they entered the dining room, Lord Wiswall gestured for Jacob to sit between his mother and Lady Elizabeth, Henry seated between Maria and the earl. On the other side of the earl sat his wife, with Simon next to the countess. Jacob couldn't help staring at Lady Cassandra as she settled in between Simon and Adeline, her head still bowed, shifting about in her chair. He could tell that she felt uncomfortable under the weight of his gaze and so Jacob tore it away, silently cursing himself for his rudeness. No doubt, with the scar she was rumored to have, she must abhor having eyes on her for long.

But with her head still bowed, even as the first course was being served, Jacob couldn't help it that his eyes were constantly brought back to her.

"Have you been in London long, Lord Charlington?" asked Adeline, starting the conversation.

Jacob tore his eyes away from Lady Cassandra, hoping that no one caught him staring. "Only a few days," he said.

"And are you happy to be back? Or do you much prefer the quietude of Bath?"

"I think you've answered your own question with that," Jacob said ruefully and made them chuckle. "I am happy to have returned to London though. It is nice to meet with old friends again, Simon included—"

"Aw, I'm touched," Simon cut in, putting a hand to his heart.

Jacob grinned "—but I will have to admit that I prefer the slow paced atmosphere of Bath to the hustle of London, especially during the Season."

"Truly?" Lady Wiswall spoke up. "I do not think I could get enough to the Season activities."

"Neither do I," Maria agreed and the two ladies shared a smile. Jacob could easily see them striking up a fast friendship. "And my, have the events started quite spectacularly. Lady Hanesbridge's masquerade ball was a hit!"

"Were you in attendance, my lady?" Henry asked Lady Wiswall, then shook his head. "Oh, what am I asking? Of course you were. You are Lady Hanebridge's sister, aren't you?"

"Even if I weren't I would have made sure to be there," the countess answered. "She always throws the best balls, you know."

Jacob resisted the urge to sigh. He didn't want to talk about the Season and was already regretting bringing it up at all. The last thing he needed was a reminder of the lady who had slipped out of his grasp like a plume of smoke.

"Are you enjoying the meal, my lord?" Lady Elizabeth spoke up by his side.

"I am," he said simply.

"That's good. I hope the evening's weather is as fair as it had been earlier today. The meal will certainly settle better that way."

"I'm sure it will." He wasn't in the mood for conversation, and certainly not with Lady Elizabeth. But he supposed he should at least *try* to talk to her. She did seem like a nice lady. "Do you read, my lady?"

"I do, now and again. Though not often, as of late."

"Then what do you do to pass the time?"

"I spend time with friends," she answered. "I also enjoy shopping."

This conversation was going downhill fast. They had nothing in common. Jacob could hardly muster up the strength to give her a response better than 'Oh'.

"What about you, my lord?" Lady Elizabeth asked when the silence stretched on a beat too long.

"I like to read. And I spend much of my time outdoors."

"Doing what?"

"All manners of things," he answered noncommittally. "Riding and hunting, mostly. But my greatest hobby is found in the library."

"Ah, I see." There was a slight pause before Lady Elizabeth said, "You are just like my sister."

At that, Jacob shifted his eyes to Lady Cassandra once more. She'd lifted her head a little, as if satisfied that no one would be looking her away. Indeed everyone else was so engrossed in conversation about the Season that they paid her no mind. And that seemed to be the way she preferred it, her shoulders a little more relaxed than they had been a short while ago.

Doubtlessly, she was beautiful. Jacob could not take his eyes off her. The elegant sweep of curls tumbling down her back seemed to shine under the chandelier above, her small jaw moving slowly as she chewed. Her posture was upright, her deep blue eyes focused on her meal, completely oblivious to Jacob's staring. He couldn't help running his eyes all over her face, noting the faint splash of freckles around her eyes and her slightly upturned nose. How could anyone look at this lady and think her anything but beautiful?

As if she finally felt the weight of his stare, she glanced up. The moment their eyes met, Lady Cassandra shrank into herself once more, lowering her head completely. But not before he'd caught a glimpse of the scar his father had spoken about. It was indeed long, a dark stain stretching beneath her chin and reaching over her left cheek. Yet it did not hide the beauty shining back at him. As a matter of fact, Jacob was having a hard time catching his breath, his heart racing in his chest.

His spoon fell out of his grasp and it clanked against his bowl. The sound had the conversation stalling as all eyes fell on Jacob.

"Pardon me," he murmured, a little flustered by how much this lady was affecting him. He could still feel her eyes on him but he didn't dare look up yet.

"Is everything all right, my lord?" Lady Elizabeth whispered to him as everyone else slowly went back to the topic of the Season.

"Yes, please don't mind me," he said softly. "I only grew distracted, that's all."

It was a pitiful excuse, he knew. And judging by the soft *hm* Lady Elizabeth gave him, she thought so as well. But he didn't bother to say anything more, waiting another few seconds before he finally gave in and looked back at Lady Cassandra.

Their eyes met once more and she quickly looked away, a blush covering her cheeks. Once again, Jacob was struck by how familiar those eyes were, how they stirred something in him. *Perhaps I'd seen her in passing once before*, he thought.

Even so, something told him that there was certainly more to Lady Cassandra than what met the eye.

## Chapter Fifteen

Cassandra wished she could just disappear altogether. She could still feel Lord Charlington's eyes burning through her, even though she didn't dare to check if he was still staring. One time had been enough for her to feel like coming to dinner had been a bad idea.

They were only at the third course. Cassandra poked at her roasted meat, barely able to muster up her appetite. She'd picked at her food from the moment she noticed Lord Charlington staring at her and she knew she would suffer from hunger pains later this evening. Even so, she could not help but entertain the thought of feigning illness and departing the dinner table early. She could deal with her parents afterward. This evening was really for Elizabeth's sake, after all.

"What's the matter, Cassie?"

Cassandra shook her head at Simon's quiet question. He nudged her in her side when she failed to answer him in time. "Nothing."

"Then why are you pouting over your meal?"

"I'm not pouting," Cassandra said as her bottom lip jutted out a little further. Realizing this, she bit it, shaking her head once more. "I am only feeling a little unwell, that's all."

"Is it the present company that ails you so?" he asked, a note of amusement in his voice. "I know Lord Charlington is not nearly as nice to look at as I am but surely it should not be enough to turn your stomach?"

Despite herself, Cassandra laughed under her breath. The duke and duchess were still engaged in conversation with her parents, Adeline joining now and again, and Cassandra had been more than content to pass the entire evening in silence. Simon's words were enough to brighten her mood just a bit, though she did not quite believe it.

Simon was handsome in his own right, but Lord Charlington...

It should be a crime to look that handsome. His voice was as deep as she remembered it, rumbling through her body and setting her heart on fire. She forced a forkful of meat in her mouth to distract herself from looking back up at him. She'd been doing a good job ignoring him as best as she could thus far.

"How did you two met?" Cassandra asked, unable to stop herself from inquiring about the marquess.

"Well, as I said before, we met while we studied in Eton. But, believe it or not, we did not get along very well at first."

"I can believe that," Cassandra said instantly.

"Truly? Why?"

"Because you are quite difficult to deal with, of course," she said simply and laughed again when Simon shook his head in betrayal. "I jest, I jest. But I'm sure you would have tried to befriend him by making a joke that only earned you a scowl and silence. Am I right?"

"Any joke I make ends in boundless laughter, Cassie. You do not give me enough credit." Cassandra raised a brow at him and he grinned, scratching the back of his head. "But yes, Lord Charlington liked to pretend as if he was austere, as if he had not smiled since he was a child."

Cassandra didn't dare to look at the marquess, even though her eyes burned with the urge to. "How did you get through to him?"

"It only took one good laugh for us to become fast friends. And once we both joined the rowing team, it was history."

"You two do seem close," Cassandra observed. "Especially seeing that you have not spoken in years and yet picked up where you left off as if no time at all had passed."

"Yes, he did write to me now and again when my father passed. I suppose it is really my fault we did not talk, though it clearly did not make a difference."

A giggle pulled at Cassandra's attention. She looked across the table to see Elizabeth laughing behind her hand at something Lord Charlington had said. Cassandra took in her sister's posture, how relaxed and engaged she was in whatever it was they were talking about. She leaned slightly to him and said something that Cassandra couldn't hear, making him chuckle.

Slowly, Cassandra fixed her eyes on the marquess. He didn't smile, but humor lit his eyes. Whatever they were talking about was clearly far more interesting than the ongoing conversation about the Season, lost in their small world.

Cassandra quickly looked away, trying to ignore the pang of jealousy that threatened to consume her.

"It seems as if Elizabeth is enjoying herself with Lord Charlington," Simon commented.

Cassandra heard the envy in his voice and resisted the urge to take his hand in comfort. "No one makes her laugh the way that you do," she told him and Simon gave her a wan smile before returning to his meal.

She was willing to let the silence sit for a while, that low hum of jealousy simmering still. Cassandra didn't dare to look back up at them, didn't dare to give in to the wishful thought that it should be her sitting next to the marquess like that. It would never be so. He'd seen her scarred face, had stared at her as if he couldn't believe his eyes. And with her beautiful sister by his side, it wouldn't take a genius to figure out who he would prefer to spend time with.

Cassandra tortured herself with that fact as she bided her time, waiting for the dinner to come to an end. When it was finally time for them to leave the dining room, however, she knew she would not have the solitude of her bedchamber just yet. Her mother began to lead the way to the drawing room while the men all lumbered after her father to the parlor. Only when she was settled in the drawing room next to Adeline did she let herself relax.

"Oh, dear, I thought we would never get away," Adeline sighed as she reclined in the chaise lounge with her legs propped up beside her. "I am so full I thought I would burst!"

"Goodness, you eat as much as a horse," Elizabeth commented with a giggle. She settled across from them in a plush armchair.

Adeline waved a dismissive hand. "Only because I am around people I know. Had it been anyone else I would have picked at my food the way Cassandra did. The way proper little ladies should."

"I wasn't picking at my food," Cassandra protested.

"You were," Adeline stated firmly and left it at that. Cassandra didn't bother to argue with her, especially seeing that she was right.

She felt Elizabeth's worried gaze on her but before Elizabeth got the chance to question her about it, Viola spoke up. "Lizzie, what do you think about the marquess?" she asked.

Elizabeth's eyes lit up and Cassandra quickly looked away. She didn't want to hear her sister's response so she fixed her attention on Adeline. "What plans do you have for the week?" she asked.

"Plans?" Adeline hummed in thought. "I haven't thought about it as yet. I was hoping to be called on by a lovely baron I met at last night's ball but I've decided not to see him."

"Why?"

Adeline smiled, shrugging. "He is not quite as handsome as I thought he was. I blame the mask he wore last night. I woke this morning realising that I would much rather spend my time alone."

"Oh, you are horrible," Cassandra declared with a laugh. "Please tell me you did not say that to his face."

"I wouldn't dare!" Cassandra only raised a brow at her and Adeline laughed. "Well, not unless he gives me a reason to."

"Well, that means you will be free tomorrow then, won't you? I'd like to get out of the house but I cannot think of what to do."

"Perhaps a picnic in Hyde Park, then?"

"Or would you rather we go to Egyptian Hall?" Cassandra offered and grinned when Adeline rolled her eyes.

"Why do you bother to ask if you already know what you want to do?"

"The illusion of choice?" Cassandra said by way of explanation and Adeline giggled.

"If you wish to be so democratic perhaps we should involve others in this decision then?" Before Cassandra could protest, Adeline spoke loudly to Elizabeth and Viola, cutting into the conversation they were having. "What would you all like to do tomorrow? Hyde Park or Egyptian Hall?"

"Those are our only two options?" Elizabeth asked and Cassandra let out a groan, knowing where this was going.

Just as she expected, the four of them delved into an oddly engaging conversation about all the things that could be done in London. And Cassandra found herself slowly relaxing, forgetting the fact that Lord Charlington was just a few doors away from her. Here, surrounded by the comforting presence of the ladies in her life, she could ignore the embarrassment tingling in the back of her mind at the fact that Lord Charlington had seen her scarred face. And she could pretend she didn't care that he'd clearly gotten along well with Elizabeth.

Above all, she could almost convince herself that everything she'd felt last night had been nothing but her own frazzled emotions. Nothing solid, nothing real, and certainly nothing that should cause this pinch of pain in her heart.

Unfortunately, Cassandra knew deep down that it would be a while before she truly believed it.

## Chapter Sixteen

"This is weird," Jacob spoke up, setting down his second glass of wine. After the dinner he'd just partaken in, he felt the insane urge to indulge in more than a few glasses.

"What is?" Simon asked, seated across from him. The viscount didn't bother looking up, the scowl on his face remaining. Jacob half-wondered if he was really paying attention at all.

"You're quiet," Jacob pointed out. "And you are never quiet."

That made Simon blink, looking up at him. They were seated in the center of the parlor, Henry and Lord Wiswall speaking in hushed tones behind them. Jacob didn't have to guess to know what they were talking about and the thought made him reach for his wine again.

Simon scratched the back of his head and the smile he fixed on his face didn't reach his eyes. "Oh, I was thinking about something, that's all."

"Business?" Jacob asked, because that was the only cause of stress he'd had in his life since lately. And since, as far as he knew, Simon was not being pressured to be married, he couldn't think of what else was bothering him.

Simon lifted the glass of whiskey he'd been nursing to his lips. "Something like that," he said after a sip. And then his eyes grew distant once more, whatever was bothering him clearly pushing to the forefront of his mind again.

Jacob didn't push him on it. He had his own share of confounding thoughts that occupied him, making it easy to slip into the silence. The dinner had been a little more pleasant than he'd expected. Lady Elizabeth was better company than he thought she would have been, even though their conversation had begun with mundane and uninteresting topics. After a while, he began to realize that she was quite excitable, gushing about small things like the tonight's meal to how often she wondered what it would be like to go on a hunting trip. She'd made an effort to talk about what *he* liked, rather than the other way around, which was quite unusual.

But the thought of her came and fled quickly. Lady Elizabeth was not who occupied his mind, despite having spent most of the night in her company. Lady Cassandra was the one he couldn't stop thinking about.

They'd barely said anything to each other all night. Yet he could not rid of the feeling that he knew her, that there was something about her he recognized. When he thought of how her deep blue eyes had locked onto his for those too-brief seconds, his heart quickened, his throat going dry. Jacob took another sip of his wine, unable to understand it.

He looked back at Simon, who had gone right back to his silent contemplation. "How do you know Lord Wiswall and his family?" Jacob asked. *Or better yet, how have you become such dear friends with his daughters?*

Simon sat up a bit straighter as he said, "My father was dear friends with Lord Wiswall. Whenever he came to visit, he would bring me and Adeline with him. I've known Cassie and Lizzie ever since I was a child."

*Cassie and Lizzie.* Jacob rubbed his fingers over his jaw, feeling oddly uncomfortable with the casual familiarity in Simon's voice.

He thought back on how relaxed Lady Cassandra had appeared when she spoke with Simon during dinner and could not help but say, "You truly do seem to be a part of the family."

"Well, I am basically the son they never had," Simon stated cockily, looking a lot like himself now. "Though for a while, Cassie seemed determined to prove that she could fill that role quite well herself."

"Oh, really?"

"She was quite fearsome as a child, I tell you," Simon continued. "Even I could not keep up, and I thought myself rather rambunctious in my youth. She wanted to do everything, go everywhere, and never seemed to run out of energy."

"Is that how she got her scar?" Jacob asked before he could stop himself.

Simon frowned at that, shaking his head. "It isn't my place to say," was all he said, clearly not intending to offer up any more information than that.

"I'm sorry," Jacob said, feeling a little guilty for talking about her scar at all. He couldn't imagine how frustrating it must be to be known for what others only deemed a flaw. "I didn't mean to pry."

"I understand why you would. Just a word of warning, though: try not to ask Cassie about it yourself. She has quite a bite and I'd hate to see you on the receiving end of her wrath…as funny as it would be."

That peaked his attention. Jacob felt as if he could sit here and talk about Lady Cassandra all night, if only to satisfy the need to know a little bit more about the lady behind the veil. But he didn't want Simon questioning him about it. So, instead he turned his focus on the other sister.

"And what of Lady Elizabeth? She does not strike me as the type easily angered."

"She isn't." Simon's smile slipped. He suddenly seemed quite interested in his drink. After downing it on one go, he rose and made his way to the sideboard.

Jacob opened his mouth to say more but was interrupted when Lord Wiswall clapped his hands. Jacob took in the broad grin on the earl's face. "Now that we've gotten a few drinks in us, why don't we begin a riveting game billiards?"

"Were you trying to get us drunk, my lord?" Simon asked as he sipped his second glass of whiskey.

"Only a little," Lord Wiswall stated, bold-faced. "It is always a little more entertaining when we are seeing double of each ball, you know."

Jacob couldn't help but grin at that as he stood and approached the billiards table.

"Would you like a glass of whiskey, my lord?" the earl asked him. "Brandy?"

"Wine is fine, thank you," Jacob said politely.

"Very well, then. Shall we?" Lord Wiswall gathered the balls, grinning unmercifully at the three of them as they crowded close to the table. "Prepare to go home as terrible losers, men!"

Jacob chuckled again. Lord Wiswall was clearly a little inebriated. And judging by the way Henry punched him playfully in the arm, some of his whiskey sloshing over his hand, his father was too.

"What do you say, Jacob?" his father said. "Shall we show these gentlemen how it's done?"

Before Jacob could answer, Simon spoke up, "Oh, are we teaming up then? If that's the case, then you two stand no chance against Lord Wiswall and I."

Jacob snorted. A wave of fierce competitiveness took hold of him as he nodded at his father. "Let's show them just how we Kingsley men do things, Father."

"That's what I like to hear!" Lord Wiswall boomed, eagerly setting the balls for the first play. And as they lost themselves in a riveting game that grew more intense as alcohol flowed freely between the four of them, Jacob forgot all about Lady Cassandra and her stormy blue eyes.

***

Jacob was far too inebriated to bid a proper goodbye when it was time to leave Wiswall Manor. So he stayed behind his parents, hands clasped behind him as his mother took care of the pleasant farewells. He didn't listen to anything, staring over all their heads and focusing his eyes on Lady Cassandra, who remained at the back.

She set herself apart from the others, once again wearing her veil. She had shifted slightly away from the others, as if she busied herself by staring idly at the painting next to her rather than pay attention to what was happening. It was the only reason Jacob felt bold enough to stare at her so. Though perhaps the five glasses of wine he'd consumed had something to do with it as well.

Before he knew it, Maria was seizing his arm, steering him out the door with Simon and Lady Adeline on his heels. Just as he was about to turn away, mumbling a hasty farewell to his hosts for the evening, Lady Cassandra turned her head his way. Jacob didn't know if her eyes watched him as he left but the idea that they might have been made his heart race.

He gave Simon a hearty hug as they parted ways, tipping his head at Lady Adeline who gave him a small smile. Then they went to their separate carriages, Jacob climbing into his behind his parents. He let out a long breath, closing his eyes and resting his head on the back of his seat. As the carriage rattled along, Jacob felt himself floating, pleasantly inebriated.

"Lord and Lady Wiswall are a lovely couple, don't you think?" said Maria. "And I have so much in common with Lady Wiswall! Perhaps I should plan to have her visit us for tea one day."

"Even more importantly," Henry answered. "It seemed you got along well with Lady Elizabeth, Jacob."

Jacob didn't bother to open his eyes. He'd known this conversation was going to happen but had hoped that his father would at least wait until they were both sober enough to think clearly. "She is a nice lady," was all he said, since that was the truth.

"Lord Wiswall is very keen on making a match between you and Lady Elizabeth," his father went on. "I think it would be in your best interest to consider courting her."

"Father…"

"Think about it," Henry continued before Jacob had a chance to protest. Jacob gritted his teeth, opening his eyes to look at his father. "An arranged marriage between the two of you will be very beneficial for both our families. Not to mention the fact that she has a substantial dowry."

Jacob slid his eyes out the window even though all he saw were moving shadows. "I shall think about it."

"I'm sure that when you do, you'll see that I am right about this. You are my only heir, Jacob. You know as well as I that this is your duty."

*It is my duty to force a marriage with a woman I do not love?* He was tempted to voice his argument but thought against it, especially since his father left it at that. At least his father was being reasonable, asking him to consider the idea rather than force the decision down his throat. Jacob was not foolish enough to assume that the latter would not happen sooner or later though.

Thankfully, no one said anything for the rest of the ride home. Jacob stumbled his way inside the manor, throwing a goodnight over his shoulder at his parents before he dragged himself to his bedchamber. His valet was waiting for him and helped him change into proper nightwear since he was far too sloshed to do it properly himself. All he wanted to do now was sleep. But once he was finally alone, the silence that hung over his head made his thoughts scream louder.

Slowly, using the moonlight shining through the window to guide him, Jacob made his way to his chest of drawers. He pulled out the top drawer and picked up the only thing he'd left inside—his grandmother's ring. He opened the small box, watching the bright ruby glint despite the limited lighting. Jacob sank onto the bed and pulled the covers over his legs, staring at it.

The sight of it brought his grandparents to mind. The love they shared was so all-consuming that it was felt by everyone around them. That was the kind of love Jacob wanted for himself, the kind that will make yearn to be by his wife's side at all times. He wanted to raise children who would one day wish to emulate their parents' decision to choose their hearts over all else, the way Jacob did with his grandparents. His parents had been lucky, falling in love with each other only after they had married. But Jacob was well aware that such things were not commonly found among the *ton*. He couldn't begin to assume that he would be as fortunate.

With a sigh, he set the ring down and sank further into the bed. Whatever decision he chose to make was one that would be done in the morning. For now, he would sleep and pretend he hadn't a care in the world.

When the morning came though, that sentiment was quickly dashed. As soon as his father sat down to have breakfast with Jacob and Maria, he asked, "Have you thought about it?"

Jacob nearly sighed. It was still too early in the day for this conversation but he supposed his father was feeling anxious about the decision he'd made.

"Not yet," he said noncommittally, not looking away from the newspaper in his hands.

Henry let out a grunt of frustration. "What else is there to think about, Jacob? All you need to do is court Lady Elizabeth. I do not see why this is so difficult for you to do."

"I do not want you to think that I have decided to marry her," Jacob stated honestly but his father's disapproving scowl deepened.

"You are thinking too deeply about this. Spend some time in her company and you shall see that she is the perfect lady for you to marry."

*How much time have you spent in her company to know this?* Jacob was tempted to ask but he was too tired to taunt his father. The truth was, Henry knew nothing about Lady Elizabeth, just like Jacob. But he supposed that *he* should at least try to get to know her. That way, he could make an informed decision about marrying her.

Jacob folded the newspaper, setting it aside. Both Henry and Maria looked at him as he rose. "Where are you going?" Maria asked him.

"To see Lady Elizabeth," Jacob said and he turned away, not needing to look back to know his father was grinning from ear to ear.

## Chapter Seventeen

Yet another sleepless night. Yet another morning waking up thinking about the Marquess of Charlington. At this point, Cassandra was starting to feel pathetic.

But she couldn't help it. She stared up at the ceiling, mulling over every single thing that happened last night. It was clear as day that Lord Charlington could never be hers and there was no use harboring hope about it. All she could hear was Elizabeth's giggling, the way she had leaned into Lord Charlington while she spoke despite the fact that it would not be deemed appropriate. Cassandra could not get the image out of her head even though it tortured her to think about it. She hadn't expected seeing Lord Charlington would affect her so deeply, would rub such strong salt into the wound that had been left exposed and bleeding after the masquerade ball.

*I should return to reality*, she thought sitting up with a sigh. Back to stuffing her nose in a book of Shakespeare where she could imagine she was one of the characters and forget her life. She didn't like pitying herself like this, but when the truth of her future stared her so blatantly in the face Cassandra couldn't stop herself. It would take all her strength not to mope about so that no one could question her.

And certainly not Elizabeth. She couldn't fathom telling her sister that she might have fallen in love with the gentleman Elizabeth would be meant to marry. Only after one night, one dance! It would sound outrageous.

Cassandra dragged herself out of bed and managed to plaster a pleasant expression on her face when Sally arrived to help her get dressed. She didn't want her lady's maid worrying about her or questioning her about last night. If Cassandra dared to open that dam, everything will come flooding out and she wasn't ready to face her true feelings just yet.

She got dressed in a simple yellow morning gown. If it weren't for the fact that Elizabeth would certainly come looking for her if she did not come down for breakfast, Cassandra would have forgotten about it altogether, locking herself in the library. It took a bit of her strength to drag herself downstairs and put that amiable mask back on her face before she entered the drawing room.

"Cassie!" Elizabeth squealed the moment Cassandra stepped past the threshold.

Cassandra managed a genuine smile. Elizabeth was a ray of sunshine on these dark, gloomy days of late. She could not help brighten a bit when Elizabeth was near. Cassandra came closer, raising a brow. "Is there a reason you're screaming my name so loudly that even our neighbours might hear?"

Elizabeth flushed, a pout adorning her lips. "Well what do you expect when you've never spent all morning locked away in your chambers? I thought you would never come down for breakfast. I had half a mind to go and get you myself."

"Perhaps I wanted to sleep in a little longer. Had that not occurred to you?"

Viola spoke next, scoffing. "You? Sleep late? I don't think you are physically capable of doing such a thing."

Cassandra chuckled as she sat between her mother and sister, her father quietly reading on the other side of the small table. "Very well. I was just being lazy. Is that what you'd like to hear?"

Even though she'd spoken in jest, Viola fixed her with a concerned look. "Are you certain you are well? You have been rather quiet lately. Surely you aren't coming down with something, are you?"

"Mother, you will be the first to know if I am." And because her words clearly hadn't assuaged her mother's worry, Cassandra laid a hand on top of hers. "I am fine. Believe me. I cannot tell when last I've gotten sick. Now *that* is something I am physically incapable of."

They laughed at that and Cassandra relaxed. She supposed she hadn't done that well of a job hiding the fact that something was wrong.

"Elizabeth." Gilbert's serious tone cut through the good cheer. Cassandra poured herself a cup of tea and reached for a scone.

"Yes, Father?" Elizabeth answered quietly.

Gilbert folded the newspaper and put it aside. His direct stare made Elizabeth squirm uncomfortably. "Did you enjoy the marquess' company last night?"

Cassandra's heart sank. She focused wholeheartedly on eating, trying to ignore the way Elizabeth perked up at the question.

"I did! It was a little uncomfortable at first. He seemed so unimpressed with me and I couldn't help but wonder if he did not want to be here. But then I began to relax a little and we actually had a nice conversation."

"What did you two talk about?" Cassandra asked before she could stop herself.

"We spoke about the weather, the meal, his hobbies. He said he enjoys reading and hunting."

"It seems as if you have nothing in common then."

Elizabeth nodded, completely unaffected by Cassandra's words. "Yes, it would appear so, but I have little in common with nearly every gentleman I've met so far. But out of all of them, I do enjoy his company the most."

Cassandra was beginning to think she shouldn't have come down for breakfast at all. The food suddenly felt like a hard rock in her throat and she quickly chased it down with a big gulp of her tea, ignoring the burn.

"I'm happy to hear that, Elizabeth," Gilbert went on, his tone pleased. "The Marquess of Charlington has sent word this morning that he wishes to meet with me. I have no doubt he wishes to ask me for permission to court you."

"Truly?" The excitement in Elizabeth's voice tore Cassandra's heart into two. Did she really like Lord Charlington that much? "How do you know, Father?"

"Isn't it obvious?" Viola gushed, her eyes shimmering with happiness. "You are so beautiful that Lord Charlington grew smitten the moment he saw you!"

"It didn't seem that way..." Elizabeth tried to counter but Viola shook her head firmly.

"You are too modest for your own good, my dear. The marquess, like every other gentleman who meets you, could not help but fall in love with you."

Elizabeth blushed furiously at that, a bright smile on her face.

"Don't you want to be courted by him?" Viola pressed.

"Well, he is more handsome than all the other gentlemen I've met." Elizabeth chewed on her bottom lip as she considered the idea. Then she shook her head. "I won't let myself think about it. If he asks for permission to court me then—"

"Will you say yes?" Cassandra murmured, hardly able to look up from the table.

Silence met her words, so draining that she didn't know what to make of it. Then Elizabeth answered, "I would."

"Wonderful!" Gilbert boomed and his first smile of the morning stretched across his face. "I'm sure the Duke of Edingdale will be pleased."

Cassandra fell quiet, nibbling on her half-eaten scone even though she had long since lost her appetite. The conversation, thankfully, moved on to other things but she couldn't find the energy to partake. She tried her best not to give in to the resentment coating the back of her tongue. It wasn't Elizabeth's fault she'd harbored hope for love she could not have, all because of one magical night that felt straight out of a fairy-tale. And it wasn't Lord Charlington's fault that he was interested in a beautiful, entertaining lady like Elizabeth.

*I will have to overcome this. One night with Lord Charlington should not make this much of an impact on my life!*

Somehow, she didn't have much faith that she could.

\*\*\*

"Cassie, stop this. You're ruining the fun."

Cassandra looked up from her book, her lips twitching at the scowl Adeline was giving her. Only ten minutes before, Elizabeth, Simon, and Adeline had found her in the library and forced her to join them in the drawing room. And since Cassandra had wanted nothing more than to wallow in her solitude—and they had given her no choice—she'd waltzed right into the drawing room, sat down in the furthest corner she could find, tucked her legs under her, and began reading once more. Simon had invited her to join them in a game of whist and Cassandra had barely glanced up at him, as if her book was far too interesting to look away.

In truth, Cassandra hardly read a thing. Her mind was worlds away, wondering whether Lord Charlington had already arrived to see her father. Was he already in his library? Would he come to see Elizabeth?

Despite the anxiousness that spread throughout her at the thought, Cassandra couldn't help feeling a little hopeful at the thought of seeing him again.

"How exactly am I doing that?" Cassandra asked as she tilted her head to the side.

"Because you won't join us," Elizabeth whined. She threw down her cards, leaning back in her chair. "And it's always better when it's the four of us."

"Lizzie is complaining because she's losing," Simon drawled and his cheeky smile stretched wider when Elizabeth narrowed her eyes at him.

"And both Simon and Elizabeth are terrible players," Adeline added. A giggle escaped Elizabeth as Simon's smile fell but Adeline's attention was focused solely on Cassandra. "You're the only worthy opponent here. These two are far too easy."

Simon shook his head, coming to a stand. He stretched his arms far above his head, letting out a groan. "One winning streak, ladies, and she thinks she's the queen of whist."

"She cannot be the queen of whist when I still stand," Cassandra mumbled.

Adeline grinned, rushing over to Cassandra's corner of solitude. "Then prove you are great at this game, won't you? Play a round with us."

Cassandra let out a sigh. She put her book aside, getting to her feet. She wandered over to the table and eyed the cards. In truth, she wanted to get out of the manor. Perhaps a bit of fresh air, a change of scenery, would help her forget about the marquess.

"I thought we were going to the Egyptian Hall today," she mentioned. "Shouldn't we depart soon then?"

"Now, now." Adeline shook her head. "We never decided between the Egyptian Hall and a picnic in Hyde Park."

"That's easy," Simon said as he leaned against a wall, crossing his arms. "Hyde Park."

"You are no fun," Cassandra stated and turned her back to him. "I say that we visit the hall instead. Perhaps indulge in a small history lesson?"

Elizabeth wrinkled her nose. "That sounds horribly boring, Cassie. I'm sorry."

"Boring?" Cassandra echoed, incredulous. "Goodness, Lizzie, I thought you would be on my side."

"That's why I said I was sorry!"

"Don't bother. I already feel betrayed. I can feel the three of you preparing to outvote me on this so I suppose we shall be having a picnic in Hyde Park, after all."

Adeline grinned victoriously. She rose, putting her hand on Cassandra's shoulders. "Just take a look outside, Cassandra. It's such a wonderful day. It would be wasted if we do not spend it outside."

Cassandra only rolled her eyes, even though her lips quirked upwards in a slight smile. "Yes, yes, you've won the battle."

"But the war is still on?" Simon questioned.

Cassandra met his stare with a twinkle of mischief blooming in her chest. "That goes without saying, now doesn't it?"

"Then it is decided then!" Elizabeth shot to her feet with an excited clap. "I shall tell the cook to prepare us a basket while I go and change. Cassie, shall we change in your chambers or—"

Before she could finish, there was a knock on the door. "Come," Cassandra called.

The butler slipped inside and bowed his head slightly. "Please forgive the intrusion, my lord and ladies. Lady Elizabeth, you have a caller."

"I do?" Elizabeth frowned in confusion, glancing at Cassandra as if she would know about this. "I was not expecting anyone. No one sent a request to call on me today."

Cassandra's heart sank, her good mood fleeing instantly. She had a feeling she knew what the butler was going to say next.

"Who is it?" Cassandra whispered, hating that her inquisitiveness made it difficult for her not to.

The butler looked at her as he answered, saying the words that both excited and dismayed her at the same time. "It is the Marquess of Charlington, my lady."

# Chapter Eighteen

"What do you think, my lord?"

"I think I would be more than happy to have you as a son-in-law."

It took everything in Jacob not to cringe at those words. He didn't like the gleam in Lord Wiswall's eyes, nor the manner in which he wrung his hands together in such a conspiratorially manner. It felt as if the earl was reading too deeply into Jacob's request and he had to make sure that he set things straight.

"My lord," Jacob began, resisting the urge to shift uncomfortably in his chair. They were in the ear's study, a quaint room that seemed to serve as both an office and a gathering room of sorts. Jacob had complimented the earl on the décor when he'd walked in, feeling complete at ease.

"Whiskey?" Lord Wiswall offered before Jacob could finish what he was about to say.

"No, thank you. I was saying—"

"Ah, I commend how well you mind your manners, my lord," Lord Wiswall gushed, grinning from ear to ear. "Elizabeth is just the same, though she has a tendency to speak without thinking. If she says anything untoward, I hope you do not take offence."

"I shan't." Jacob straightened, waiting a moment to see if the earl would say anything else. When he did nothing but take a quiet sip of his whiskey, Jacob continued. "I do not wish to cast the impression that I will be asking for Lady Elizabeth's hand in marriage, my lord."

"Oh, don't worry about that. You two have the entire Season to enjoy together. We could plan the wedding—"

"I wish to court her to get to know her," Jacob stated firmly. "Nothing more than that."

Those words managed to get through to him at last. Lord Wiswall's smile fell, a slight frown marring his brow. "I do not understand."

"I think Lady Elizabeth is a lovely lady, my lord. I'm sure I will find her swell to be around. And of course, if I wish to have her as my wife, you shall be the first to know about it."

Emphasis on the if. Jacob watched as his words sank in and the earl nodded. "I see. Well, I still extend my permission for you to court Elizabeth. She is a lovely girl. I'm sure you will come to care for her in due time."

Jacob didn't bother to grace that with a response, not wanting to give him any hope. Lord Wiswall got to his feet, his excitement returning. "I believe she is in the drawing room, my lord. Why don't you go and see her right now?"

"It was my intention to take her for a ride in the park, once you gave me your permission."

"Wonderful! Come, my butler will take you to her."

"Thank you, my lord," Jacob said, trying not to feel as if he was being given a chore. He left the study, grateful that the earl didn't follow him. The butler, who had been hovering on the other side of the door, gave him a swift nod and began leading Jacob to the drawing room. Each step he took felt like he was sinking deeper into this, as if the expectations that had been placed on his shoulders were soon to become reality. And there was nothing he could do about it.

Jacob held back a sigh, watching and waiting for the butler to enter the drawing room. He eyed the hallway that he knew would take him back to the manor's front entrance, wondering just how rude it would be for him to leave right now. Before he could act on the mad thought, the butler returned, leaving the door wide open for him to enter through.

Jacob gave him a nod of thanks before he swept into the room. The moment he did, his gaze landed on a pair of blue eyes as dark and smoldering as a thunderstorm. The emotions behind those eyes swirled furiously, stirring something in Jacob. And for those few seconds, it felt as if they were the only two people in existence.

Once again, Jacob was struck with the sharp disbelief that anyone could look at Lady Cassandra and think she was anything short of perfect. She wore no veil today, her cheeks flushed pink and her lips parted slightly as she stared back at him. That odd sense of familiarity pricked him once more, urging him to cross the distance to her.

"My lord," someone breathed. Jacob blinked, coming back to himself. Right, he had come to see Lady Elizabeth.

She was standing next to her sister, looking just as surprised to see him standing there. That surprise quickly faded as she smiled.

"I came to see you," he said, realizing suddenly that the sisters weren't alone. Simon and Lady Adeline were with them, all eyes on him. "But I was not aware that you would have company."

"Is there something you wanted to say to me?" Lady Elizabeth asked, stepping closer. She looked lovely as well.

"It was more of an invitation for a ride through Hyde Park."

"You're a minute too late," Simon spoke up before Lady Elizabeth could give her response. He was standing by the window, arms folded tightly across his chest. His jaw was tight.

Jacob frowned at that, especially since Simon offered no more explanation than that. But before he could question further, Lady Adeline said, "We just made plans to have a picnic in Hyde Park. You are welcome to join us if you'd like."

"I do not want to intrude..."

"No, it would be no intrusion," Lady Elizabeth said quickly, her smile as bright as the sun. "We would love to have you with us. I was just about to go to ask the cook to prepare a basket for us and it won't take us long to fetch our things."

"I see. Then perhaps you would not mind riding in my carriage," Jacob offered.

Lady Elizabeth nodded eagerly. "I would enjoy that."

"I shall come with you two." Jacob's heart leaped as he looked at Lady Cassandra. Whatever he'd seen in her eyes a few seconds ago was gone. She stared coolly back at him, as if she could not care less whether or not he came with them.

Jacob nodded. "Very well."

Lady Cassandra hardly waited for the words to leave his lips before she tucked her arm through her sister's and pulled her out the door, leaving him alone with Simon and Lady Adeline. Lady Adeline glanced at her brother, who was staring at the floor, before she hurried after the sisters.

Jacob let out a breath the moment they were all gone. "I know you said you were close with the family but I still find it surprising that you're here."

"Oh?" That steely look on Simon's face disappeared and the jovial man Jacob knew returned. "Afraid that I might be shirking my duties?"

"I would not put it past you," Jacob said with a grin.

Simon chuckled at that, the sound dying a second later. He seemed to want to say something and Jacob waited for him to get the words out.

"Do you fancy Lady Elizabeth?" Simon asked at last.

Jacob shook his head. "I don't. She is a nice lady though and my father is already looking at her as if she's his daughter-in-law."

"Then do you plan on marrying her?" Simon asked softly.

"I plan on marrying the woman I love," was all Jacob gave as response. If that was Lady Elizabeth was to be determined.

Simon's lips tightened. But then he changed the topic to the horse races that had occurred two days ago. Jacob indulged himself in the conversation as they were waiting for the ladies to return.

They did after nearly twenty minutes. Lady Adeline did not look much different, since she'd already been wearing her gloves, but had fetched her bonnet and parasol. Lady Elizabeth had done the same, though it seemed as if she'd let down some of her hair to fit under the parasol.

But Lady Cassandra...

He couldn't take his eyes off of her anymore. She'd stepped back into the room with matching white gloves and bonnet, clutching her parasol in one hand. And a thin, silky layer of yellow fabric veiled her face. Jacob was hit with the urge to stalk over to her and pull it away, to tell her that she had no need to hide her beauty from the world.

With much effort, he tore his eyes away from her and focused them on Lady Elizabeth. "Are we all ready?" he asked. Lady Elizabeth and Lady Adeline nodded. Lady Cassandra remained quiet.

He offered Lady Elizabeth his arm and she quickly slid hers through. As he turned to the door, he saw Simon approach Lady

Cassandra offering his own arm with a broad grin. Jacob couldn't see if Lady Cassandra grinned back but he caught the way Lady Adeline rolled her eyes good-naturedly.

A maid met them at the foyer with a picnic basket and blankets in her hands. She fell in step behind them as they made their way outdoors. Simon led Lady Cassandra all the way up to Jacob's carriage before he patted her hand and swept into a low bow before leaving. Jacob didn't see Lady Cassandra's smile behind the veil but he did hear her soft giggle. His heart twisted with envy, which just didn't make any sense to him.

So he once again tried to focus on the lady on his arm. Lady Elizabeth gave him a grateful smile as he helped her into the carriage. Then he turned to Lady Cassandra, offering her his hand.

She didn't move and he thought she was going to refuse his help. But then she took his hand. The moment she touched him, a jolt went through his body.

"Thank you, my lord," she murmured, climbing into the carriage. Her voice washed over him, his body tingling from the slight contact. Even the sound of it made him feel as if he knew her, as if that voice was ingrained in his very soul.

He looked over at Simon's carriage to see that the maid with the basket and the blankets was climbing into the carriage behind Lady Adeline. Nodding at Simon, Jacob made his way around his carriage and climbed in next to Lady Cassandra. It took every ounce of his strength not to look at her, even though it felt as if his entire body had been set on fire. He wanted to talk to her, to ask her everything under the sun if that meant he could understand why he felt like this. But his father's words echoed through his head and he remembered his purpose for being here.

If only he was interested in talking to Lady Elizabeth as he was in her sister, he thought. But Jacob knew Lady Cassandra was not on the marriage mart, and was only sitting next to him because she wanted to act as chaperone for her sister.

He knew he shouldn't feel disappointed by that yet could not help that he did.

# Chapter Nineteen

Cassandra could feel Lord Charlington's lingering touch burning through her gloves. She left her hand limp in her lap, staring down at it under the cover of her veil. Her heart was yet to recover, butterflies chasing each other in her stomach. She was sitting next to him. She had not been this close to him since the masquerade ball.

She murmured a quiet prayer that she would be able to keep her emotions in check during this picnic. Now that Lord Charlington was joining them, Cassandra knew she stood no chance of enjoying herself. She would never be able to relax around him, not when his attention was focused solely on Elizabeth. She was the reason he'd come to Wiswall Manor in the first place, after all. And Cassandra was only here because she could not leave Elizabeth alone with a gentleman, lest her reputation suffer a grave hit.

Lord Charlington cleared his throat, dragging her from her thoughts. "I must be honest with you Lady Elizabeth. I had asked your father for permission to court you."

Elizabeth blushed, giving Lord Charlington that demure look that usually had men eating out of the palm of her hands. Cassandra glanced anxiously at Lord Charlington but he did not seem to notice it all. "Then I must be honest with you too, my lord. My father already told me he believed you would come today to do just that."

"Then I have not surprised you. I shall make a greater effort a next time. Do you like flowers, perhaps?"

"What lady doesn't? But since you ask that, then should I be expecting to receive some in the future?"

"I shan't say. It is a surprise, remember?"

Elizabeth laughed and Cassandra's heart twisted in her chest. She stared out the window, wishing she'd opted to travel with Simon and Adeline instead, leaving Elizabeth in the company of her lady's maid for a chaperone.

"So," Jacob continued and Cassandra could tell he was directing his words to the both of them. "What made you all decide on an outing to Hyde Park?"

"Well, we decided to vote on what we should do and the decision rested on the picnic."

"What were the options?"

"Cassandra had suggested Egyptian Hall."

Cassandra's toes curled in her shoes when she felt the marquess' eyes on her. "Is that so? Do you have an interest in Egyptian history, my lady?"

Seeing no way out of not joining the conversation, she nodded. "I do."

"And what, may I ask, had first piqued your interest?"

"The pyramids," Cassandra answered without hesitation.

Lord Charlington shifted slightly. "Now, don't leave me in suspense," he urged. "What do you mean by that?"

Cassandra was grateful he couldn't see her blush. Every time he looked at her so directly, she forgot how to breathe. "It is foolish, the sentiments of a child."

"I'll be the judge of that."

"Well..." Cassandra glanced at Elizabeth but she did not seem bothered by the conversation so she went on. "When I was a child, all I could think about was climbing things. Once it was taller than me, I would climb until I reached the top. The banisters of the staircase, the bookshelves in the library, and certainly every tree in our garden. And when I first saw an image of the pyramids, in one of the paintings in the main hallway, I'd wanted to visit them."

"To climb to the top?" Lord Charlington probed, his voice tinged with humor.

Cassandra looked away. "I told you it would sound foolish."

He laughed and the sound loosened the tension in her limbs. "Not at all. It is far more interesting than my reasoning."

"Do you enjoy Egyptian history as well, my lord?" Cassandra asked as if she didn't already know the answer to that.

"I do, though my interests do include other areas of history as well."

"Tell me about how your interest came about. And I do hope it is as embarrassing as my own."

He chuckled again. "Don't worry, my lady. You've won on that front."

Cassandra scoffed, the sound sounding a lot like laughter. "It is not a competition, my lord."

The moment the words were out of her mouth, Cassandra's smile fell. She caught the curious look Lord Charlington was giving her and she knew he was thinking the same thing.

*It is not a test, my lord.*

She'd said those very words the night of the masquerade ball, while they spoke about the same topic. Cassandra stared at him, wondering if he would realize who she was now. Her heart was in her throat as she waited for him to reveal the truth.

Suddenly, he looked away, clearing his throat. Cassandra quickly looked away as well, trying to get her breathing back under control.

"And what of you, my lady?" Lord Charlington asked Elizabeth. "I recall that you told me of your interest in spending time with friends and shopping. Is there anything else that interests you?"

"Well I do love playing the pianoforte," Elizabeth answered. "And I enjoy painting with watercolors."

Lord Charlington nodded at that as if it was the most fascinating thing he'd ever heard. "I would love to hear you play one day."

"And I would love to play for you, my lord. Perhaps when we return to the manor, you will be able to spare a few minutes to listen."

"Perhaps. I would not want to take up too much of your time..."

"Oh, it would be no bother at all!" Her excited eyes shifted to Cassandra. "What do you think, Cassie? Would you like to sing with me while I play for Lord Charlington?"

Cassandra opened her mouth, her protest on the tip of her tongue, but Lord Charlington spoke before she had the chance to voice it. "Do you sing, my lady?"

His attention was on her once more and Cassandra was no better at handling it. Pounding heart, her stomach doing somersaults, her throat growing dry. It was a wonder she could muster up a single coherent thought when he looked at her so intently.

"I do not anymore," she said after a long while.

She expected him to ask her why and she readied herself to tell him that it was none of his business in the most ladylike manner she could manage. Instead, he smiled brightly, the sight so exceptionally handsome that the walls Cassandra had built up came crashing down around her.

"How can I convince you to give me the full Matthews Sisters experience?" he asked.

"Matthews Sisters experience?" she repeated, not knowing whether to frown or to laugh. She managed a mixture of both.

"Yes, I'm sure I know what it would feel like," he said with a grin. "One sister who plays the pianoforte beautifully while the other sings with the voice of an angel."

"And what shall you do then, my lord?" Cassandra asked before Elizabeth had the chance to say anything.

Lord Charlington tilted his head at that. "What do you mean?"

"Well, surely you do not expect to receive such marvelous entertainment without offering us something in return." She looked at Elizabeth. "What would you like for Lord Charlington to do, Lizzie?"

Elizabeth hummed in thought. "I'm not sure," she said with a small smile. "What do you think, Cassie?"

"I shall have to give it some thought as well," Cassandra stated and Lord Charlington shuddered.

"Why do I get the feeling I was outmatched just now?"

"Because you were," Cassandra and Elizabeth said at the same time. But Lord Charlington's smile was focused on Cassandra a second longer than necessary, making her own grin fall as her heart thundered in her ears.

"So, my lord," Elizabeth spoke up again. "Why don't you tell me about what it was like living in Bath."

Lord Charlington indulged her and Cassandra bit on the insides of her cheek to keep from joining the conversation. She shouldn't get too comfortable, she reminded herself. Lord Charlington had come here for Elizabeth, not her.

But she couldn't help but think about the way his eyes had lingered on her, how it had somehow felt as if he'd been more interested in talking to her than he had been in speaking with Elizabeth. But that couldn't be. Elizabeth was every gentleman's dream. Gentle, amiable, beautiful, and capable of engaging in all sorts of conversations. Meanwhile, Cassandra knew she could be a little too defiant in her speech, her droll tone not often taken as a jest the way it should be. She found that, whenever she spoke to someone outside of her family, Simon, or Adeline, she had to watch what she said so that she did not offend. But her words had fallen off her tongue at ease while she spoke with Lord Charlington and she could have sworn he was truly intrigued by all that she was saying.

Just like the night of the masquerade ball.

Cassandra bit her lip, chasing away that horrible hope slowly creeping up in her once more. She needed to forget about him, not imagine what it would be like to hear him say that he'd asked to court *her*.

She tried her best to ignore the conversation, which was slowly dwindling down to nothing as they drew nearer to Hyde Park. By the time they'd arrived at the park, the carriage following behind Simon and Adeline's as they led the way across the many beaten paths at the park, there was nothing but silence in the air. Cassandra didn't dare to break it, didn't dare to look back at Lord Charlington.

Before long, the carriage came to a halt. Lord Charlington exited first, then jogged around to the other side. Cassandra still pointedly refused to look at him, even when he'd helped Lady Elizabeth exit and extended a hand to her once more. She took his help without hesitating this time, still not prepared for the way her stomach seemed to leap and sink at the same time from that single touch.

"I shall speak with Simon about where we should set up the picnic," he said and gave neither of them a chance to respond before he walked off.

The moment he was out of earshot, Elizabeth let out a wistful sigh. "Isn't he so charming?" she asked Cassandra, eyes still following Lord Charlington.

Cassandra forced herself to nod. "You two would certainly make a lovely couple."

"I'd rather not think that far ahead," Elizabeth said with a blush. "But I am enjoying my time with him. I find that I do not have to fake my laughter with him."

"You do not have to fake it with Simon either," Cassandra pointed out but Elizabeth was quick to dismiss her comment with a wave of her hand.

"Simon is different," she said simply. "He is like my brother. And the marquess is most certainly not."

Cassandra finally let her gaze wander over to him, her heart twisting painfully. "You're right. He isn't."

This time, there was no hiding the hurt in her voice but she walked off before her sister had a chance to question it, more determined than ever to forget about the marquess and all that she felt for him.

# Chapter Twenty

Simon chose to have the picnic under one of the looming willow trees that adorned Hyde Park. They were a decent distance away from the main path, the one that was often traveled by other visitors to the path. But they were close enough to the main throng of visitors that it would not be deemed unusual.

Jacob stood by the rough bark of the willow tree with his arms crossed, the maid who had traveled with them quickly setting everything up. To the left of him, Simon was talking to Lady Cassandra, while she idly brushed her fingers against the petals of blooming purple peonies by her. Jacob wasn't close enough to them to hear what they were saying but he felt something pinch within him at the broad grin on Simon's face. Lady Elizabeth had wandered towards the small pond hidden within a cluster of shrubbery, smiling at the ducklings wading in the water.

"It is a beautiful day, Lord Charlington. And that frown you are wearing does not quite match our surroundings."

Jacob wiped the scowl off his face as Lady Adeline came to stand beside him. He hadn't realized that he had been frowning. "Forgive me, my lady. It is a sad consequence of a man of my status. There is always something to scowl about."

"Ah, and yet my brother laughs as if he hasn't a care in the world." Jacob noticed that her attention was also drawn to Lady Cassandra and Simon, who seemed so engrossed in their conversation that they didn't care about anything around them. What could he be saying that was so interesting?

"Simon has always been like that, I'm afraid. Even when we were in school together, he treated his studies as if they were optional, like it didn't matter if he did well or not."

"So I've heard from a few of his others classmates I've met," Lady Adeline said with a breathy laugh. "I'm sure you couldn't believe that he graduated nearly at the top of his class."

"Had I not been the one to graduate at the very top, it might have angered me as well," Jacob agreed and Lady Adeline laughed again.

"I wonder when he will settle down," she mused aloud. "He is young still, so he has time. But it does not seem as if he intends to take the matter of his heart into his own hands."

Jacob looked at Lady Adeline, noticing how her gaze shifted to Lady Elizabeth and then back to her brother. "What do you mean, matters of his heart?"

"Nothing, really," she stated noncommittally.

She continued to stare at Simon and Lady Cassandra and, after a moment, Jacob followed her. Even though he could not see Lady Cassandra's face beyond the veil, he could tell by her posture and the way she turned slightly to Simon that she was comfortable with him. Happy, even. And it was clear as day that Simon was enjoying her company as well, even though his eyes kept darting towards the pond now and again.

Something coiled within Jacob, coating the back of his tongue. It felt suspiciously like envy…but what was there to be envious about? Simon had nothing that Jacob didn't already have, or couldn't get himself.

Except perhaps the friendship of Lady Cassandra. Jacob tore his eyes away, looking over at the younger sister as she approached the picnic with a smile on her face. And Lady Elizabeth, he supposed.

"Seems like everything is ready," Lady Adeline commented, already moving away. "Good. I am famished."

Jacob said nothing as everyone began to gather close and the maid disappeared to one of the carriages. He watched as Lady Cassandra sank onto the blanket first, his teeth grinding a little when Simon took her side. Lady Adeline sat on her other side, forcing Jacob to sit next to Simon's sister while Lady Elizabeth sat between both him and Simon.

The blanket was laden with sandwiches, small cakes, and tea. Jacob watched as Simon poured the tea for the ladies, starting with Lady Cassandra. She murmured something to him that Jacob couldn't hear and Simon sniggered.

"You chose a lovely spot, brother," Lady Adeline commented aloud, picking up a small cucumber sandwich. "Do you come here often?"

"Not at all," Simon responded. "I only have an eye for beauty."

"Yes, I'm sure it had nothing to do with the fact that this willow tree could be seen a mile away," Lady Cassandra drawled, her tone tinged with humor. "And it was the easiest choice."

"A choice you would not have thought to make," Simon countered.

"That is because I am not predictable," she shot back and Jacob could almost hear the smile in her voice.

"Predictable or not, it is a perfect spot for the picnic," Lady Elizabeth spoke up. "And there is even a small path extending beyond the pond where we can go for a walk after this meal."

"Do you hear that, Cassie?" Simon's chest seemed to grow broader as he grinned. "That is Lizzie's way of saying that I made the right choice."

"No, I agree with my sister," Lady Elizabeth said simply.

Simon's smile fell and the three ladies descended into giggles. Jacob felt a smile tug at his own lips, even though he didn't like the way his chest burned at how easily Simon bantered with Lady Cassandra.

"I must admit that it is quite refreshing watching you all talk," Jacob confessed. "I can tell that you have all been friends for quite a long time."

"Like family," Lady Adeline corrected with a prideful smile.

"Though some of us would like to forget that, I'm sure," Lady Cassandra stated, but before anyone could question what she meant, she moved on. "Adeline, will you be joining us for the theatre?"

"Oh, I was not extended an invitation," Lady Adeline responded.

Lady Elizabeth shot Simon a stern look. "What does she mean by that, Simon? Did you not ask her to attend with you?"

"I do not need my sister following me everywhere I go," Simon complained and Lady Adeline rolled her eyes.

"That is because you fear that I will outshine you, as I tend to do without trying." She looked at Lady Cassandra with a mischievous smile. "Even though my brother thought to leave me out of the planning, I will be attending as well."

"Don't mind me," Jacob spoke up. "I am content to listen. I do not feel jealous at all. Nor do I have the sudden urge to attend the theatre."

They all chuckled but it was Lady Cassandra's laughter that captured his attention. Jacob felt his heart bloom with pride at the sound. "Do you enjoy attending the theatre, my lord?" she asked.

"As much as I am enjoying having this picnic with you all," he said honestly. "Which is quite a lot, if that was not already obvious."

"Beware, my lord. It will take quite a lot to join our small band of friends."

"Will I be put to the test before, then?"

"Yes." Jacob longed to see her face, longed to know if her face was filled with humor as it sounded. "But don't tempt me or I shall make it quite difficult for you."

"Question me on ancient history," he challenged. "And I promise I shall greatly impress you."

"That isn't nearly enough," she laughed.

"Oh? Then perhaps I shall climb this tree and show you just how high I can get."

Lady Cassandra tilted her head to the side. "Now that sounds a little better."

He was grinning like a fool. Jacob didn't realize just how hard until his jaw was beginning to hurt. And then Simon cleared his throat and he realized that he was still staring at her with that sappy smile on his face.

He suddenly remembered the reason he was here and turned to her. Lady Elizabeth was daintily sipping her tea as if she didn't care much about the conversation. "I take it you will be in attendance as well, my lady?"

She shook her head. "I much prefer operas to plays."

"Ah, I shall remember that for another day then."

Her eyes glittered with surprise and pleasure. "Do you intend on inviting me to the opera soon, my lord?"

Did he? The thought didn't appeal to him much but he did make a promise to himself that he would at least *try* to get to know her better. And a night at the opera would be a good way of doing that.

He only gave her a smile. "We shall see, shan't we?" he answered, a subtle reminder of their earlier conversation in the carriage.

Lady Elizabeth grinned, clearly understanding what he meant.

Jacob reached for a cake, not knowing how to continue the conversation as Lady Adeline, Lady Cassandra, and Simon continued talking about the theatre. He knew he should try to engage Lady Elizabeth in a personal conversation, but his gaze was constantly drawn to the lady across from him. The elegant way she sat bespoke her upbringing, the whimsical tone in her voice filling him with excitement. This wasn't the same lady who had hesitated to speak to him, and had seemed unwilling to touch him. She was more relaxed now and seeing her personality come to surface made him want to see more.

Jacob found himself wondering how to engage Lady Cassandra in conversation, rather than the younger sister, and he shook the thought from his head as he reached for another cake. At that moment, he caught sight of a leather-bound book sitting near the teapot. He picked it up without thinking.

"Romeo and Juliet?" he read aloud, the words inscribed on the front of the book.

He looked at Lady Elizabeth with a question in his eyes but she shook her head. "It is not mine," she said. "That book belongs to my sister. Romeo and Juliet is her favourite book."

Without a sliver of hesitation, he looked up at Lady Cassandra. And from how still she sat, he could have sworn she was looking at him too. And for a moment, it felt as if the world had slowed to a stop, his heart thundering in his chest.

*History and Shakespeare. Just like the lady in gold. Is this all a coincidence?*

## Chapter Twenty-One

Truly, this day could not get any worse, could it?

Cassandra tried not to sigh as she caught the intense stare of the marquess. She didn't have to ask to know what he was thinking. Between their conversation about history, her slight slip of the tongue, and now what Elizabeth had just revealed about her, Cassandra knew he was thinking about the night of the masquerade ball.

Her breath quickened at that realization. She knew she shouldn't think about him this way, knew that she shouldn't give in to the way her heart reacted to him. But it filled her with something unimaginable at the idea of Lord Charlington thinking about that night the way she had. She could see the question in his eyes, the frown adorning his brows. When he opened his mouth, she was almost certain he was going to ask her something she could not answer. And, for a brief and insane moment, Cassandra was almost ready for it.

But then Elizabeth continued speaking, completely oblivious to what was passing between Cassandra and the marquess. "I didn't even notice that she'd brought it with her. Cassie takes that everywhere with her."

"Ah, so it was in my reticule all along," Cassandra sighed, pointing a gloved finger at the reticule lying shortly away. "I thought I had lost it forever. I suppose it makes sense since I've searched everywhere for it and hardly used my reticule since the Season began."

"Do you enjoy Shakespeare, my lady?" Lord Charlington asked, his tone a bit breathless.

Cassandra licked her lips and tried to remember that they were not alone. "That is a bit obvious, don't you think, my lord?"

For a second, she could have sworn his cheeks colored before he nodded, setting the book down. "Ah, yes, I suppose it is."

"I do not fancy it much," Elizabeth cut in, adorably unaware of the slight tension simmering between Cassandra and the marquess. "I think I might have said this before but I do not fancy reading that much. Which is quite odd, since I do not fancy spending much time outdoors either. Though this day is quite perfect for a picnic, so I am happy that I came."

"That is because you have not engrossed yourself with Shakespeare's tales," Cassandra answered her, clinging to any opportunity she got to turn her attention away from the marquess. It didn't help that she could feel his eyes burning into her, though.

"Oh, Cassie, I do not think it will matter either way."

"On the contrary, Elizabeth," Adeline spoke up. "Perhaps you are not giving your sister enough credit. She knows you quite well, I'm sure. And considering how hopeless you are when it comes on to matters of the heart, Romeo and Juliet seem like the perfect tale for you to enjoy."

Elizabeth wrinkled her nose. "Doesn't it end with both of them dying?"

"It does," Adeline confirmed with a small nod and a smile. "But that is not what you should focus on. It is their love persisting despite their circumstances that I'm sure you will enjoy."

"I am not sure how," Elizabeth protested. "To love someone but have everyone tell you that you cannot be with them is more heartrending than beautiful, don't you think?"

Cassandra quickly nibbled on a small sandwich, hardly tasting it. That sounded far too close to her own situation right now and she didn't need a reminder of it. But she didn't do anything to stop the conversation as Adeline spoke again, shaking her head determinedly.

"Don't you see, Elizabeth?" Adeline pressed. "That is exactly what makes it so wonderful! And I'm sure if you were to see it for yourself, you would understand."

Elizabeth chewed on her bottom lip as she thought about it. And then her eyes shifted to me. "Is that why you adore this book so much, Cassie?"

The attention was on her now, but only Lord Charlington's silent stare mattered. She tried her best not to look at him, fearing what she might see there as he studied her. "Not entirely," she answered her sister.

"What do you mean?" Simon asked, as if he was genuinely interested in what she would say.

Cassandra straightened, sensing that she would not be able to get out of answering properly. "On the one hand, I do understand Adeline's point of view. The passionate love those two hold for each other is quite endearing, despite everything trying to force them apart. But what truly makes me enjoy this tale is its inevitable ending."

"You mean, their deaths?" Lord Charlington asked and Cassandra could not ignore him any longer.

Her heart skipped a beat when their gazes met. She could have sworn he was staring right into her eyes, as if he could see through to her soul despite the veil that she wore. "Yes," she breathed.

Lord Charlington cocked his head to the side. "I'm afraid I do not understand what you mean. Surely you are not praising such a depressing ending?"

"I am. I know how odd that must sound, especially coming from a lady. But it only helps us see that we cannot escape the reality of our situation. Though they might have fallen in love, the stars were against them from the very beginning. And no matter how hopeful they might have been, it was never meant to be."

"Are you saying they never should have tried?"

"Precisely. Perhaps then they would have met a better end."

"And live in discontentment and unhappiness for the rest of their lives?"

"Is it better than dying an early and painful death, where they believe they had lost the one they loved? Would it not be better to know that the person you love is living a healthy life?"

"Though perhaps not a happy one."

Cassandra shrugged. She was very aware of the others watching their small back and forth. She was also conscious of the fact that she was revealing her darkest thoughts, ones she did not make a habit of showing. They were borne from the bitterness that had filled her heart after her scar set and she became truly aware of the future ahead of her. "There are other ways of finding happiness."

Lord Charlington hummed in thought, rubbing the side of his face as he observed her. Cassandra felt a glimmer of unease, afraid of what he would find. Certainly, her words were not very proper of a lady to make, though she did not think he was the kind of gentleman who resented ladies with opinions.

"While I do understand your opinion on this piece of literature, my lady," he began again, "I cannot say that I agree."

"What is your take on it, then?"

"Beware, Cassie," Simon interjected, his tone laced with mirth. "Lord Charlington here will not hesitate to spend hours talking about the way of the heart and how we should all succumb to our deepest emotions."

Lord Charlington's lips quirked up into a slight smile and he shrugged. "Not exactly. But I do believe that Romeo and Juliet is a perfect example of what we should all try our best to do to put ourselves first. True happiness is often found in the arms of the one you love."

"Even in death," Cassandra said slowly, unable to believe what she was hearing.

He nodded, utterly serious. "It is unfortunate. But many of us will not meet such a tragic fate. If we take the principles laid out in the tale, however, we may very well find ourselves on the path to true happiness."

Cassandra tilted her head to the side. She had to admit that she was intrigued by his thoughts, but she couldn't very well agree. At least, it was not a sentiment that she could apply to her own life. For someone as beautiful and kind as Elizabeth, or a lady as witty and lovable as Adeline, it may be possible. But not for her. Not when she was fated to live her life as a spinster, wearing a veil to every function she attended, and pretending the slow bitter poison of her life would not eventually consume her whole.

For a second, she was tempted to reveal that all to Lord Charlington. And he stared at her with a challenge in his gaze as if he could tell that she wished to debate with him on the matter. But that was a wound she had no intention of poking.

Thankfully, as if she sensed that Cassandra did not know what to say, Adeline spoke next. "It sounds as if that is your intention for this Season, my lord. Are you hoping for a love match?"

Lord Charlington stared at Cassandra for a beat longer before he turned his attention to Adeline. "Aren't we all?"

Elizabeth nodded at that. "That is my hope as well. And I must say, the way you've explained yourself makes me very interested in seeing it for myself." She slid her gaze towards Simon, a blush filling her cheeks. "I know I said I didn't want to go before, but I've changed my mind. Is there still a spot—"

"You don't even have to ask!" Simon boomed, bringing a genuine smile to Cassandra's face. He couldn't hide his enthusiasm if he tried. "In truth, I thought that Cassie would have—"

"Me?" Cassandra cut in.

"Yes, *you*. I thought you would have convinced Lizzie to come with us from the day I asked you two."

"You put too many expectations on me," Cassandra answered with a shrug.

Simon just grinned at her as if he'd been knighted by the Regent himself and Cassandra laughed under her breath. Elizabeth was staring at Simon with a small smile on her face, her eyes glowing. Cassandra wondered if she even knew just how much of her heart she wore on her sleeve sometimes.

"I am feeling restless all of a sudden," Adeline announced. And Cassandra gave her her full attention so that she didn't have to look at the marquess across from her.

"Oh, we should go and take a look at the rose hedges I saw nearby!" Elizabeth suggested. She was already rising, brushing her skirt off. "They seemed to be in bloom. Perhaps we shall see a hummingbird as well!"

She was off before anyone could say anything. Simon and Adeline got to their feet as well. "So excitable," Simon muttered, unable to hold back his smile. And Adeline stared after the two of them, shaking her head as if she couldn't handle either one of them.

It took Cassandra a second too late to realize that she hadn't moved. In fact, the thought hadn't even occurred to her. Perhaps, deep down, her limbs had remained frozen because she knew Lord Charlington had not moved either. Perhaps she wanted to be alone with him.

And when she caught his eyes once more, she thought he might want that too.

## Chapter Twenty-Two

Jacob thought the heavens had opened up and had shone down upon him at that moment. He had been staring at Lady Cassandra, wishing he could have a moment alone with her so that he could ask the question pressing on his mind. And as soon as the thought occurred to him, Lady Elizabeth had suggested that they all go and look at the blooming rose hedges nearby.

Jacob didn't know why Lady Cassandra didn't go with them and he was not going to question it. He didn't take his eyes off her, studying her rigid posture and how she twisted her head to the side as if she were trying her hardest not to meet his pointed stare. He knew that what he was doing bordered on inappropriate, not to mention the fact that if anyone were to find them alone together her reputation might be compromised. Never mind the fact that she didn't have much of a reputation in the first place. Jacob didn't care about the consequences. He only wanted to know one thing.

If she was the lady he could not stop thinking about.

He cleared his throat and her fingers twitched as if the sound had frightened her. Jacob scratched the back of his head, the silence quickly growing uncomfortable. The question was stuck on the back of his tongue. He couldn't come out and say it, could he?

"Is there something on your mind, my lord?" Lady Cassandra asked before he could figure out how to break the quiet.

Her boldness inspired him to do the same. "Yes."

"Perhaps I may be able to relieve you of any stress you may be feeling." Her tone was a little curt. Almost forcefully so. "Does it have anything to do with our earlier conversation?"

"A little," he admitted, though it wasn't entirely the truth. Her words had stuck with him, but his concern rested on something else entirely. "I just find what you've said quite interesting...and concerning."

"Concerning how?"

"For a young lady like yourself, having such a mindset may not put you in a favourable position when it comes on to future marriage prospects."

"What future marriage prospects, my lord?" She looked around, then faced him again. "I do not see any gentlemen lining up to ask for my hand in marriage."

"And yet I find it hard to believe that that is not the case, my lady. You are quite..."

She remained silent, waiting.

"...captivating."

For a few seconds, Lady Cassandra said nothing. An uneasy silence followed Jacob's words and it took all his strength to say something to cover up what he'd last said.

Just as he'd opened his mouth, Lady Cassandra tilted her head back and let out a hearty laugh, one bordering on unladylike. She even had to hold her hand under her veil as her laughter shook her body. Jacob felt his lips twitch, though his brows were twitching with confusion.

"I'm sorry, is there something I said?"

"No, no, it's nothing," she told him between giggles. "Only that I do not think I have ever received such a heartfelt compliment before. It is rather refreshing."

"Surely it is not the best one you have heard," Jacob responded with a grin. Lady Cassandra only shrugged, leaving it at that. Jacob reached for the leather-bound copy of Romeo and Juliet and held it up to her. "This is my favourite book as well."

"Is it now? I could not tell."

Her sarcastic tone was enough to bring a laugh out of Jacob. "Yes, well, I have to say that is my first time hearing someone say that they enjoyed the ending."

"I have been known to be a little grim at times."

"And I like that. Because I've always been told that I am a little too optimistic."

"Are you bragging, my lord?" she teased and Jacob shook his head as he chuckled.

"Only sharing a part of myself with you. I hope you can do the same with me too."

She tilted her head to the side at that. "It sounds as if there is something you'd like to know."

"There is...but I wonder if now is the right time to ask it."

"Now that your intentions are clear, there is no use holding back." Lady Cassandra seemed to straighten her spine a bit as she continued, "Go ahead. Ask."

It was now or never. Jacob could feel his confidence slipping, draining at the very thought that she might not be the lady who had followed him into his dreams every night since the masquerade ball. He didn't want to consider how it would feel if she did not give him the answer he was hoping for.

"I know this might be very sudden for you," he began. "Or perhaps it may not. I suppose it all depends on your answer to the question, honestly, so there is no guessing—"

"You're rambling," she observed and he could have sworn her he heard a smile in her voice.

"I guess I am," he responded with a sheepish grin, rubbing his jaw as if that would be enough to relieve the tension seizing his body. "I will just come right out and ask it then. My lady, are you perchance the lady I danced with the night of the masquerade ball?"

Slowly, Lady Cassandra tilted her head to the side. He could feel the weight of her stare, even though he could not see her eyes. He tried not to shift uncomfortably, hoping that the silence that drifted between them was not because of what he feared.

For a moment, he wondered if he should give her more details about the lady. But if she truly was the same person, then there should be no need. The intensity of their meeting, how it felt as if a piece of him he didn't know was missing had finally fallen into place. Those few minutes together had felt so perfect that, now that it was over, Jacob wondered if he would ever feel such peace and bliss again. And while he danced with her, he could have sworn she felt the same.

It didn't matter that she'd run off at the end without revealing who she truly was. All that mattered was the connection he'd felt—and that he was determined to find her.

"My apologies, my lady," Jacob started again when she still did not answer him. "I hope I did not offend you with my question—"

"You did not," she cut in, lifting her chin slightly. "Yes, I am her."

His heart thudded in his chest. All of a sudden, it felt as if the world was slowing, the wind on his face tingling every nerve in his body. The pounding heartbeat and the somersaulting stomach was expected. But the way his body relaxed, finally at ease, made Jacob realize just how much he'd been hoping to hear those words.

"Why?" he breathed.

"Why what?" Lady Cassandra asked, her tone far colder than he'd hoped it would be. But he didn't care. Not right now.

"Why did you keep your identity a secret? You knew who I was from the moment I came to your manor, didn't you?"

"I did."

"And you didn't reveal who you were." It took all his strength not to go closer to her. She held her behaviour so stiffly that he couldn't tell how she felt about this conversation. "Why didn't you? Didn't you want to see me again, the way I longed to see you?"

"I did not want you to know who I was," she answered simply.

"But why?" he asked, desperation lacing his words.

"Isn't obvious, my lord?" she asked. Jacob blinked at the sudden sharpness to her tone, but he had no chance to respond when she suddenly lifted her veil, revealing her beautiful face and fiery eyes.

Except, she was gesturing to the left side of her face—where the scar was. Her voice was tinged with bitterness as she said, "Look at me, Lord Charlington. Why would I ever dare to ruin such a moment when I look like this? When I have such a horrid scar that makes it certain that I can never have any sort of connection with—"

He wouldn't let her finish the thought. He caught her hand, pulling her so close that their faces were just inches apart, close enough for him to lean in and kiss her at long last.

***

Cassandra thought her heart was going to beat right out of her chest. The marquess wasn't just holding her hand, squeezing it gently to his chest. He was so close that she could feel his breath against her lips. It would only take a single move for him to kiss her. Only to lean just an inch closer and their lips would meet. Cassandra knew that she should pull away from him, lest they be caught in this compromising manner. But her body wanted to lean in and let him wrap his arms around her.

He stared into her eyes, squeezing her hand. "You should not allow that scar to define you, Cassandra."

Cassandra tightened her lips, but she didn't pull away from him. She knew she shouldn't let him call her by her given name, knew that she shouldn't dare to let him get too familiar. But now that she'd revealed who she was, she supposed they were long past that.

"It is not something I wish for, Jacob," she murmured. "I am not the one who is defining myself because of this scar. It is society."

"Then society is a fool if they cannot see how beautiful you are."

She frowned, trying to pull away. He only tightened his grip, keeping her from moving. Though she supposed she didn't put up much of a fight. "You're just saying that," she protested.

"It is the honest truth, I swear to you. It feels as if I could get lost in your eyes, and listen to you voice your opinions on various matters all day. The way you speak, the way you carry yourself, even the way you look at me turns me into a lovesick sap that cannot think about anything but you."

Her throat grew thick with tears. Cassandra shook her head. "Don't mention that word," she whispered. "You don't know what you're saying."

"But I do. Now that I have found you again, Cassandra, everything is clearer to me now."

"Jacob, I..."

His other hand lifted gently to her face, making her go rigid. Cassandra forgot how to breathe, unable to tear her eyes away from his tender gaze.

"Don't you feel it too, Cassandra?" he asked her. "This thing between us?"

She swallowed harshly. She wanted to say yes. So desperately did she want to tell him that she hadn't stopped thinking about him from the night of the ball, that she feared she might have succumbed to the fabled idea of love at first sight. Cassandra had already convinced herself that she was just thinking too deeply about their connection, that the lack of romance in her life led her to wanting more than she could really have. But now that he was saying the exact same things she wished she could, she wanted it to be real.

Cassandra opened her mouth, her response right on the tip of her tongue. But then the sound of laughter broke through their small moment. She quickly jerked back, scrambling to her feet as quickly as she could. She shifted the veil to cover her face again, so that they wouldn't see how red her cheeks had gotten from the urge to cry.

It had been Elizabeth's laugh. Her dear younger sister who was excited at the thought of being courted by the Marquess of Charlington. Her beautiful sister who was her family's only chance of being joined to another's through marriage, since Cassandra was fated to live the rest of her life as a spinster.

She couldn't do this to her.

And she couldn't forget the lonely future she was destined to have.

"Cassandra—" Jacob started again but she shook her head.

"No," she pushed out, valiantly holding back her tears though she knew she was bound to fail soon. "We cannot."

"But—"

"It isn't meant to be!" she hissed just as Elizabeth, Simon, and Adeline came back into view. "You and I can never be together. And there is nothing either one of us can do about it."

The pain and dejection that filled his features was enough to tear at her already crumbling heart. For a moment, it took all her strength to throw caution to the wind and throw her arms around him, to accept his affection. But then Elizabeth ran up to them, an excited smile on her face and Cassandra remembered where her loyalties should lie.

"Why didn't you two come with us?" Elizabeth asked as she collapsed onto the blanket with a flushed face.

Under the cover of her veil, Cassandra stared at Jacob, watching as he schooled his expression and gave Elizabeth a tight smile. "I was not feeling too well," he lied. "And Lady Cassandra was kind enough to keep my company."

"Oh, what's wrong?" Simon asked as he sat between Cassandra and Jacob once more, a grin on his face. "Did you eat too many sweets?"

"I think that might be it, in truth," Jacob admitted, returning the smile though it didn't quite meet his eyes. "I would hate to be the boring one of the lot, especially when you all kindly extended your invitation to me, but I think it would be best if I returned home."

"Oh, of course," Elizabeth was quick to say. "It wouldn't do if you got sick because of us."

"You needn't blame yourself, my lady. It is only my weak stomach that is the cause." He offered her another smile but it died quickly. Elizabeth didn't seem to notice.

Simon, Elizabeth, and Jacob joined Cassandra and Adeline on their feet, who had stayed standing silently when they returned. Adeline stared at Cassandra, then shifted her gaze to Jacob with a slight frown. Cassandra didn't think she could stay around for any question the observant lady might have.

She didn't bother to wait for them. She turned on her heels, making her way back to the carriage. Now she was regretting coming with Elizabeth and Jacob earlier, since she would be forced to return with them. If she dared to change places with someone else now, they were bound to know that something had happened.

Deep down, she'd wanted to be near him. That was why she'd chosen to travel with her sister, using the excuse of a chaperone as a disguise. And she would have to suffer the ride home with his last words playing over and over in her head.

It was bad enough that she was fated to be alone for the rest of her life, because of this stupid scar. But now, she would pine for a man she could never have because of it.

# Chapter Twenty-Three

Another few days went by while Jacob suffered from thoughts of Cassandra. She followed him everywhere, her image torturing him at nights until the morning came and he had no sleep. Three days disappeared in the blink of an eye since he'd gone to the park with Cassandra and the others and he was yet to recover from the rejection that had torn into him.

He understood why she did it. He harbored no resentment, no anger. Only bare-faced disappointment that she'd denied herself what she so clearly wanted. And because of what? A scar that only accentuated her beauty? The fact that she did not know how breathtaking she was what truly infuriated Jacob.

Jacob dragged his hand down his face as he descended the staircase, heading to the dining room for breakfast. He was in no mood to be around others, but his mother had protested at last night's dinner that he was not making time for them anymore and he did not want them prying into what made him so sluggish lately. If only he could get one night's sleep...but that would only happen when both his mind and heart were at ease.

"Oh, there he is!" Maria exclaimed the moment Jacob walked through the doors. He gave her a small smile, a pale comparison to the bright grin that she offered him. "I thought you wouldn't come. Breakfast is almost over, you know."

"I had trouble waking up," he told her, instantly reaching the pot of coffee in the center of the table.

Henry, sitting at the head of the table, frowned at Jacob. "Are you having trouble sleeping?"

"I am," Jacob answered, because there was no use denying the obvious. But then he added, "There is a deal I am trying to secure and the other gentlemen involved are making it quite difficult for me, that's all. But I'll handle it in time."

"As you always do," Henry said, his voice filled with smug pride.

Jacob didn't have the energy to feel good at his father's unwavering belief in him. He wouldn't be saying that if he knew the direction Jacob's thoughts had been going in for a while now.

"Have you heard from Lady Elizabeth?" Maria asked suddenly, her voice filled with excitement.

Jacob tried his best not to sigh. "I have not."

"Why not? Hasn't she written you?"

"She hasn't."

"I wonder why that is." Maria sounded quite confused by that. "Have you written to her then?"

He paused, waiting for the flood of energy from the coffee to fill him whole before he answered. "I have not."

"Why not?" Henry demanded. "Hasn't it been three days already since you've last seen her? If you take too long to reach out to her, Jacob, she will think that you do not think highly of her."

"I did not know that you are the expert in winning the hearts of ladies, Father," Jacob teased, hoping it would be enough to bring a genuine smile to his face. It was, but not for long.

Henry, however, did not look like he was in the mood to jest. "If I didn't know better, Jacob, I would think you are not taking this seriously. Surely you understand how important it is that you marry soon."

"I understand."

His simple response left them in silence. Jacob hoped that it would last for the remainder of breakfast, but those hopes were dashed when his mother turned slightly to him.

"Well?" she probed. "Will you write to her?"

"I will." *Though it will contain the word you hope I will say.*

"Oh, I just love the thought of the two of you together," Maria gushed. "Lady Elizabeth is such a lovely lady, don't you think, Jacob? So beautiful, and demure, and well-spoken."

Jacob only gave her a slight nod. All those things he could agree with. Lady Elizabeth truly was the epitome of what a lady of England should be. But even though he could not deny his mother's words, he also knew that those things were not enough for a lasting marriage. Not if he did not feel any affection towards her at all.

But Cassandra...

*She* was the lady he yearned for. Now that he knew who she truly was, it felt as if the clouds hanging over his head had drifted away, revealing the glorious rays of sunshine that made his mind clearer. He understood what he truly felt for her, even though it was outrageous to think that he could feel this deeply for a lady he'd only seen three times. Jacob didn't care about the logic. He only cared about her. And he wanted to prove to her that what he felt was nothing to ignore.

He glanced at his mother, half-listening while she continued to gush about how lovely Lady Elizabeth was. Both her and his father would be upset to learn that Jacob had no interest in her, and that he did not plan to pursue to the courtship any longer. He could only hope that he did not upset Lady Elizabeth too much by cutting their courtship short so quickly. But he planned on following his heart.

"Oh, goodness!" Maria said suddenly, clapping her hands together. "How could I have forgotten? I received an invitation for a dinner ball from Lady Wiswall early this morning."

"Did we?" Henry probed with interest while Jacob's heart lifted in his chest. Though he knew why his mother was so excited about the invitation, all he could think about was the fact that he might see Cassandra again.

"Oh, this is perfect, Jacob," his mother continued. "When we go, you could spend some time with Lady Elizabeth. Though I would like to speak with her myself. I think she would make such a lovely daughter-in-law and I cannot wait to get to know her better."

*Daughter-in-law?* Unease drifted through Jacob at that word. He couldn't bring himself to answer and his mother continued, going on about future wedding plans and the grandchildren she was hoping to have. Any chances of eating anything went out the window, his stomach in knots.

*I have to put an end to this.*

Jacob endured breakfast as best as he could before he excused himself. He left with his mother's worried protests following him out the room and he knew she would find him later to fuss over him. But that was a problem for later. For now, he needed his courage, knowing the conversation he was going to have later.

*** 

Later came within a couple of hours, after Jacob returned to his chambers for a short nap. It helped to shed some of the fatigue that plagued him since the morning began but as he made his way to his father's study, he knew that whatever strength he had would be sapped in an instant.

He knocked and a moment later, he heard his father's brusque voice beckoning him to enter.

Henry's eyes followed Jacob from the door all the way to the armchair where he sat. Jacob suddenly wished he'd poured himself a glass of whiskey for this conversation.

"What is it, son?" Henry asked, putting his quill pen down to give Jacob his full attention.

"I have made a decision about my current courtship," Jacob stated.

Henry raised a brow. "Oh? I pray it is what I hope?"

"Unfortunately, Father, it is not." Jacob waited, watching how his father narrowed his eyes. "I know you and Mother have grown enamored with the idea of my marriage to Lady Elizabeth, but I do not think I can continue courting her."

"And why is that? You've only called on her once."

"Once is enough to know that I feel no affection towards her."

"That is something that can come with time, Jacob," Henry stated, sounding exasperated. "Lady Elizabeth is the diamond of the season. You will not find a better match than her. It wouldn't make any sense for you to reject your union only because you feel no affection, especially seeing that you know you can feel affection for her over time."

"And what if I do not, Father? I do not wish to be shackled to a lady for the rest of my life on the thought that I *might* come to care for her."

"Love is not important when it comes on to marriage, Jacob. I do not know how many times I have to explain that to you. All that matters is that your union is capable benefiting your future generations. If you two are able to become friends along the way, that is wonderful. Even more so if you fall in love. But what is important for your future comes first."

Jacob stubbornly shook his head. "I do not need to hear the same lecture, Father. I have already made up my mind."

Henry's jaw ticked with annoyance. He rested his elbows on his desk, lacing his fingers. "Then what do you plan to do instead? Surely you have another person in mind if you wish to reject her so soundly."

"I do." He straightened in his chair. "Lady Elizabeth has a sister, Lady Cassandra—"

"Enough!" Henry barked, shocking Jacob into silence. "If you are about to say what I think you will, I do not want to hear any more. That is not an option."

Jacob frowned, anger surging in him at the quick dismissal. "And why not?"

"Lady Cassandra? She is nothing but a scarred spinster! Courting her would only damage your reputation, let alone a marriage."

"Father, how could you—"

"Enough, I said!" Henry bellowed. His face was growing red with anger. "You know better than to come to me with such nonsense. Under no circumstances are you to even consider tarnishing the family name by your desire to pursue such a lady. She will do nothing but ruin us."

"You hardly know her," Jacob protested. "She is the most beautiful lady I know and I find it foolish for others to judge her because of a scar that—"

Still, Henry would not listen. "Jacob, you will do the honourable thing and continue courting Lady Elizabeth."

The order tugged at his last tether of restraint, his anger spilling through him. It trembled throughout his body and it took all his strength not to lash out at his father, not wanting to be disrespectful.

"And what if I do not?" Jacob asked in a low voice.

Henry narrowed his eyes. "It is not up for discussion, Jacob. Now leave me be and stop bothering me with such nonsense."

With that said, he picked back up his quill pen and continued what he was doing. Jacob could only stare at him, his mind racing with all the things he wanted to say. But he knew his father would not budge on the matter. Pushing back right now would only make them both more upset.

As much as he hated the thought of doing so, Jacob knew he had to retreat for now. He'd already suspected that his father would not take kindly to his decision, which was why he had been dreading the conversation in the first place. But he thought it would be because of his unwillingness to court Lady Elizabeth, not because of his desire to turn his full attention to the older sister instead.

Jacob wanted so badly to put his father in his place for daring to offend Cassandra in that manner. But he stood, drawing in a deep breath to calm himself before he turned and stiffly made his way out of the study.

His father was only another person he'd have to convince to let this match happen.

The first was Cassandra herself.

## Chapter Twenty-Four

"Everything is happening so quickly, don't you think?" Viola asked, resting a hand on Cassandra's arm.

The touch was enough to pull Cassandra from her deep thoughts, vaguely nodding at her mother. "Yes, but you are quite skilled mother, so I am not surprised."

"I agree," Elizabeth chirped. They were traveling in the open-topped carriage today, so the wind brushed against Elizabeth's curls and the sun brought a lovely flush to her cheeks. She looked particularly lovely on this fine afternoon, while Cassandra felt like she'd been dragged through the street.

"Oh, you two, don't flatter me too much," Viola gushed, waving a hand at her daughters. "But I will admit that it is quite a feat to plan a ball in so little time."

"I'm sure it will be lovely, Mother," Cassandra murmured, hardly hearing herself speak. She gazed out at the side of the road as they neared Bond Street. She hadn't wanted to leave the manor today. Her plan had been to wallow in bed for the entire day, trying to banish the memory of Jacob and his heart-racing words from her mind. Every day she attempted it, she failed.

"Have you invited many people, Mother?" Elizabeth asked.

"Not as many as you would think," Viola explained. "It is supposed to be an intimate ball, my dear. It isn't as if I need as many gentlemen there as possible for you to find your match. You're already courting Lord Charlington, after all."

Cassandra could have sworn Elizabeth's smile grew a little tighter. "That's true. So I assume you have invited him then."

"Of course I have! Why wouldn't I invite your future husband and his family?"

Cassandra's heart sank. They were on their way to Bond Street to do final fittings for their dresses for the ball. She didn't want to go to the ball at all and now that she knew for a fact that Jacob had been invited, she was filled with both trepidation and eagerness. She hadn't seen him since that day at Hyde Park. Since he revealed his heart to her and all but begged her to do the same.

Only, Cassandra still could not believe that he truly wanted her the way he'd expressed. What man in their right mind would want a scarred woman like herself, when he had the option of having such a beauty like Elizabeth?

Her mind drifted as her mother and sister continued to talk about the ball that would be happening tomorrow. Every time she thought of how he'd looked at her, at the way he'd held her hand and pulled her so close to him, Cassandra thought she might combust. Her face would grow so hot that it was a wonder she didn't pass out from the heat.

It didn't make any sense, she told herself. All the things he'd said, the emotions he'd expressed to her...coming from a man so handsome who could have any woman he wished, why did he want her?

*Oh, goodness, there's no need to be so self-deprecating*, she thought depressingly, resisting the urge to heave a great sigh.

For now there was no use lamenting what had happened between them, and the things that could never happen. If he continued courting Elizabeth, that meant she could not ignore him forever. He was bound to come around. And she would have to be cordial and forget her feelings if she wanted to stand a chance at being happy.

"Oh, we're here!" her mother chirped suddenly, pulling Cassandra from her dour thoughts. It took much effort to drag herself out of the carriage, a fleeting smile appearing on her face when Elizabeth linked her arm with hers. It was destined to be a long day, she knew. And she didn't know how long she'd be able to wear this mask.

The moment they entered the modiste's shop, Madame Henri rushed at the door, her eyes glistening with excitement.

"Well, if it isn't the diamond herself!" she gushed as she pulled Elizabeth from Cassandra's side. "How long it has been since I've last seen you! What are you all here for today?"

Cassandra watched as Madame Henri swept her gaze over her as if she didn't exist and came to rest on the viscountess. She tried not to let it bother her. Besides, she much preferred being ignored to open stares at her veil.

"We are hoping to have a few dresses tailored for a ball tomorrow evening," Viola said, already scanning the shop for fabrics and colors she might like.

"I'll take care of you both, don't worry!" Madame Henri quickly ushered Viola and Elizabeth over to the large rolls of fabrics and bespoke dresses she had in one corner of the room. Elizabeth glanced over her shoulder at Cassandra, gesturing for her to follow.

Cassandra trailed quietly behind, a little annoyed by how easily the modiste was pretending she wasn't there. There were a few other ladies already browsing the shop, being assisted by who Cassandra assumed was the modiste's assistant. She felt them staring at her but she didn't pay them any mind, keeping her back straight.

"My eldest daughter will be having a dress fitted for her as well," Viola announced, reaching out to grasp Cassandra by her hand and pull her forward.

Madame Henri looked at Cassandra as if it were her first time noticing her. "Oh, is she?"

"Why would I not be, madam?" Cassandra spoke, her voice chilly. "I intend to enjoy this Season like every other lady in London."

"Ah, of course, of course." Clearly flustered, Madame Henri rushed to her side, steering her forward. "Then let us start with you first, shall we? Oh my, what a lovely figure you have."

Cassandra didn't answer, trying to tamper her annoyance at the modiste. While she stood still as Madame Henri took her measurements, Elizabeth and Viola drifted to the side to chatter about the ball and what colors they should wear. Their excitement was palpable and Cassandra felt a twinge of guilt at the fact that she could not muster up the same.

"Are you enjoying the Season thus far, my lady?" asked Madam Henri.

Cassandra mulled over whether she should answer her or not, and decided at last that she should at least take the high road. "I am."

"I'm happy to hear that! It is an important time in a lady's life, you know. To meet many gentlemen who come from all around England—sometimes from other parts of the world!—to find herself a husband."

"Yes, I suppose that's true."

"And what of yourself? Is there any gentleman that catches your eye?"

Cassandra was suddenly glad for the veil that shielded her expression. "I only wish to support my sister's coming out."

"Ah, I understand. Though it is a pity that you are unable to take part yourself. There is nothing more fulfilling for a lady than to have a family and a home they can take care of."

"I'm sure there is more to life than such things," Cassandra murmured, though she was having a hard time thinking about anything but Jacob right now.

"Is there?" the modiste mused aloud. She stepped away before Cassandra could respond, giving Cassandra a look of pity before she wiped it off her face and gestured to one of the changing rooms. "Why don't you get undressed and I'll bring you something I think might fit."

Cassandra nodded stiffly, moving off to the dressing room. As she neared, she heard the other ladies present giggling, but she couldn't hear what they were laughing about. Nor did she care to right now. The only thing she wanted was to go home, bury her nose in a book, and forget about the world around her.

Except, now even reading brought on the vivid memory of Jacob and all he had said at Hyde Park. She could not even read her favorite Shakespearean story without thinking about him and all he'd said to her. It was now tainted, but in the most bittersweet manner possible.

Alone in the dressing room, Cassandra drew in a soft breath and let it slowly out her nose. It did nothing to calm her. She didn't like being in public with her veil on, didn't like having to face the curiosity and questions about why she had to step aside while her younger sister participated this Season. Alone in her manor, she could deal with the idea of becoming a spinster. But now that she was faced with the possibility of true love...

*No! I cannot entertain such an idea! Elizabeth has grown smitten with the marquess and I cannot interfere with their courtship.*

Cassandra squared her shoulders, hating the pain that laced her heart at the thought of the two of them being married.

"Are you ready?" Madame Henri called from the other end with a soft knock.

"Yes," Cassandra answered. The quicker they were done with this, the quicker they could be home. Though, knowing her mother and sister, they would want to wander around Bond Street a little longer.

The modiste entered bearing three lovely ball gowns that swept the floor. Cassandra barely looked at them, not caring what she wore to the ball. In all honesty, she'd prefer a drab brown gown if that meant she could be a fly on the wall, where no one paid her any mind.

"Do you need any he—"

"I'm fine, thank you."

"I'll give you some privacy then," Madame Henri murmured as she slipped out of the room.

Cassandra listened as the modiste happily went back to Viola and Elizabeth, gushing about how beautiful Elizabeth was. Holding back her sigh, she reached for her first dress.

It was a lovely number in truth, with puffed sleeve the color of primroses and a dark pink satin belt around the waist. Cassandra donned it quickly, then turned to the tall mirror behind her.

She looked...lovely. The dress was a little different from her usual styles, yet simple enough that she didn't think she was standing out. It settled nicely on her figure, emboldening Cassandra to lift her veil.

The scar sat starkly against her left jaw, slicing awkwardly into her cheek. But this time, Cassandra didn't recoil at the sight. She didn't turn away. She tilted her head to the side instead, observing the way the dim light above her head cast shadows on the angles of her face, how her eyes seemed as dark as midnight. Her heart didn't twist in her chest at the horrible scarring because...well, was it really that horrible?

She came closer to the mirror, brushing her fingers against her jaw. She'd always hated this mark on her face no matter how many times she willed herself to come to terms with it. But this was the first time she'd ever felt...acceptance. Perhaps even a smidgen of appreciation for the way it added depth to her face.

*Then society is a fool if they cannot see how beautiful you are.*

Cassandra felt heat rush her cheeks at the memory of Jacob's words. Could it really be true?

"Did you see her?"

"Of course I did! With that horrid veil she always wears, she's quite difficult to miss."

Cassandra felt sharp dread slice through her at the voices on the other side of the door. She knew without a doubt that they were the ladies she'd seen earlier. Shame washed her at the fact that they were standing so close to her dressing room, as if they didn't care if she overheard them or not.

"Why does she even bother?" said one of the girls in an excited whisper. "No one is going to notice her anyway. It must truly be so terrible having a younger sister who outshines you in every way."

"I know! I pity her, honestly. If I were her, I would never leave my home."

Anger surged in Cassandra, seizing her so sharply that she had to clench her jaw to keep from bursting through the door and forcing them to say it to her face. She tightened her fists, trying to tamper the rage. How cowardly of them to gossip about her when she was standing so close by.

She acted without thinking, gathering her skirts and marching to the door. Just as she reached for the handle, one of them whispered, "Have you see her scar?"

Cassandra froze. The anger rushed out of her, leaving her with a stark sense of defeat.

"No, I haven't," the other whispered back. "But I can only imagine how terrible it makes her look. That's why she is destined to live the rest of her life as a spinster, after all."

The girls giggled, the sounds fading as they walked away. Cassandra lifted a trembling hand to wipe at the tear that had escaped her eye. She hadn't cried about her state in years and she wasn't going to fall back into that terrible habit now. She was stronger than that.

And smarter. Smart enough to know that they were right, and that it was useless thinking she could ever be anything but the scarred lady who would never be married.

# Chapter Twenty-Five

Wiswall Manor seemed larger than usually on this particular night. Jacob supposed it had something to do with the way the moonlight struck the imposing home, partially hidden as it was behind a large cloud. Even so, it was a lovely evening, with a gentle breeze that chased away Jacob's trepidation, filling him with determination instead. He had a goal in mind today and he wasn't going to allow anything get in the way.

"I take it you have given some thought to what we've decided," came Henry's voice, breaking into Jacob's thought.

Jacob looked away from the dark sky, narrowing his eyes at his father across from him. The carriage shook and rattled as it traveled over the cobblestone driveway, bringing them closer to the front of the long line waiting to be attended to.

"We did not decide anything," Jacob responded.

"Jacob, do not test me," Henry growled. "Not tonight of all nights."

"Father, I cannot imagine what you are referring to," Jacob drawled, turning his attention back out the window even though he focused on nothing.

"Is something the matter?" Maria asked to Jacob's left.

Jacob left it up to his father to answer, who only mumbled, "Nothing you need to concern yourself about, dear," before they all settled into silence. Jacob knew his mother would confront Henry about it later, but for now she didn't press the issue. Which Jacob was glad for. The last thing he wanted was to sour his mood with an argument when he was already minutes away from seeing the lady he loved again.

His excitement mounted when they finally came to the front and the carriage was approached by two footmen. The footmen opened the door for them but Jacob hardly took note of them. His body was thrumming with eagerness now, itching with the urge to run ahead himself.

It had been four days since he'd seen Cassandra and it felt as if he was about to go mad. He hadn't tried to contact her since their talk in the park, sensing that she might have needed her space. But he couldn't go another day without seeing her.

And tonight, he would convince her to accept his love.

Jacob walked slightly ahead of his parents as they were led into the manor and towards the dining hall where the ball was being held. It was meant to be an intimate event, according to the invitation, but the decorations were lavish enough to make him wonder just how true that was. Most of the guests congregated in the center of the dining hall, with tables and chairs tucked away to the side. The tables were laden with refreshments, a few ladies already occupying some of the chairs.

And in the one in the furthest corner of the room was Cassandra.

She was wearing a pale pink veil that matched her primrose-colored gown, her head turned away from the door. Jacob's heart thudded in his chest at the sight of her, his excitement mounting. She had her hands clasped in her lap with her back straight, the picture of perfection. Yet she was clearly separating herself from the festivities.

Jacob separated himself from his parents before they had a chance to say anything to him, heading straight towards her. In the corner of his eye, he noticed Lord and Lady Wiswall as he went by and he made a mental note to greet them later. For now, the only person he cared about seeing was Cassandra.

She noticed him when he was almost to her. She quickly got to her feet, looking as if she was about to take a step towards him. But then her sister—whom Jacob hadn't noticed before—touched her arm and Cassandra froze.

Jacob slowed as he neared. He hadn't expected Lady Elizabeth to be there. He wanted to talk to Cassandra alone.

But it was too late. Lady Elizabeth had noticed him and gave him a wide smile. "Lord Charlington," she greeted warmly, sinking into a perfect curtsy.

"My lady," Jacob murmured, glancing at Cassandra. That annoying veil made it difficult for him to know what she was thinking.

"It is lovely to see you again," Lady Elizabeth said. "I had enjoyed our time at the park and had hoped to hear from you again."

"My apologies, Lady Elizabeth. I suddenly grew busy with work I had been putting aside for some time now."

Lady Elizabeth nodded, accepting the lie with ease. "I understand. A man of your stature must have quite a lot on his plate."

"Yes, I suppose." He glanced at Cassandra again. He simply couldn't help himself. "Good evening, Lady Cassandra."

"Good evening, my lord," she answered easily, her voice aloof.

"I trust you have been well?"

"I have. And you, my lord? Last we saw you, you were ailed by the sweets you'd eaten."

He might have been mistaken, but he could have sworn he heard a twinge of humor in her voice. "Yes, well, you would think I'd learned not to indulge too much at my age."

"I suppose, but it's never too late to learn. In other news, would you like a slice of cake?"

Jacob chuckled. The tension that had been sitting like a knot in the base of his skull eased instantly when she laughed in return. "Are you laying a trap, my lady?"

"It was a test. And I think you passed. It will only get harder from here on out."

"And I welcome them all."

He grinned from ear to ear. At that moment, only the two of them mattered. Jacob didn't care about Lady Elizabeth, or his parents, or the expectations that had been placed on the both of them. And now, more than ever he was determined to leave here this evening knowing that he had Cassandra as his own.

Cassandra turned her head to the side and it broke the moment, bringing him back to the present. Before he could say anything, Simon approached.

"Well, if it isn't my two favourite ladies in the world," he greeted with a broad smile. "Don't tell me that Lord Charlington here has already taken the first place on your dance cards."

Lady Elizabeth shook her head, a blush staining her cheeks. "He hasn't, actually..."

"But I was about to," Jacob said quickly. "If you had not interrupted."

Simon's eyes sparkled with mischief. "Then you'd better hurry. You're standing with the two most beautiful ladies in the room. Already every other gentleman in attendance is staring at you with envy."

"Oh, stop it, Simon," Lady Elizabeth chastised, though a smile played around her lips. "You might make him feel bad when he did nothing wrong."

"He should feel bad. He'll have to stay alert lest another gentleman comes along and sweeps you away."

For a moment, Jacob could have sworn he heard a hint of seriousness in his tone but it was quickly covered up with a laugh. He didn't bother to answer to Simon's taunts, stepping forward to write his name on Lady Elizabeth's dance card. He did it because he knew it was expected of him, and he didn't want his parents to question him about why he hadn't been her first dance.

But he couldn't stop himself from turning quickly to Cassandra, just as Lady Elizabeth turned to Simon. Jacob could feel Cassandra's eyes boring into him as he scribbled his name. He took his time, savoring their closeness, how lovely she smelled. He wanted nothing more than to lift her veil, if only just to see her eyes.

When he was done, he didn't step away. He opened his mouth to tell her how lovely she looked when the first chord of music struck, cutting into his words.

"Ah, the first set is beginning," Cassandra said, taking a step away from him and breaking the connection. "You two should take your positions."

"Then, shall we dance?" Simon asked, sweeping in between Jacob and Cassandra with his hand held out to her. Jacob frowned at them, feeling a sharp stab of jealousy.

Cassandra easily slid her hand into his. "Do not step on my feet this time," she warned, laughter in her voice.

"I make no promises," Simon answered. And then he led her away, leaving Jacob and Lady Elizabeth staring after them.

The jealousy kept simmering in him even as he forced himself to face the sister he was meant to be courting. She was staring after Cassandra and Simon as well, a look of longing in her eyes. The moment Jacob held out his hand, however, the look cleared and she gave him a smile.

Silently, he led her to the center of the room where the other dancers had taken up their positions. Thankfully, the first dance was the cotillion which meant he found himself next to Cassandra again. But her head was turned away from him, focused pointedly on Simon who was making an odd expression that made her laugh. Jacob's jealousy deepened to something almost tangible.

The dance began. Jacob tried to focus on the steps, on his main partner. But at points, he came in contact with Cassandra and it took all his strength not to forgo what they were doing and pull her into his arms. The dance seemed to last a lifetime, with Cassandra so close and yet so terribly far.

At long last, it came to an end. But still Cassandra ignored him, curtsying to her dance partner while Jacob tried his best not to stare at her. He didn't want to seem rude to Lady Elizabeth, but for some reason, it seemed as if she was more focused on something else as well.

The next set began nearly instantly. And lo and behold, it was a waltz. Jacob thought the heavens might be shining down on him.

Cassandra turned to him, saying nothing. So neither did he. He only took her hand and pulled her close as the music began, noting vaguely that Simon did the same with Lady Elizabeth.

"Have you been well, Cassie?" Jacob whispered.

Her hand tightened in his hold. "Please don't call me that," she whispered back.

"Why? I thought it would be cute, though I suppose I am not the sort of gentleman who tries to act adorably."

"Don't joke about it," she was quick to chastise. "You know exactly why I'm saying that. We can't be too familiar with each other."

"And why not?" he asked as if he simply could not understand why.

Cassandra lifted her head to him. "Don't pretend to be dense."

"I am not pretending. I am actually very dense. I only pretend to be smart to save face."

She stared silently at him for a moment, then huffed a laugh under her breath. "You're unbelievable."

Jacob chuckled. "So will you tell me why I cannot call you Cassie or not?"

"You know why, Jacob. You are courting my sister and we are not close enough for others to think it's normal."

"Who cares what others think?"

"I do," she answered softly. "As much as I hate to admit it, I care deeply about what others think because whatever I do reflects on my family as well. And I cannot allow their names to be tainted by my own any more than it already has."

Now it was his turn to chastise her. "You're being hard on yourself. Would it make you feel better if I let you call me 'Jakey' then?"

"Jacob!" she hissed under her breath but there was no hiding the thread of humor in her voice.

Jacob laughed, letting it die a little later as he prepared himself for what he was going to say next. "I'm so happy to see you again, Cassie. You're all I've been thinking about since we last parted ways."

"You shouldn't—"

"You say that but that doesn't stop what I feel. The only reason I cared to come to this ball was because I knew I would see you again."

She was quiet for a moment. Again, Jacob found himself wishing he could see her face, just to know where her thoughts were heading.

"I thought about you as well," she murmured at long last.

Jacob thought his heart was about to beat right out of his chest. He tried and failed to keep the broad, happy grin off his face. "Have you now?"

"Yes, nearly every second of the day," she breathed, sounding defeated. "Even though I know that I shouldn't. Even though I am well aware of my position—"

"Which should be by my side," he told her instantly.

Cassandra looked sharply at him. "That is something you should say to my sister. Not me."

"It's something I should say to the lady I love," he answered determinedly. "Which is you."

Cassandra shook her head. "Jacob, we can't—"

"Is it Simon?" he asked suddenly. "Are you hoping that he will wish to court you instead?"

"No, Simon is only my friend," Cassandra answered without a moment of hesitation, easily dissipating the mountain of uncertainty that had been building in him. He relaxed, even though she continued to shake her head. "Both our parents are committed to the idea of your marriage with my sister and there is nothing that can be done about it."

"You don't have to worry about that, my love. Say the word and I shall handle it."

Jacob waited. The dance was coming to an end, which meant their conversation would be as well. And he knew it would draw unwanted attention to them if they dared to dance again tonight, especially if he didn't do the same with Lady Elizabeth. Jacob didn't care about what others said, but Cassandra had made it clear that she did and he didn't want to put her in an uncomfortable position.

*What a hypocrite I am*, he thought to himself as he continued to wait for her to respond. A second dance he was willing to put aside yet he knew the pressure he was putting on her with his question. Yet, he couldn't help himself. He knew his heart and knew very well what she was denying herself in order to put her sister and her family first.

"Cassie?" he probed gently.

"I..." she began. But she never finished. Instead, she stepped away from him, clearing her head. Whether it was at him or at herself, he didn't know but it didn't matter. She'd already decided to step on his heart one more time, pain shooting through him.

"Cassandra, wait," Jacob called but she was already turning away. He nearly gave chase, not wanting her to disappear again. But then Simon called to him and it forced him to stop, staring after her instead.

Simon said something to him, leading him away from the other guests preparing for the next set. But he didn't hear what he said. He only focused on Cassandra's retreating frame, fearing that he was fated to do just that for the rest of his life.

## Chapter Twenty-Six

"Do you like it?"

"I do," Cassandra answered absentmindedly. She hardly noticed that she'd nodded, her gaze directed out the window.

"You know I am far more likely to believe you if you were actually looking at me," Elizabeth said with a sigh.

Cassandra looked at her sister, who was giving her a frown, her hands on her hips. She gave her a small, apologetic smile. "I was looking," she protested. "And you needn't ask because you know you look good in anything you wear."

Elizabeth flushed, rolling her eyes. "You're exaggerating."

"No, I'm not but your modesty is part of your charm."

"Oh, goodness, whatever you say," Elizabeth responded, sounding a little exasperated. "Your mind has been wandering a lot lately, I know. I wouldn't be surprised if you hadn't heard a single word I'd said."

Cassandra felt a twinge of guilt at the observation. She couldn't deny it. All of last night into this morning, all Cassandra's thoughts would drift towards Jacob. No matter how many times she tried to banish him from her mind, he plagued her, filling her with such acute longing that she was tempted to throw caution to the wind. But every time she began to ponder her own true feelings towards him, Cassandra didn't let it go any further. She knew she had feelings for him but she didn't dare to explore just how deeply those feelings ran.

Or at least, she was willing to pretend that she didn't know.

"Is something the matter?" Elizabeth asked, coming to her side. She took Cassandra's hand, eyes filled with worry. "Did something happen at the ball last night?"

"Nothing happened, Lizzie," Cassandra answered with a smile on her face. Elizabeth's frown only deepened at the sight.

"Are you sure?" Elizabeth squeezed Cassandra's hand. "Did anyone say something to you last night? Because, if they did, just tell me their names and—"

"No one said a word to me," Cassandra told her, hating how bitter she sounded. She drew in a breath and tried again. "What I mean to say is that you don't have to worry about that."

"You know I can't help myself. I know you tend to let those rumours upset you."

"I am the big sister, you know. You don't need to be overprotective of me. I can take care of myself."

"I know that, I know. But I can't help myself. And it upsets me whenever anyone says anything because no one truly knows how beautiful you are."

Cassandra's smile dimmed a bit. She appreciated the kind words but she could only think of one thing. "You overheard those ladies at the modiste's shop, didn't you?"

Elizabeth gave her a sad nod. "I did. And all I wanted to do was give them a piece of my mind!"

"They're right, though—"

"No, they're not! And neither are you if you are foolish enough to think such a thing."

Cassandra rarely ever saw her sister get so upset and she didn't like that it was at her expense. Tonight was to be a happy occasion. Soon, they would be heading to Covent Theatre to see the play with Simon and Adeline. And Jacob. But Cassandra wasn't going to let her mind linger on *him*.

What mattered was that she wanted her sister to be happy, not frustrated at the fact that Cassandra brought nothing but bad rumors wherever she went.

"Never mind that," Cassandra said in a placating tone. "You should continue getting ready. It will soon be time for us to leave."

Elizabeth tightened her lips, looking as if she was ready to argue further. But then she let out a sigh and Cassandra relaxed, knowing that her sister would let it go for now.

Elizabeth stood and made her way back to her vanity table. "I am almost ready," she said, reaching for her jewelry box. "I just need to find the right necklace and then I'll be fine to leave. I don't want to keep Lord Charlington waiting."

Cassandra turned her attention back out the window, happy that Elizabeth couldn't see the look of pain that crossed her features at the mention of the marquess. She didn't want to think about him, didn't want the conversation to shift to him even as she asked, "Are you excited to see him again?"

"I am," Elizabeth answered simply. She was too busy sorting through her necklaces. "I enjoy his company."

"I'm sure he enjoys yours as well." Cassandra paused, biting her lip to hold back her next question. It didn't work. "So…if he asks for your hand in marriage, will you accept?"

Elizabeth stopped what she was doing as she thought about it. And then she nodded slowly, each move of her head tearing Cassandra's heart to smaller shreds. "I suppose I must have to."

"You don't have to do anything," Cassandra murmured but Elizabeth heard her.

"It is what Mother and Father wants. And if he asks, it must mean it is what he wants as well."

"What about what you want?"

This time, Elizabeth took a long moment to answer. Then, she mumbled softly, "I only want to be happy."

"I want you to be happy as well," Cassandra said to her, blinking away the traitorous tears that filled her eyes.

"As do I for you, Cassie." Elizabeth found the necklace she wanted to wear and as she clasped it on, she turned to Cassandra. Cassandra schooled her features, hoping that her sister wouldn't notice that she'd started crying. "I want to see you happy and in love and raising a family of your own."

Cassandra gave her a smile that she knew didn't quite meet her eyes. "What if what I want is to spend the rest of my days alone and unmarried?"

"Then I would support you," Elizabeth answered without missing a beat, "but I know that isn't the case."

Cassandra opened her mouth to answer, a light-hearted excuse on the tip of her tongue, but she was interrupted by a knock on the door.

"Cassie? Lizzie?" called Viola on the other end. "Lord Charlington has arrived to escort you two to the theatre."

"Oh, wait, I cannot leave yet!" Elizabeth wailed suddenly. "I wish to change my gown. My necklace doesn't match."

"Then change the necklace," Cassandra suggested just as Viola came into the room.

"No," Elizabeth pouted. "The necklace is beautiful and I want to wear it tonight. I'm sure I can find another dress that will match."

"Oh, dear," Viola sighed, hands on her hips. She shook her head as if Elizabeth just couldn't be helped. "Cassie, could you go and tell Lord Charlington that Elizabeth will be down shortly? I don't want him to think we're being rude. I'll stay and help her with her dress."

Cassandra gaped at her mother, staring at her as she joined Elizabeth by her wardrobe. Protests rushed to the tip of her tongue but none of them were good enough to be voiced. So she stood, heart pounding with anticipation as she quietly left the room.

Each step towards the drawing room had her palms sweating. Cassandra tried to tuck her feelings into a box in her heart, locking them away, but the thought of seeing him again had them bursting free and filling her whole. After all he'd said last night, she began to think about what it would be like to call herself Lady Charlington. To wake in the morning with him by her side, to bear him an heir while he promised to stand by her side and protect her until the end of her days.

She hated imagining those things, the longing too strong to ignore. It was torturous, a life she could never have.

Outside the door of the drawing room, Cassandra took a deep breath, steeling her nerves. Then she entered.

Jacob was sitting by one of the bay windows. He rose when he saw her enter, a ghost of a smile on his lips. "Cassie..." he breathed.

"I thought I told you that it's best you don't call me that," Cassandra said, her tone far softer than she'd wanted it to be. She needed to be colder, to solidify the walls she was trying to erect between them.

"I can't help myself." Then he ran his gaze down the length of her, bringing a burning blush to her cheeks. "You look breathtaking."

"Thank you." She looked away because she couldn't handle the intensity of his eyes. "Mother asked me to tell you that Elizabeth will be down in a few minutes."

"I didn't come to see Lady Elizabeth. I came to see you."

Cassandra drew in a breath, closing her eyes as if that was enough to block out his words. When she opened her eyes again, she noticed him coming closer and instantly side-stepped his advances, not daring to allow him to come closer.

"Why do you insist on ignoring everything I'm telling you?" Cassandra demanded to know, putting another few feet between them.

Jacob paused, his brows knitting together. "Because I know you don't really mean what you're saying, Cassie. You say one thing but then the way you look at me."

"The way I look—" She broke off, realizing suddenly that she'd forgotten to pull her veil down. She instantly brushed it over her face. "It doesn't matter what you think I'm feeling for you, Jacob. What matters is that you're courting my sister!"

"I'm sure Lady Elizabeth will not mind if I decide I no longer want to court her anymore."

"You don't know that."

"You know her better than I do and you aren't very convinced by it either. She is a beautiful lady. I'm sure she has scores of men longing to court her in my stead."

"And then what will you do? Will you tell the world that you've decided you like the scarred sister more? What will your parents say when they learn of that?"

Jacob's jaw hardened. "I can handle my parents. They will just have to understand."

Cassandra shook her head. She knew very well what that meant and though it hurt her to know the truth, she also savored it. If only to help her get over him faster. "I don't believe that, Jacob. They will never approve of you and I. I am nothing but a blight on your pristine reputation."

"Don't say things like that, Cassandra!" Jacob said sharply, making her blink in surprise. "It pains me to know how easily you will push yourself into a corner and pretend as if you are nothing but a mistake when you are quite literally the most beautiful, most compelling lady I have ever met. What I feel for you can hardly be explained in words, but I am willing to spend the rest of my days telling you how much I care for you if that is what it means to have you in my life."

"Jacob, please..." She couldn't hold back the tears this time. Jacob was by her side in a second, pulling her into his arms. Cassandra went still when his arms wrapped around her but she couldn't find the strength to pull away from him.

"I know. I know it must be hard. I know you are thinking about your sister's welfare over your own and you have already committed to a life of spinsterhood because of a scar. But if you would only give in to what your heart is telling you, Cassie, I promise to make you the happiest lady on this earth."

It was tempting, so tempting to give in. But all she could think about was her conversation with Elizabeth earlier. Her sister's happiness was what mattered.

Before she could try to say that again, Jacob lifted her veil, revealing her tear-streaked face. Cassandra tried to pull away from him. No one had ever seen her scarred face so closely and she knew she must be quite a sight now that she was crying. But Jacob tightened his hold, his eyes growing tender.

"I love you, Cassandra," he murmured.

Cassandra's lips parted but no words came forth. She savored those three beautiful words. Over the next few seconds, she let his love wash over her, allowed herself to believe everything he was saying. That she was beautiful, that she would be happy, that she was loved.

But then, when the moment was over, Cassandra firmly tugged herself out of his hold, taking a step away from him. She wiped her face but didn't pull the veil back down. "I'm sorry, Jacob."

The pain on his face was enough to deepen her own. For a moment, it looked as if he was going to pull her into his arms again and Cassandra knew she would let him. But instead he walked away, dragging a hand down his face. Cassandra released the breath she was holding, hating how much it hurt to watch him walk away from her.

"This doesn't make any sense," she murmured, loud enough for him to hear. But he didn't turn around. "It was only one night."

Cassandra left it at that, knowing he understood what she was referring to. That fated night they'd met, the night neither of their hearts could recover from.

For a long while, nothing was said. Cassandra only stared at him from behind, as she was destined to do for the rest of her life. She didn't know what he was thinking and she was afraid to ask. As much as she wanted him to let go of all he'd said, she also knew it would tear her already fragile heart into a million pieces if he said so aloud.

Finally, Jacob moved, stalking back over to the window he'd been sitting by when she'd walked in. He sat heavily and then looked at her after a moment. "Are you excited about tonight's play?"

The change in the topic had her heart twisting in her chest. Cassandra couldn't understand why it hurt so much, but it helped her to put aside her emotions and focus on what she needed to do. Which was getting over him.

"I am," she admitted after the long moment she used to gather herself. "I've always wanted to see my favourite Shakespearean tale in theatre. I couldn't be more excited."

"Then I hope I did not ruin your night already," he said with a sad smile.

"You did not," she told him in a low tone. Jacob nodded then turned his attention to the window. Cassandra began making her way back to the door, not wanting to give him the chance to continue the conversation. The longer she stood here with him, the more it felt as if her heart was tearing out of her chest. "I shall go and see what is keeping Elizabeth so long."

"Cassie—"

But she left without giving him the chance to continue, chest heaving as the tears assaulted her once again.

# Chapter Twenty-Seven

Cassandra gathered her skirts and marched back towards her sister's bedchamber. Once she was outside the door, she wiped her tear-streaked face, squared her shoulders, and then entered.

"Lizzie? Are you ready—"

Elizabeth was in the process of grabbing her reticule, Viola watching her impatiently by the door.

"We're coming!" Elizabeth called then gave Cassandra a broad, excited grin, tucking her reticule under her arm as she brushed at her skirt. Cassandra could barely match her exuberance, steeling herself for the night ahead of her. She wasn't prepared to see him again. She knew very well that it would be quite difficult being around the man she couldn't have. But she had to. She had to prepare herself for the future she would have.

"Oh, truly, this girl will be the death of me," Viola sighed, shaking her head as she led the way out the door.

Cassandra stepped to the side as her mother and sister brushed past her, not noticing that she was still slowly falling apart. Neither of them seemed to notice that she was dragging her feet. Cassandra trailed behind them, feeling a rush of relief when Viola and Elizabeth began to talk amongst themselves. They weren't paying Cassandra much mind, leaving her free to torture herself with the memory of her conversation with Jacob.

He was still in the same spot she'd left him in. Cassandra was suddenly glad she had her veil. It was her one saving grace, so that he couldn't see the longing that would inevitably fill her eyes.

"My lord!" Elizabeth gushed once they entered the room. Cassandra stayed by the door, watching as Elizabeth hurried up to Jacob, who was slowly getting to a stand.

"Good evening, my lady," Jacob greeted with a polite smile. He took Elizabeth's hand and kissed the back of it. Cassandra looked away. "You look positively radiant this evening."

"Why, thank you, my lord," Elizabeth giggled. "And you look quite dashing yourself. I'm glad you decided to escort us to the theatre."

"Well, I couldn't just allow two beautiful ladies such as yourselves to be seen without an escort now, could I?"

"Did Simon come along with you?" Elizabeth asked, her tone high. Perhaps a little hopeful.

Cassandra still didn't let herself look at them. Her mother was standing by her side, grinning from ear to ear as she watched them converse. The happiness in Viola's eyes was so poignant that Cassandra had to look away from her too.

"Simon?" Jacob repeated, sounding confused. "No, he told me that he and Lady Adeline would meet us there. I thought he would have told you too."

"Oh." Elizabeth sounded slightly disappointed. "Perhaps he did tell me and I simply forgot. Anyway, shall we be on our way?"

Jacob didn't answer, though Cassandra saw movement in the corner of her eye which indicated that they were approaching her. She steeled herself, but nothing could prepare her for when he spoke to her.

"Lady Cassandra, it is good to see you again."

"Good evening, my lord," Cassandra murmured, keeping her eyes on the floor as she curtsied.

Jacob lingered for a moment. She could almost feel the weight of his stare burning through her veil.

"Let us go then, shall we?" he spoke at last and Cassandra blinked at the tears that suddenly stung her eyes. His voice was cold, aloof. A stark difference from the man from earlier. Maybe he had come to accept their positions, which should be a good thing. Her heart will learn that in time.

She gave them a stiff nod, turned, and walked out of the room. Thankfully, when she did, she took note of the fact that Jacob and Elizabeth were not standing arm in arm. She didn't realize just how much she'd been afraid of seeing that until it was no longer a reality.

She took the lead. Behind her, Viola began to engage Lord Charlington about mundane topics like the weather. He answered diplomatically but there was no denying the palpable excitement with which her mother spoke. She couldn't make it any more obvious that she was happy to have Jacob as a potential son-in-law.

Cassandra helped herself into the carriage before Jacob got the chance to offer his assistance. She knew he was staring at her but she didn't dare to give in to the urge to look at him. Instead, she stared out the window as the carriage took off.

"Are you ladies excited for the evening?" he asked at last. Cassandra knew the question was directedly mostly at Elizabeth, since he already knew her response, and that he was only trying to be polite by including her.

"I am!" Elizabeth said excitedly. "After hearing you and Cassie talk about Romeo and Juliet at the park, I'm eager to see what all the excitement is about."

"I'm sure you will not be disappointed."

"Have you seen this play already, my lord?"

"I haven't had the pleasure, no. It will be my first time."

"Then I am happy that we get to experience it together. Though I suppose I am much further behind than you are."

Cassandra didn't think she could take it any longer. She didn't want to hear them flirt with each other, even if she could tell it was done mostly out of politeness. Would it have really been that bad if she'd gone to the theatre without an escort?

Cassandra didn't realize that she was gripping her skirt tightly until Elizabeth's hand covered hers. She looked at her sister, who was frowning worriedly at her. "Are you all right, Cassie?" Elizabeth whispered.

"I am," Cassandra answered tightly but she knew she wasn't convincing.

Elizabeth leaned closer, dropping her voice to a whisper. "Does it hurt?"

Before she could shake her head, Jacob spoke, his voice sharp, "Does what hurt?"

They both looked at him. Cassandra was ready to shut him down, telling him that it was none of his concern, but Elizabeth spoke before she had the chance.

"Cassie's...injury tends to hurt now and again," she murmured.

"Elizabeth!" Cassandra hissed.

"It's all right, Cassie," Elizabeth told her in a gentle tone. "Lord Charlington won't judge you for it, I'm sure. If Simon trusts him, then I'm sure we can as well."

"When you mean injury, you're referring to..." Jacob's eyes darted to where Cassandra's scar was, though it was under the veil.

She felt her face grow red with embarrassment. Stiffly, she turned to the window. "You needn't worry about it."

"But if you're in pain—"

"I'm not."

She thought that the coldness of her voice would end the conversation there. At least, that was what she hoped. But then after a few seconds of tense silence, Jacob spoke again.

"How did you get the scar?"

Cassandra bit her lip. She didn't know why, but the answer rushed to the tip of her tongue. "It was a foolish accident involving a horse. Mother told me never to go riding without supervision and I did not listen."

"She snuck out during the night when we'd both been sent to bed," Elizabeth added in a soft voice. "And when she lost control of it, it threw her off its back. We didn't know what had happened until the next morning."

"So you'd laid there all night?" Jacob asked, his voice filled with horror.

The memory came rushing back to her. The pain, the tears, believing that she was going to die alone and afraid. She hadn't dared to move, her face sticky with blood and her breathing so shallow that she thought her lungs might have collapsed on her. Hours had passed by before anyone found her and by that time, she barely had any energy left.

"The physician said that it was a miracle I am still able to walk," Cassandra added in a hollow tone. "I spent months on bed rest but no matter what he did, there was nothing he could do to heal the scar that formed along my face. All he'd managed to do was reduce the intensity of it."

"Sometimes it still hurts her," Elizabeth explained. She squeezed Cassandra's hand gently.

"It hasn't in a while, though."

"I see." Jacob rubbed his jaw. Cassandra dared to look at him and she didn't miss the pain that filled his eyes. "I'm sorry to hear that."

"It is in the past," she said dismissively, though the way he said that while looking at her did unspeakable things to her chest. She patted Elizabeth's hand. "Thank you for your concern, Lizzie. But I'm fine."

Elizabeth nodded, giving her a small smile. Cassandra didn't know how convincing she'd been but her sister seemed content to let it drop for now. She turned back to the window, letting Elizabeth strike up another polite conversation with Jacob about his day. Now and again, she glanced at Jacob and found him already staring at her, eyes unreadable.

The ride to Covent Theatre was achingly long. Cassandra was glad when they finally pulled up in front, which was an unusual feeling. She normally preferred not being in public where others could whisper about her veil, but the sight of the theatre brought back her excitement at tonight's play. Jacob was the perfect gentleman, assisting them both out of the carriage while Elizabeth looked around with wide eyes.

"You all took your time," came Simon's drawl from behind.

Cassandra whirled to greet him, relieved by his presence. He would easily make tonight less uncomfortable for her. Adeline was by his side, looking lovely in a cornflower blue gown and white gloves.

"Were you waiting long for us," Jacob asked him.

"Oh, don't let him fool you," Adeline said, waving a dismissive hand in her brother's direction. "We've only just arrived ourselves."

"Even so, the play will begin soon," Simon defended. Cassandra watched as he drank Elizabeth in, who blushed lightly at his open stare. He seemed to realize that he was in public however and plastered that smile on his face once more. "Shall we?"

Cassandra smiled sadly at that. She supposed Elizabeth being courted by Jacob didn't lessen the feelings Simon had for her. She couldn't help but wonder if Elizabeth had gotten over her own emotions, or if she harbored any longing for their friend. It was certainly a sad state of affairs.

But as Jacob took Elizabeth's arm and led her into the theatre, Cassandra reminded herself that nothing could be done about it. Their paths had been laid out before them and, before the Season was over, her sister and the man she loved would be married.

She blinked back tears as she accepted Simon's arm, with Adeline on his other, and entered the theatre. Candlelight washed the lobby, which was already teeming with people. Lords and ladies chattered in their small groups and Cassandra noticed more than one of them looking at her. She ignored them. As long as she wasn't hearing what they were saying, she could handle it. But she was already feeling so fragile today that she was a little afraid that anything else would only set her over the edge.

They wasted no time heading into the theatre hall. Simon led the way to the box seats he had secured, which they thankfully had to themselves. Simon let go of her arm and instantly began making her way to the end so that she didn't have to sit with Jacob.

"Wait, I want that seat," Simon complained with a pout. He tugged on her hand, forcing her out of the way.

"Goodness, you are such a child," Adeline chastised lightly with a roll of her eyes and instantly sank into the chair next to Simon. Which left the chair next to her available. Cassandra sat in it, praying that Elizabeth would take her side which would put her between Cassandra and Jacob. But he chose the seat next to her as well and Elizabeth happily sank by his side, though Cassandra didn't miss the frown she gave Simon.

And just like that, she found herself next to him, the last yet only place she wanted to be.

# Chapter Twenty-Eight

Her scent was driving him insane.

Jacob didn't know how one person could affect him so completely, but the living proof sat next to him, paying him absolutely no attention. He'd looked at her more than ten times since the play began and Cassandra kept her face straight the entire time. She sat stiffly, hands in her lap, and the smell of her hair perfume wafting over him until he could focus on nothing else.

All he could think about was how perfectly she'd fit in his arms. It was not like when they danced, when they had to keep a few inches of distance between them to remain proper. Having her flush against his chest, feeling the rapid beat of her heart echoing against his own, only deepened the feelings he had for her. And it only bolstered his determination to have her, even though her constant rejection was wearing down on him.

"Oh my, who is that?" Lady Elizabeth whispered aloud, drawing Jacob's attention back to her. He felt a slight pinch of guilt at the fact that he hadn't been paying her much mind, merely going along with the motions.

"That is Romeo," Jacob whispered back, a little confused as to how she did not already know that even though the play was well underway.

"Ah." Lady Elizabeth nodded her understanding—and then began sweeping her eyes across the room as if she was bored with what was happening on stage. He noticed her fiddling with her fan and, soon enough, she turned her attention to it, like a child entertaining herself.

Jacob left her to it. He looked back at Cassandra. That irritating veil was back in place so he was left wondering what she was thinking, wondering if she was looking at him as well. Just as the thought crossed his mind, Cassandra leaned over a little as if she was trying to capture everything happening on the stage. The sight made him smile.

"You will hurt your back if you keep sitting like that," he whispered to her.

Cassandra slowly leaned back and for a moment, he thought she wasn't going to say anything. Jacob was racking his brain for some other way of conversing with her when she finally acknowledged him. "I can't help it," she murmured. "They are capturing everything so perfectly."

"I agree." *Though I can't say that I'm paying attention to much of it with you by my side.* "So, I was thinking about what you said at Hyde Park."

"You'll have to expound. I said a lot at the park."

"About the play and your take on it."

"Are you ready to admit that I was right?"

Jacob chuckled softly. "I was not aware that there was a wrong or right answer. Opinions are opinions for a reason, after all."

She inclined her head slightly in his direction. "Look at the way Juliet looks at him," she whispered.

Jacob did, but his attention quickly turned back to the more beautiful lady by his side. "Yes?"

"Isn't it painful to see the love in her eyes? When you know that it will end with nothing but her heartbreak and her death?"

"A tragic ending it may be, but I'm sure you can see the beauty in it all the same."

"To an extent," Cassandra conceded after a moment.

Jacob couldn't help grinning. "Are you admitting that I might be right in that regard, then?"

"Don't let it go to your head," she said, her voice light enough for him to take it as teasing. At least, he was willing to convince himself of it. He'd much prefer this to the tension that constantly sat between them.

"Then I suppose I can admit that it is a beat disheartening to know that this will end in nothing but failure," he told her.

This time, Casandra turned her head fully to him. Though he could not see her eyes, he knew she was staring into his own. "It was meant to be."

"It doesn't have to be," he responded gently, knowing that they were talking about something else now.

Cassandra just shook her head, looking away. "Perhaps we should focus on the play for now."

Jacob let out a low breath of frustration. He tried to but he couldn't stop thinking about her, constantly glancing at her hoping that she would pay him a smidgen of attention. It hurt knowing that she was constantly shutting him out like this. Jacob understood why, just as much as he understood that the intensity of these feelings were a little hard to believe when they haven't even been given the chance to court. But those things didn't matter to him. All he cared about was her.

Slowly, Jacob reached under the armrest, his fingers brushing against her leg. She stiffened instantly and Jacob paused, waiting for her to scold him. But she said nothing so he pushed further, reaching out until he touched her hand. Her fingers twitched and he paused once more, expecting her to slap it away.

His heart raced in his chest, the drone of the actors fading to nothing. They were the only two people in existence, this simple touch enough to drive him insane with longing. Cassandra allowed him to push his fingers under her tight fist, prying her hand open and then sliding their palms together. He gripped her hand tightly in his own, brushing his thumb against the back of her hand.

Anyone looking their way would notice what they were doing. But Simon and Lady Adeline were paying keen attention to the play while Lady Elizabeth seemed as if she was on the verge of falling asleep. They were in their own world, with this forbidden act driving him to the edge of destruction.

They stayed like that for the rest of the play. Even when it came to an end and applause rang through the hall, Jacob did not let go of her hand and Cassandra did not pull away. Only when everyone got to their feet for a standing ovation did she snatch her hand away from him, rising as well. Jacob slowly stood, staring at her as she clapped. He didn't care if anyone noticed him. Right now, he was willing to risk it all.

"What a wonderful play!" Lady Adeline gushed as the curtains were pulled closed. Jacob forced his gaze away from Cassandra, who took a discreet step away from him as if that was enough to sever their connection.

"Yes, I thoroughly enjoyed it," Simon agreed. His eyes were trained on Cassandra. "What about you? Was it up to your high standards?"

"It was pleasing enough," Cassandra managed to tease. How she was capable of joking right now was beyond Jacob, seeing that he was still having a hard time recovering from what had just happened. "I would certainly come again, if given the chance."

"And you?" Simon asked, raising a brow at Lady Elizabeth. She'd only just gotten to her feet, blinking wearily at him.

She looked rather bemused, as if she was still trying to wake up. "I liked it..." Lady Elizabeth murmured and they all chuckled at that, knowing that she'd barely watched a thing. Even Jacob managed a smile but it fell from his face when everyone—including Cassandra—began to leave the rented box.

"Come here, young one, let me explain all that happened to you," Simon called, easily pulling Lady Elizabeth to his side. She offered no protest, nodding along as Simon began to recount all that happened while Lady Adeline jokingly chastised him about being annoying. The three of them went ahead, leaving Cassandra and Jacob at the back of their small group.

"That cannot happen again," Cassandra murmured to him. "It was far too risky."

"I am willing to risk anything for you," Jacob whispered back to her.

She didn't say anything for a long moment. They were quickly nearing the lobby and Jacob found himself getting a little impatient. Soon, they would have to get back into the carriage and he would have to endure the short ride to Wiswall Manor trying not to stare at Cassandra. He wished this night could last forever.

"Are you always this...persistent?" she asked suddenly. Her tone was light enough that Jacob felt his spirits lift a little.

"Only when it comes on to the things that are important to me."

"I can only imagine how frustrating it must have been for your governess growing up."

"Yes, she never failed to tell me that I could be quite a handful at times. Though I find it one of my more redeeming qualities."

Cassandra huffed a low laugh. "Well, I must admit that I do not hate it."

Her words struck him dumb, his steps faltering. Cassandra didn't pause to let him catch up, but she did turn her head as if she was looking over her shoulder at him. Though the veil had not shifted out of place, he could almost imagine the teasing look in her eyes.

Butterflies swarmed his insides, his limbs buzzing with the urge to rush forward and pull her into his arms. He had to fight that longing and once he was certain he'd gotten ahold of it, a broad smile pulled at his lips as he quickly followed after her.

Jacob joined her side just as they stepped out into the lobby. Simon, Lady Adeline, and Lady Elizabeth were already standing around waiting for them, but were so engrossed in their own conversation that they didn't seem to care that they had fallen behind.

"Did you see her?"

"Oh goodness, why would she ever come out in public with that horrid thing on her face?"

Jacob froze. The voices were coming from the left, from a group of men who didn't seem to care that they were being overhead.

Their eyes were trained directly on Cassandra, lips curled and their eyes mocking. "Can you imagine how ugly she must be to wear a veil like that all the time?"

"Haven't you heard? She has a terrible scar that makes her the ugliest thing in London, which is why she will never be married. And with a sister as pretty as hers too..."

"I pity the gentleman who ever gets shackled with her."

A harsh laugh. "How bold of you to assume that she will be married at all."

Rage flooded Jacob so forcibly that it coated the back of his tongue. The room grew red, his mind filling with furious thoughts that urged him to take action. He didn't stop to think, swiveling on his heels, eyes trained on the men to the left.

"Don't!" Cassandra whispered under her breath. She wasn't moving, standing too still.

Jacob halted, curling his hands into fists. "But—"

"It's only going to make it worse. For me, you, and Elizabeth."

But that wasn't enough to stop the need to act on his rage, to teach those men a lesson. He knew the consequences well enough. If he dared to lash out, gossip would spread throughout London like wildfire. Everyone would be talking about how the Marquess of Charlington attacked another gentleman for Cassandra's honor, even though he was courting her sister. And it would inevitably do more damage to the sisters' reputations than it would his own.

Not to mention the attention it would bring to Cassandra, who clearly did not want to be noticed. He didn't want to make her any more uncomfortable than she already was.

But it was already too late for that. The gentlemen had spoken loudly enough that others were taking notice of her too and there was suddenly a loud hush of chatter as nearly everyone in the lobby began talking about the lady with the veil. Jacob didn't know what to do with himself, wanting to defend Cassandra to everyone who dared to speak badly about her. He wanted to pull the veil from her face and show them all that she was beautiful and that their evil rumors were baseless.

But right now, it wasn't his place. And that was felt like the worst part about this all.

## Chapter Twenty-Nine

The words whispered about seemed to burn her skin, eating away at the buzz of happiness she'd felt during the play. She'd allowed herself to sink too deeply into what could have been and forgot what the truth was—that she was a scarred lady who would always be the subject of gossip.

But this...this was more than she could handle.

The eyes she'd felt on her before now seemed to tear through the last shreds of confidence she had left. They were vicious and the people gossiping didn't seem to care that she could overhear them. Those words were meant to lash at her, not caring the damage that was being done. They didn't care about the truth. Even Cassandra wasn't certain what was true anymore.

"Cassandra..." Adeline came to her side, Elizabeth taking her other. Simon stood in front of her and the three of them easily blocked her from the eyes of others. She wished she could tell them that they didn't need to protect her, but the tears burning the back of her throat made speaking impossible right now.

Elizabeth's hand took hers. "Cassie, we should go."

She didn't want to rush home just because of the horrid gossip being spread about her while she was here. She truly didn't want to let them win. But if she was being honest with herself, they already did.

She didn't say anything, only squeezed her hand back. Tears blurred her eyes so much that she could no longer see Simon's angry expression, his jaw set. She knew he wouldn't say anything because she didn't want him to. She couldn't count on one hand how many times she'd had to talk him down from defending her—or worse, attacking someone—for her honor. He was a kind friend to her, but that was the last thing she wanted.

Not to mention the man currently standing behind her. She could almost *feel* the waves of fury coming off him. God only knew what would happen if she hadn't stopped him when she did.

"Come," Simon grasped her elbow, gentle yet firm. "We should leave. We have no business staying here."

Cassandra barely had the strength to nod in agreement. They all moved in unison and she went along with them, feeling like a coward for hiding behind them like this. She didn't dare to look behind her at Jacob, fearing what she might see on his face. What if he was disgusted because of the comments? Or embarrassed that she brought nothing but bad gossip everywhere she went? What if he'd only wanted to act as a gentleman protecting her reputation and not because of the feelings he said he had for her? Right now, she was reconsidering everything, wondering if she was truly worthy of any modicum of affection if she was really as ugly as they said.

Cassandra bit her lip, fighting against the shame that took ahold of her. She heard laughter and had to keep herself from lowering her head.

"I can walk on my own," she murmured loud enough for Simon to hear her. He gave her a concerned look but didn't fight it, letting go of her elbow. Cassandra raised her chin, holding on to the last thread of pride she had left to at least leave the theatre without cowering behind her friends and her sister. She could feel their concern, could almost hear the tremble of tension that hung over them all. Cassandra knew that they wanted to say something to console her but couldn't find the right words.

But nothing would be good enough right now. The only thing she wanted to do was to curl up in bed and have a good cry where there was no one around to see her.

The exit neared. People stepped out of their way as they went but no one cared to hide the fact that they were whispering about her, or at least watching her. A silent sob caught in her throat as tears blurred Cassandra's eyes. Thankfully, Simon opened the door for her so she would only need to keep walking.

As soon as the first gentle breeze of the evening hit her veil, Cassandra's foot twisted. A cry of alarm escaped her throat as she felt herself falling. Simon's hand brushed her arm but he wasn't quick enough to catch her.

She landed harshly on the steps, pain ricocheting throughout her body as she tumbled down to the landing. The last thing she heard was Jacob's voice ringing through the whoosh of collective gasps before blackness crowded her vision.

***

In what felt like the blink of an eye, Jacob flew down the steps, barking at everyone who was in his way. He might have shoved Simon to the side, but he didn't care. His only concern was Cassandra, who was lying still on the ground.

"Cassandra," he breathed, sinking to his knees next to her. His heart was in his throat, blood rushing in his ears. Her eyes were closed but he could tell that she was breathing, at least. "Cassandra!"

"Let me see." Simon was suddenly on her other side, trying to pry Cassandra from Jacob's arms. He didn't give him the chance. He rose, scooping her up with ease.

Without a word, he made his way to the carriage. Vaguely, he took note of the fact that Lady Elizabeth was following behind, her eyes filled with tears. Simon and Lady Adeline were trailing him as well.

"What are you doing?" Simon demanded to know.

"I'm taking her back to her manor," Jacob answered him, voice clipped. "She needs to see a physician immediately."

Jacob expected a retort but Simon didn't say anything, nodding. Then he gently steered Lady Adeline in the direction of their own carriage. Jacob knew they planned to go to Wiswall Manor as well.

"Oh, Cassie," Elizabeth murmured as she climbed into the carriage. Jacob laid Cassandra down on one side, fighting the mad urge to rest her head in his lap. He wanted to take her hand, to stroke the back of it and murmur to her that everything was going to be all right. If only to console himself into thinking that as the truth.

But he patted Lady Elizabeth's instead, her worry for her sister palpable. "She'll be fine," he said to her. "I believe that."

Tears streamed down her face. She didn't bother to answer him, only biting her lip and giving him a slow nod. He understood that she wasn't capable of words right now. He was hardly managing it himself.

Watching her tumble down the steps of the theatre had been like someone had punched him directly in the throat. He'd reached out to her but had been too late, too far. If only he'd stayed closer. If only he'd gone with his instincts and pulled her close to his side while she escaped the ton's scathing remarks.

Now, Cassandra's face was deathly pale. Lady Elizabeth lowered her head with a sob when a thin line of blood began to trickle down the side of Cassandra's face. More blood stained her temple, wisps of her hairline matted to her skin. Jacob could hardly breathe, fear and apprehension coiling in the pits of his stomach. They couldn't make it to the manor fast enough.

By the time they were pulling into the driveway, Jacob was sitting on the edge of his seat. He leaped out of the carriage before it fully came to a stop, bellowing for the footmen. Despite the late hour, the butler came rushing out of the manor.

"My lady!" the butler called, rushing to Lady Elizabeth's side and helping her out of the carriage.

Jacob already had Cassandra in his arms, marching inside. "Fetch the physician now," he ordered over his shoulder.

"I'm fine," Jacob heard Lady Elizabeth say. "But Cassie, she—"

He didn't hear what else was said, already heading into the manor. Jacob didn't pause, making his way up the grand staircase even though he hadn't a clue where Cassandra's bedchamber was. The first chamber he found would suffice. Just as long as she had a soft place to rest her head.

"My lord!" Lady Elizabeth called from behind. Jacob gritted his teeth, forcing himself to stop, to quell the rage of anxious energy smoldering in him.

With her skirt clutched in both hands, she rushed by him, almost running. "Her room is this way," she called and left Jacob to follow.

Her room smelled like her. Jacob realized that the moment he entered, like the same hair perfume she often wore. But he didn't take the time to look around, heading right to the bed. As gently as he could, he laid her on top of the covers.

"Where is the physician?" he demanded to the butler hovering by the door.

"I have sent someone to fetch him, my lord," he answered, chin cocked. "He should be here shortly. Perhaps in the meantime, you could wait in the parlor."

That was the last thing he wanted to do. He didn't want to leave her side, not until he knew for certain that she was fine. But he also knew that it would not bode well with the family if he lingered like this.

Jaw set, he gave the butler a tight nod, leaving Cassandra alone with her sister. He was halfway down the hallway when Simon and Lady Adeline came rushing up to him.

"Is she all right?" Simon asked him, breathless.

"She hasn't woken yet," Jacob said, trying to keep his tone as neutral as possible. "The physician is on his way."

Simon barely waited for him to finish before he charged down the hallway. Jacob had to fight the urge to go after him, feeling a knee-buckling wave of jealousy wash over him at the fact that Simon could so freely do as he pleased.

"Are you all right, Lord Charlington?"

Jacob looked at Lady Adeline. He'd almost forgotten that she was there. He managed a nod. "It is Lady Elizabeth you should be worrying about," he said softly.

"That may be true, but you seem beside yourself as well. Come, let us wait in the parlor until we hear good news."

She didn't wait for him to answer, turning and heading back the way she came. Jacob forced himself to follow, realizing after a moment that the butler had disappeared. They said nothing as they went down the hallways, Lady Adeline expertly navigating her way to the parlor.

The moment they entered the small resting room, Jacob made a beeline for the sideboard, pouring himself a glass of whiskey and downing it in one go.

"I thought you did not drink such harsh liquor," Lady Adeline commented from behind.

Jacob only poured himself another one. "Tonight is different."

"I can see that. You are quite worried about her."

"Aren't you?"

"I most certainly am," she answered calmly, despite the bite in Jacob's voice. "But I have known her for nearly all my life. She is one of my closest friends. How long have you known her, Lord Charlington?"

Downing his third glass in one go, Jacob set the glass down and whirled to face her. "What do you wish to ask me? Just come out and say it."

She tilted her head to the side, moving over to one of the chaise lounges. "Do you have feelings for Cassandra?"

Jacob clenched his jaw. The truth rushed to the tip of his tongue but he quelled the urge, knowing it would only make things worse. "You are imagining things," he said instead.

"Am I? You basically shoved me out of the way at the theatre trying to get to her. And I have never seen you quite this…agitated."

"I am only concerned for a lady's welfare. As a gentleman should be. I am the one who escorted her and Lady Elizabeth, after all. They were in my care."

"Hmm," Lady Adeline hummed and Jacob knew that she wasn't convinced. But thankfully, she didn't seem inclined to pursue the matter any further. So as silence descended within the room, Jacob took to pacing back and forth, unable to quell the anxiousness that simmered within him. He hated having to wait, hated not knowing what was happening. He didn't know when the physician arrived—or if he'd arrived at all—and it was killing him not knowing whether or not she'd woken up.

After what felt like ages, the door opened and a tired-looking Simon walked in. Jacob shot out of the chair he'd been sitting in. "How is she?" he asked, breathless.

Simon leaned against the wall by the door, running a hand down his face. "The physician has treated her head wound and says that it won't scar. But she is yet to wake."

"Then is he still there? What about smelling salts? Has he used that?"

"He's done all that a physician could," Simon stressed. "But he says that Cassie will wake when it is time and there is no use worrying about when that will be. Otherwise, she is fine."

That didn't make Jacob feel much better but at least it was something. He swallowed harshly, wishing that he could be by her side right now.

"We should go," Simon murmured. "The hour is late. We should leave them be."

Jacob knew Simon was talking to him as well but he didn't answer. Not until Lady Adeline had made her way to her brother's side did Simon address him again. "Jacob?"

He didn't want to leave. He couldn't bear the thought of going back to his residence, going to sleep alone, and unable to know if Cassandra was all right.

Yet, he couldn't think of a single reason he could stay. So he gave Simon a stiff nod, ignoring the way Lady Adeline stared at him, and left the parlor.

Lord Wiswall was already in the foyer by the time they made it to there. He looked haggard, lines of stress dragging down the corners of his mouth. He gave them a tired bow as he said, "Thank you, Lord Charlington, for your quick assistance. Simon told me how you took charge of the situation and that it was you who brought my daughter here."

"It was nothing, my lord," Jacob answered, a lump forming in his throat. He hesitated, then added, "I shall visit in the morning to see if she is doing better. And Lady Elizabeth, of course. I know she is quite distraught about what happened."

"I doubt Elizabeth will be leaving her sister's side tonight, that's for certain." Lord Wiswall heaved a sigh. "But your concern is appreciated. Please, take care on your way home. You two as well, Simon and Adeline."

Simon clapped Lord Wiswall on the shoulder, then stepped aside before Adeline swept in for an embrace. The tension in the earl's shoulders seemed to lift at the comforting gestures but he said nothing more, walking with them onto the porch.

Every step away from the manor tugged on Jacob's heart. He tried not to look back, climbing into his carriage and resting his head on the back of his seat as it took off. He would try to sleep tonight, if only to make time pass quicker.

And then in the morning, he wouldn't waste a single second before coming to see Cassandra again. This time, he would not be turned away.

# Chapter Thirty

Pain drummed in Cassandra's ears, slowly pulling her from her deep sleep. The more awake she became, the more intense the pain grew, until she could not hold back the small groan that escaped her lips as she pried her eyes open.

Tears already blurred her vision and it alarmed her to know that she had been crying in her sleep. Even more than that, her entire body ached, a pounding megrim holding her in its grasp. It took her a moment to realize that she was in her bedchamber, though she couldn't remember how she'd gotten here. She didn't remember arriving home last night, nor climbing into bed. As a matter of fact, the last thing she could recall was being at the theatre...

"Cassie?" Elizabeth's tiny voice sounded at Cassandra's left. "Are you awake?"

Cassandra tried to look at her but attempting to move only made her head pound harder. With extra effort, she managed to sit halfway up before Elizabeth put a hand on her shoulder, forcing her to lay back down.

"Don't sit up," she said gently. "The physician said that you need to stay rested."

"Why?" Cassandra croaked. She desperately needed water. "What happened?"

"You...you mean you don't remember?"

Cassandra tried not to frown at Elizabeth's tone. Just what happened last night?

"Lizzie, what aren't you telling me? Why does it feel as if someone had hit me over the head with something?"

"Well, not hit per se..." Elizabeth bit her lip. "You fell."

Suddenly, it all came rushing back to her. The gossiping, her tears, the moment she'd twisted her foot and went crashing down the steps of Covent Theatre. As the memory assaulted her, her ankle began to throb, as if bothered by the reminder of what had happened.

Shame seized her. Cassandra squeezed her eyes shut, bracing herself against the pain and the sheer horror that took hold of her. She couldn't believe that, in the midst of all that had been happening, she'd gone and tripped in public. Now the ton would never leave her alone. Her name would fill the scandal sheets, what little shred of reputation she had left dragged through the streets. They would talk about her in Seasons to come. Mothers and matrons would use her as an example of what not to do.

And worse of all, she'd gone and embarrassed herself even further in front of Jacob. Cassandra wished she could just dig a hole and bury herself in it.

Elizabeth took her hand, tears rimming her eyes. "The physician said that you should be on bed rest until your head wound and your ankle heals. He doesn't want you putting any more undue stress on yourself."

"It cannot be any more stressful than lying in bed all day thinking about what happened," Cassandra murmured. "They will not let me rest."

She didn't have to tell Elizabeth who *they* were. "Don't worry about what the ton has to say," Elizabeth said gently. "It doesn't matter that you might have caused a scandal."

"Why doesn't that matter, Elizabeth? Because I never stood a chance at being married? At having a proper life where I am not constantly hiding my face?"

Elizabeth shook her head, holding Cassandra's hand tighter despite the ice in Cassandra's voice. "No, of course not! I am only worried that you will begin to overthink. It was a mere accident, Cassie. They will forget about it in a matter of days."

Cassandra only let out a huff of disbelief, turning her head towards the window despite the pain it caused. She didn't want to take her frustration out on Elizabeth, who had obviously spent all night by her side. But every time she thought about how gracelessly she'd fallen, how Jacob had shouted her name right before everything went black, the shame was impossible to ignore.

"Lord Charlington seemed quite worried about you," Elizabeth murmured after a long moment.

Cassandra's heart skipped a beat at the mention of Jacob, her hand curling into a tight fist beneath her sheet. "How kind of him."

"I think it was more than just kindness. He was quite beside himself, you know. He was by your side in an instant and seemed unwilling to leave. Not to mention the fact that he stayed nearly the entire night while you were being treated."

Cassandra thinned her lips. "What about Simon and Adeline? I'm sure they stayed as well."

"Of course they did. Simon would not stop pacing the room and refused to leave when the physician asked him to. Adeline waited with Lord Charlington in the parlor. But, the marquess' worry seemed…different."

"He was the one who escorted us to the theatre. He must have felt guilty that something like that happened under his watch."

"Perhaps…" Cassandra could hear the doubt in Elizabeth's voice. "But it didn't seem like that to me. It seemed more…"

"More what?" Cassandra dared to ask.

"More heartfelt. I couldn't help but wonder if Lord Charlington fancies you."

"He does not," Cassandra stated instantly. "He's courting you. And as your sister, he is only extending his kindness to me as well."

In the corner of her eye, Cassandra saw Elizabeth bite her lip, frowning. "If you say so…" she said. "But right now, that doesn't matter. You cannot leave this bed for a few days so you'll have to have your breakfast here. I'll go and have the maid fetch you something."

Cassandra said nothing, listening as her sister got to her feet and left the room. Only then did she let her tears go free, released a burdened sigh. She was honestly sick and tired of everything going wrong. From the moment this Season began, it felt as if she hadn't gotten a chance to rest, the mental strain she'd had to endure being the scarred and hideous elder sister who could not marry.

But to have the man she loved just out of reach…

To hear her sister's confusion at the mere thought of Jacob fancying Cassandra instead of her...

Cassandra closed her eyes. Right now, she wished she could just go back to sleep, if only to keep these thoughts at bay. She couldn't handle it any more.

Sadly, sleep didn't come, but by the time Elizabeth returned with Cassandra's breakfast in tow, she'd at least gotten out most of her tears. She managed to sit up despite the pain, picking at the meal of toast and sausages, a steaming cup of hot chocolate waiting to be consumed. Elizabeth had carried a book of Shakespeare to read to Cassandra and Cassandra let her be, grateful that her sister was trying to make her feel better in any way she could.

Nearly an hour had passed, with less than half of her meal consumed, when there was knock on the door.

"Come," Elizabeth called. Cassandra didn't bother to look up. Her parents had come to her bedchamber shortly after Elizabeth had returned with her breakfast but Elizabeth had chased them away when she noticed how flustered Cassandra was becoming as they fussed over her. She hoped they had not come to fuss again.

But it was the butler. He bowed deeply before saying, "The Marquess of Charlington has come to see you, my lady."

Cassandra's heart thundered in her chest. She didn't dare to show it, but Elizabeth's attention remained solely on the butler.

"Tell him that I will be down shortly to see hi—"

"Pardon me, my lady," the butler said to Elizabeth, his tone sheepish. "But he stated that he was here to see Lady Cassandra."

Cassandra thinned her lips. She didn't dare to look at Elizabeth now, even though she could feel her sister's surprised gaze burning into her skin. "I am unable to see anyone right now," Cassandra told him. "Please tell him that."

"Lord Charlington insisted," the butler pressed.

"And so am I," she pushed back. Then she dismissed him, turning her attention to her half-eaten meal though she had no appetite.

She listened as the butler murmured his understanding and left the room. The silence that followed was thick, weighted by Elizabeth's stare.

"I'm sure he only came because he is worried about you," Elizabeth murmured after a moment.

"I am grateful for that. A letter would have sufficed."

"Surely it wouldn't be too difficult for you to see him?"

"Lizzie." Cassandra took Elizabeth's hand in hers, twisting slightly to face her. "Don't worry about me so much. This is your Season, you should be enjoying it with the gentleman who's courting you. You don't have to worry about me. Leave a few of Shakespeare's work here and I will be quite content." Because Elizabeth only frowned at her words, Cassandra plastered a smile onto her face. "Trust me when I say that I feel much better, Lizzie."

Elizabeth only thinned her lips, frowning at Cassandra as if she didn't believe a word that she was saying. Thankfully, she didn't question her on it. She only nodded and stood, saying, "I will go to see the marquess then."

"Run along now," Cassandra urged with that false smile against her teeth. She watched as Elizabeth silently slipped out of the room, then she released a heavy sigh, letting the smile fall. It hurt to push her sister in the arms of the man she loved, knowing that she wished to take her place. And the guilt that assaulted her at those feelings pained her even further. It was best to ignore it, to do what she did best and ensure that she stayed in her sister's shadow where she belonged.

Cassandra couldn't stay in bed any longer. Despite the fact that her head was still hurting, she set her meal aside and pulled herself to a stand, padding over to the her window. She leaned over the sill and drew in a deep breath, willing it to calm her. Being alone should help, at least. If only to calm her mind and help her come to terms with all that happened.

"I'm sure you shouldn't be standing."

Cassandra gasped, whirling at the familiar voice. There Jacob stood, looking as handsome as the day she'd first met him, his brow creased with concern.

"What are you doing?" she breathed. "You shouldn't be here."

"You should be on bed rest," he continued, ignoring what she'd said. "And you most certainly shouldn't be putting any weight on your ankle."

"Jacob—" Cassandra broke off, feeling overwhelmed by all the emotions coursing through her. She focused on the frustration, tucking aside the pure pleasure at the sight of him. "Please leave."

"No," he answered stubbornly. "I wanted to see you. I needed to make sure that you were all right."

"And now that you know that I am, you can go."

Jacob only crossed his arms, stepping closer into the room.

"Don't—" she began but he already closed the door, leaving them alone together.

"I don't have much time. Lady Elizabeth has gone to the kitchens to tend to a few snacks for us and she will be expecting me when she returns to the drawing room. I left her ladies' maid there. She thinks that I've gone to relieve myself."

"I don't need an explanation, Jacob. I need to you to leave. Please."

"Don't push me away, Cassie. I'm tired of you constantly trying to make me leave your side."

"Because you shouldn't be by my side in the first place! You are courting my sister!"

"Who has no more feelings for me than I have for her, and you know that. You and I both know what is really stopping you from doing what your heart wants and—"

"And that's enough. My insecurities, my shame, the fact that what was left of my reputation has now been ripped to shreds in one night. There are all valid reasons for me to know that we can never be."

He took a step towards her and Cassandra took a step back, even though there was still some distance between them.

"Leave," she ordered, her voice cold. "Now."

Pain filled his features but he didn't come any closer. After a moment, he retreated to the door, his hand reaching out behind him for the handle. He lingered there for a moment, a plea in his eyes. Cassandra had to turn away to keep from giving in to it.

"I'm happy to see that you are well, Cassandra," he murmured after a very long moment. And then he was gone, the door clicking shut behind him.

Cassandra didn't move away from the window for a while. Even as her parents and her sister came and went, trying to keep her company and realizing that she would much rather be alone. Jacob's face was ingrained in her face and this time, she knew that this was it. The final nail in the coffin. There was finality in his tone, a quiet indication hat he would not chase after her any longer.

And for some reason, that hurt more than anything else.

## Chapter Thirty-One

"Have you seen this, Jacob?"

Maria floated into Jacob's study waving something in his hand. Her eyes shone with intrigue and she came straight to his side, putting the sheets of paper down in front of him despite the fact that he had been so clearly writing a letter.

It was a scandal sheet. Jacob didn't dare to read it, sensing he already knew what his mother was referring to. Without saying a word, he pushed the papers to the side and continued what he was doing.

That wasn't enough to deter Maria however. "Oh, this poor thing. Isn't she Lady Elizabeth's sister? I've heard about a lady amongst the ton who goes everywhere with an odd veil on her face. Apparently, she was scarred as a child and is absolutely hideous. It's bad enough that she has to live with such a reputation but now this! Absolutely scandalous!"

"Is this truly what you wish to bother yourself with on such a morning?" Jacob asked her, hardly able to keep the chill from his tone.

But if Maria noticed it, she didn't make it clear. She pranced over to the other side of the desk, planting the sheets directly in Jacob's line of vision. "Look at what they'd said here. Oh, how could they be so cruel? What if she were to see this? How would the young thing feel?"

Jacob snatched the papers off his desk, ripping them in two in one quick motion. Maria gasped as he tossed them to the floor, angrily returning to his work even though he knew that he stood no chance of focusing.

"Jacob, what has gotten into you?" she whispered as if she was afraid that he would snap at her next.

"I do not want to hear about the new trendy scandal, Mother."

"Is it because you were with them that evening? Because they did not mention you in the article, save to briefly state that

Lady Cassandra's more impressive sister was being courted by the Marquess of Charlington."

Jacob paused, fixing her with such a heated glare that his mother cowered at the sight. "What did I just say?" he growled slowly.

Maria frowned, then squared her shoulders. "I do not understand how I have offended you," she stated stubbornly. When Jacob didn't offer an explanation, her frown deepened. "Is it because Lady Cassandra is related to Lady Elizabeth. Because—"

"No, Mother. It has nothing to do with Lady Elizabeth."

"But everything to do with Lady Cassandra," Maria realized with widening eyes.

Jacob held his silence. It didn't make any sense to admit his feelings now. Cassandra had finally laid to rest whatever hope he'd harbored that she would one day choose him over that sad life she thought she was fated to have. When he'd gone to visit her yesterday, Jacob had been fraught with worry. Seeing her by the window, a warning in her teary eyes, helped him realize that they were never meant to be. Not if she continued to fight him like this.

And it hurt. God knew it pained him to know that he had to leave her alone. Even right now it was taking Jacob everything in his power not to spring out of his chair and head straight to Wiswall Manor. He wanted to pull her into his arms, bury his face in her hair, kiss her on those lovely lips, watch her eyes smile before her mouth did. Jacob wanted to spend the rest of his life with her by his side and it tore him to shreds to know that that would never happen.

"Jacob, what aren't you telling me?" Maria asked, gentle now. She came closer, resting a comforting hand on Jacob's shoulder.

He let out a breath of frustration, putting away his quill pen since he knew he stood no chance of focusing anymore. "I am only sick and tired of hearing about them, that's all."

"Why does it bother you so much? I thought you were beginning to fancy Lady Elizabeth. You took her to the theatre, after all, and I know you well enough to know that you wouldn't spend so much of your time on something if you do not plan on getting invested."

"I didn't go for her. I went because I wanted to be close to Lady Cassandra."

Maria only stared at him like she couldn't understand what he was talking about. Jacob ran his hands down his face, shooting out of his chair, disgruntled. He wanted to take his frustration out on something, in some way, but for now he supposed it would be best to simply talk about it.

"What do you think of her, Mother?" he asked, his back to his mother as he faced the window. "You've met her before, when we joined her family for dinner. What was your impression on her?"

"That she was rather quiet. And I found it quite odd that she wore that veil, even in her own home."

"That is perhaps what most people think. They judge her on the veil she wears, not caring to know what truly laid underneath. And because of that, she believes that she has to shut herself out, as if the veil was the armor that would protect her from the rest of the world."

"It sounds as if you have grown rather close to her yourself," Maria commented and Jacob knew that she'd already come to her own conclusion.

"I have fallen hopelessly in love with her, Mother." Unable to keep the pain from his voice, he rested his hand against the windowpane, staring unseeingly out into the garden. "And I do not know what to do with myself."

Seconds stretched endlessly. Jacob knew his words had stunned his mother. He'd expected as much and had planned on keeping these feelings to himself since they were no longer of use. But the mere thought of Cassandra pulled them out of the vault he'd locked them in.

Suddenly, Jacob felt a hand on his back. Without a word, Maria pulled him into her arms. Jacob hadn't been held like this by her in so long that he had forgotten how comforting it was, the urge to let everything out filling him whole. Instead, he rested his forehead on her shoulder, letting out a painful shudder as she stroked the back of his head.

"I understand, my dear," she cooed gently.

"I cannot imagine that you do," he murmured, though not unkindly. "You have never cared to marry for love."

"Didn't I?" Maria let out a soft laugh. "There are many things that happened before you were born, Jacob. Many things that you don't know."

Jacob pulled slightly away, frowning at her. She rested a tender hand on his cheek, smiling gently at him as if she knew that he was on the verge of tears.

"Your father was not the only option I had when it came time for me to marry, you know," she explained. "I was in love with someone else, the third son of a baron. He had no title, a man who would be forced to make something of himself. As you can imagine, my father did not think him a good match for me. But I loved him."

"What happened?" Jacob whispered.

"I told him exactly what I wanted—to become his wife. And I thought he would have been brave enough to at least ask my father for my hand in marriage. If he disapproved, well, that was something we could deal with afterwards. But he did not even try. He decided that I was too good for him and decided to leave me be."

That sounded a lot like what was happening between Jacob and Cassandra. His heart thudded painfully in his chest as he asked, "What did you do then?"

"I waited for him. Until the end of the Season, I waited to hear from him, hoping that he would listen to his heart rather than to what others were saying around him. But when the Season began drawing to a close, I knew that we had run out of time. He had no intentions of marrying me and I could not wait around forever. So when your father asked for my hand, I accepted."

"Did it not bother you that you would be marrying someone you did not love?"

"At first," Maria admitted. "But as I began to fall out of love, I began to develop feelings for your father. We grew to care for each other. It made me realise that perhaps marrying someone I did not fancy at first might not be such a terrible idea."

"Which is why you have no issue with me asking Lady Elizabeth to be my wife, even if I do not love her."

"You could grow to love her," Maria explained. "But..." She took his hand, squeezing gently. "If you love someone else, I do not think you should make the same mistake that man did. Do not be a coward."

"I have tried, Mother," Jacob sighed. "But she wants nothing to do with me. It does not help that everyone believes I intend to marry her sister."

"Worry not about what others say. Follow your heart."

Jacob gave her a look of surprise. "I thought you would have agreed with Father on this matter."

"Henry is a stubborn man," Maria said with a shrug. "He will not listen to reason until it is staring him in the face. Perhaps you could be the one to do that."

"So you think I should not give up on her then?"

"I think you should do whatever you think is best for you," Maria corrected. "That may mean that you will continue fighting for her. Or that you will protect your heart and peace of mind and let her go."

Jacob studied his mother's face for a second before he huffed a laugh. "Thank you, Mother. Somehow, your words—and your story—makes me feel much better."

"I'm happy to hear it, dear," Maria said with a smile. "Have you decided what you will do then?"

He shook his head. It would not be so simple, he knew, to separate his heart from his mind. All roads led to Cassandra and the mere thought that he might have to give up entirely felt like thorns tearing into his flesh. But she had not given him much choice. If he kept pressing, she would continue pushing him away, throwing walls up so that he could never get close enough. Was it truly worth the heartache, when he wasn't sure he'd ever get through to her?

"I have a lot of thinking to do," Jacob said at last.

Maria nodded. "I understand. In the meantime, I will try to keep your father from bothering you too much on the matter. He already believes that you intend on defying him and so he's watching you rather closely."

Jacob pulled his mother into his arms, holding her gently. "Thank you, Mother. Your support means the world to me."

"You're welcome, my dear."

With that, she gave him another smile before she left the room, leaving Jacob to his thoughts once more. He faced the window, his mind wandering to the small box that sat untouched in his room. His grandmother had entrusted it to him with the idea that he would one day give it to someone who deserved it, someone who held his heart the way he held hers. Jacob couldn't fathom the thought of handing it over to a lady he did not feel this deep affection for.

It was meant for Cassandra. She was the only person for him. He could grow old with her, could sit and talk with her for hours or lay around in utter, comfortable silence. Jacob knew from the moment she revealed herself to him that she was his other half. Just how could he survive without her?

Remembering the cold look she'd leveled on him, the constant demands for him to leave her alone.

Again, Jacob didn't think he had much of a choice on the matter any longer.

## Chapter Thirty-Two

"Such a dreary frown. Seeing you without a smile is almost as unsettling as the dawn coming without the sun, Lizzie."

The smile Simon commented on did not show at his words. She only turned slightly as he and Adeline entered the drawing room of Wiswall House, her brows dipping into a deeper frown.

Simon hovered by the door, resting his hip on an end table nearby as Adeline swept forward to Elizabeth's side. The fact that Elizabeth didn't care to smile, or respond with a quick quip, meant that she was clearly bothered by something. Adeline rested a gentle hand on her shoulder in comfort. Simon could only watch from afar.

He didn't take his eyes off her for a second. Her hair fell down her face in perfect ringlets. The grass green morning gown she wore gripped her tiny chest easily, draping lightly over her waist to brush the ground. As usual, Elizabeth was a vision and Simon's breath was taken away at the sight of her.

"What's the matter, Lizzie?" Adeline asked gently. "Your letter seemed so urgent that we rushed over here the moment I received it."

Elizabeth thinned her lips and Simon's worry deepened. Had something happened to Cassandra? Was there something wrong with her parents? Did Jacob ask for Elizabeth's hand in marriage?

His head swirled with the possibilities, each more horrifying than the last, as he watched her grasp Adeline's hand tightly in her own and steer her over to the set of couches in the center of the drawing room. Simon was tempted to go nearer, but he knew that being near Elizabeth in any capacity was never a good idea.

"It's about Cassie," Elizabeth said at last.

Simon's worry spiked. He narrowed his eyes, straightening. "What happened? I thought the physician had taken good care of her and that she was well on to recovery? Is she not feeling any better?"

"No, she is physically healing," Elizabeth said quickly, noticing Simon's agitation. "Though, emotionally, I fear she might be in terrible pain."

"Ah," Adeline sighed. A pitying look brushed over her features. "I see."

"You see?" Simon frowned. "What do you see exactly? Clearly I seem to be missing out on something."

"Considering your own situation, Simon," Adeline drawled, "I am not surprised in the slightest."

Simon narrowed his eyes at his sister. There was something about her tone that told him there was more to what she was saying, but she turned her attention back to Elizabeth. "Why do you think that?" Adeline asked her.

Elizabeth heaved a sigh strong enough to rock her body. "She refuses to leave her bedchamber at all. The physician did tell her that she needed to remain on bed rest, but it has already been four days and Cassie seems content to waste her days away by the window! Any attempt I make to coax her out to the gardens, at least, has been futile."

Simon's chest panged at the pain in Elizabeth's voice. Tears swam in her eyes but they didn't fall down her cheeks just yet.

"And no matter how many times I try to get her to talk about what is making her feel so down," Elizabeth continued with a sad shake of her head, "she simply will not open up to me. Mother and Father are nearing their wit's end as well."

"Could it be because of what happened?" Adeline asked, glancing at Simon. "Cassie has always been rather brave but being made the subject of gossip and scandal overnight must be weighing on her."

Simon began nodding, opening his mouth to agree. But before he could speak, Elizabeth shook her head determinedly. "That does bother her but I'm sure it's far deeper than that."

"Then pray tell," Simon urged. "You clearly have an idea about what it is."

Elizabeth lifted her beautiful eyes, which were now devoid of tears, to meet his. Simon swallowed and willed himself to focus on the conversation at hand. "It is because of Lord Charlington."

Adeline sighed, relaxing into the couch. Simon frowned, looking between his sister and Elizabeth. "You do not seem surprised, Adeline," he commented.

"You are the only person here who seem to be, Simon," Adeline said. "Isn't it obvious?"

Simon ran his hand over his face, suddenly frustrated. He caught himself before he could cross the distance and sink into his favorite spot—which was usually just next to Elizabeth. Distance, he had to remind himself. Distance between them was best.

Agitated now, he avoided Elizabeth's eyes as he deepened his frown at his sister. "Goodness, woman, out with it already."

Adeline sighed. Then she revealed what Simon had apparently missed, while Elizabeth gazed sadly at the floor. The revelation only brought more confusion, however. If that had been the case, surely he would have noticed? Surely he would have seen something to indicate such? Or Cassandra would have at least told him, wouldn't she? She was his closest friend and he was hers. They told each other everything.

But then...

Simon let his gaze rest on Elizabeth, his silence being ignored. The two ladies began to discuss what had been brought out to the open while Simon just stood there reeling, unable to believe what he'd just heard.

Relief mounted in him in steadying waves, his body sagging under the overwhelming weight of it. Simon didn't tear his eyes off Elizabeth for those long, agonizing seconds, his mind filling with all the betraying thoughts he'd never allowed himself to linger on. For a moment, the bitter taste of hope assaulted his tongue before he swallowed it and tore his gaze away, not allowing it to grow any stronger. He'd made his decision after all.

But that decision had been on the helm of a union he had no control over. And the implications of what he knew now...

"Simon, are you listening?"

Elizabeth's voice broke him from his haze. He blinked rapidly. "I'm afraid I might have missed all that you've said..."

Adeline sighed in slight frustration. "We were trying to figure out what to do to help Cassie."

"Why not leave them to handle this matter themselves?" Simon asked and when he saw the look exchanged between the ladies, he realized he might have said something foolish.

"Heavens, he will be useless," Adeline said dismissively. Elizabeth only buried her face in her hands, clearly distraught.

Simon racked his brain for a solution. He straightened suddenly as an idea began to dawn on him, a smile tugging at his lips. "I think I might be able to help."

"Pray tell—"

"But, I have to speak with Cassie first," he continued, cutting into his sister. Without waiting for either one of them to respond, he left the drawing room in hurried steps. The plan began to form as he made his way to the grand staircase that would take him to where he knew Cassandra's bedchamber was. If everything went well, then Elizabeth would certainly feel much better, wouldn't she? Not to mention the fact that Cassandra wouldn't be suffering the way her sister made it seem as if she was.

He was at the door of her chamber within a matter of minutes. Simon knocked, waiting only half a heartbeat before he entered the room. He supposed, at their age, it was improper for him to waltz into a lady's room without even waiting for her to respond, but he'd know Cassandra for so long—and had spent many afternoons in this room in his youth—that he hardly thought about it anymore.

Cassandra was sitting in the armchair by her window. She barely turned her head to look at him before saying, "I wish to be alone."

"Yes, yes, so I have heard," he drawled, wandering closer. She was dressed, her hair styled simply over her shoulder. What struck him as odd was the fact that she wore her veil, even though she was at home.

He saw her jaw tick, though she kept her gaze out the window. "Then what are you still doing here?"

"I just have a question to ask. Or rather, I need to confirm something."

Cassandra released a sharp breath of air from her nose, clearly frustrated. "What?" she demanded.

"Are you in love with the Marquess of Charlington?"

Cassandra's head whipped around, eyes narrowing to slits. "What are you talking about?"

"It's a rather simple question, Cassie. Yes or no?"

"You cannot be serious. The marquess is courting my sister."

"Does that mean it's a no?"

"Of course it does!"

Simon grinned. She was a marvelous liar. Without hesitation, her words came out with a conviction that would have easily assure someone else that she was telling the truth. But Simon knew better. He'd known Cassandra nearly his entire life so he knew when she was lying.

The stark blush on her cheeks said it all. Perhaps he could have mistaken it for anger, but Cassandra was not as adept at hiding what she was truly feeling as she thought. At least, not from him.

"Where did that even come from?" she continued, scowling at him.

"Nowhere," he lied with a casual shrug. "Only curious. Now, I shall leave you to wallow in peace."

"Wait a second, Simon." Cassandra lurched to her feet just as he began to walk away. "Tell me why you asked me that."

"Remember to rest your foot now," he called over his shoulder, not breaking his stride. "I wouldn't want you to damage your ankle any further."

"My ankle is more than fine now and you are avoiding my question."

"That I am." At the door, he sent her a wink that only made her scowl deeper. "You should get some fresh air, Cassie. You're worrying your sister."

"Simon—"

Simon closed the door on Cassandra's words, knowing that she wouldn't come out of her room. His grin widened as he made his way back to the foyer.

Now, it was time to put his plan into action.

\*\*\*

"Jacob."

Jacob glanced up from the cup of coffee he hadn't realized he had been staring into. Sleep had evaded him for the past few days and the dark, hot liquid was the only thing capable of bringing him throughout the days. Only now, he was quite aware of how cold it had gotten while his mind wandered.

Henry stood at the door of his study, his brows knitted together in stark anger and disappointment. Jacob resisted the urge to sigh, bracing himself for whatever it was he was about to endure.

"What is it, Father?" he sighed, pushing the cup of coffee away and getting to a stand. He hadn't moved from the chair behind his desk for some time now and the kinks that had set into his body while he attempted to lull himself to sleep last night was finally beginning to hurt.

"I just returned from the club," Henry began, his words slow and deliberate. "And I saw Gilbert there. He just informed me that he no longer approves of the courtship between you and Lady Elizabeth."

Surprise washed Jacob, though he didn't have enough energy to show it. Truth was, he hadn't been to Wiswall Manor for a few days now. As a matter of fact, he hadn't been in contact with anyone other than his mother, and the butler now and again. Jacob hadn't even considered the fact that he still had a courtship that he was obligated to.

"Is that so," he drawled, pinching the bridge of his nose to assuage the headache he could feel forming. He knew his father was displeased and was already bracing himself for the argument that would ensue.

Henry seemed to be trying to keep himself together as much as he could. He ventured deeper into the room, each step calmer than he truly was. His hands flexed then tightened at his sides, his lips thinning to nearly nothing.

"Would you care to tell me, Jacob," Henry began again, "why the Earl of Wiswall no longer wishes for his daughter to be courted by you?"

"I'm afraid that is a question for the earl himself?"

"Do not be cryptic with me! There must have been a reason why he decided that so suddenly! He was as ecstatic as I was to merge our families and now he has come out and said that he no longer believes you two will be a good fit. You must have done something."

Jacob sighed, his headache spiking at his father's shouting. "I assure you, Father, I do not know what Lord Wiswall is referring to."

"Nor do you seem to care."

Jacob met his eyes. The past few days had been utter torture for him. Between longing for Cassandra, resenting the distance she'd put between them, and wondering what he should do next, he had no patience for his father and this conversation. "You're right. I do not. I made it no secret that I do not intend on pursuing a marriage with Lady Elizabeth if I do not feel any affection for her. It is you who do not wish to listen to me."

"I don't want to hear it," Henry hissed. Anger tightened the veins in his temples, his face growing red. "You'd better go to see Lord Wiswall and beg for his forgiveness. Take Lady Elizabeth out for a stroll through the park. Let them both see that you still wish to court her and that you are serious."

Jacob opened his mouth to protest. But the thought of going to Wiswall Manor—and maybe catching a glimpse of Cassandra while there—suddenly appealed to him. He had no intention of doing what his father said. But the thought of seeing Cassandra again, even if she had no wish to see him, filled him with a sudden urgency that he could not contain.

"I shall go to speak with the earl," Jacob announced and left it at that. His father would assume what he wanted to and when he found out what Jacob had done, he would only grow more furious. But that was a problem for another day. There was only one thing on Jacob's mind right now.

Henry looked satisfied. "Good. He was leaving the club the same time I did, so he must have returned to Wiswall Manor by now."

Jacob said nothing in response, stalking by him and out the door. The carriage his father had taken home still lingered outside, thankfully, so he didn't have to wait long for his transportation. He only clipped an order to the coachman and climbed aboard, agitated.

He imagined Cassandra the last time he'd seen her as the carriage went on its way. The determination in her eyes, the hint of fear. And the longing he'd seen tucked far behind it. No matter what he did, he could not get past the walls she put up between them. Even as she flashed that longing at him, even as she made it clear to him that she truly wanted him the way he wanted her, she would not give him the chance to come closer. And the incident at the theatre had only made it worse, he knew.

The ton was ruthless. Hearing all those things said about her had stoked such fury in him that, had he endured it any longer, Jacob knew he would have lashed out and put them all in their places. They didn't know how beautiful she truly was. They saw a mask and assumed that she must be quite horrifying to look at underneath. No one cared to see the beauty that was actually hidden behind the veil and Cassandra seemed content to let the world continue seeing her that way. She'd even let them convince herself of it.

Just the memory of it was enough to make Jacob's agitation smolder within him. But that was no longer his concern. She'd washed her hands of him and had no plans of letting the love between them persist.

Jacob shook his head, though it didn't succeed in banishing his line of thought. This wasn't what he'd set out to do today, but it seemed wallowing in his pain was unavoidable today as well.

It took far too long—in Jacob's anxious opinion—to arrive at the manor. But when he was there, he didn't leave the carriage immediately. He sat and stared, picturing Cassandra within the massive homestead and praying that he would be fortunate enough to glimpse her.

With a sigh, he alighted from the carriage and made his way to the front door. The butler made quick work of ushering him in and asking that he wait until he informed Lord Wiswall of his arrival. Jacob thought his heart was going to race right out of his chest being here again. Waiting felt like torture, every sound making his eyes dart around hoping that he would glimpse the lady he wished to see.

"My lord." Jacob glanced up at the earl's pleasantly surprised tone. Lord Wiswall blinked bemusedly at him. "To what do I owe the pleasure?"

"I'd hoped to speak with you on a sensitive matter, my lord."

"Of course." Lord Wiswall stepped aside, gesturing for Jacob to enter his study. Jacob hovered dawdled near the door as he watched the earl return to his massive mahogany desk and sit.

Lord Wiswall frowned at him. "Is something the matter, my lord? You seem distressed."

"I am merely a little confused, Lord Wiswall," Jacob began. "My father returned home and informed me that you no longer approve of my courtship with Lady Elizabeth."

"Ah." Lord Wiswall leaned back in his high-back chair. "I thought that would have pleased you."

"Pardon?"

"Do you fancy my daughter, Lord Charlington?"

Jacob swallowed. He couldn't bring himself to lie and yet, he didn't know how to tell the earl that he felt absolutely nothing but platonic affection for his youngest daughter. His eldest, however...

He raised his chin. "I am in love with her."

Lord Wiswall tilted his head to the side, eyes filling with surprise. "Is that so? And you have not come to see her? You do not write to her or show her your affection in any manner?"

"That is because...I..."

"You seem very uncertain now. Do you care for her or not?"

"My Lord, I—" Jacob broke off, not knowing how to respond. If he did, he would only dig a large hole for himself to be buried in. Why had he answered in the affirmative at all? Clearly the earl would not assume that Jacob was talking about Cassandra.

Lord Wiswall shook his head. "I'm afraid I do not wish to have my daughter's heart played with while you try to figure out what you wish to do, my lord. I respect you greatly but my family and what is best for them comes first. If you do not think yourself brave enough to confess your feelings, then perhaps I shall look elsewhere to find them a husband."

An odd sense of relief flooded him at those words. He did not want to be shackled to Lady Elizabeth, that he knew for certain. He hadn't come here to convince the earl to allow them to continue courting. He'd only wanted clarity on why Lord Wiswall took such a decision in the first place. And now that he knew, perhaps it was best he took a step back once and for all. From everyone.

Jacob bowed his head courteously. "I understand, my lord. And I respect your decision."

"Very well. Is that all?"

"I..." He hesitated, but the words could not be contained. "How is Lady Cassandra doing? Has she recovered?"

Again, Lord Wiswall tilted his head, regarding Jacob curiously. "Physically, she is doing fine."

Jacob's heart thudded against his chest. "You imply that she is not doing well in some other manner?"

"I'm afraid you would know far better than I would, my lord." Jacob frowned at that, but before he could question what the earl meant, Lord Wiswall stood, clapping his hands. "Forgive me, my lord, but I have pressing business to finish. Is there anything else you wished to speak with me about?"

Yes, I need to see Cassandra. If only for a second.

Jacob willed away the urge to say those words aloud, shaking his head. "That is all, my lord."

"Then I shall leave it to my butler to see you out. Travel safely home." Lord Wiswall approached, grasping Jacob's hand in a firm handshake of farewell before he turned to make his way back to his desk. Jacob left the study, his mind swimming with everything he'd just been told. On the one hand, he was relieved that he no longer had any expectations weighing on him—save for his overbearing father—but on the other, he was more worried about Cassandra than ever now. What did Lord Wiswall mean by what he said?

Jacob stalled as he came to the staircase that led to the second floor, where Cassandra's bedchamber was. He curled his hand into fists, feeling like he was being pulled by an invisible rope and, he wouldn't be able to fight it any more.

"You look horrible."

Jacob turned at the voice, frowning when he saw that it was Simon. "What are you doing here?"

"Looking for you." Simon crossed his arms, a lopsided grin on his face. "Something told me that I would find you here."

"Why are you looking for me?"

Simon approached, a mischievous glint appearing in his eyes. "Why don't we go to the drawing room and talk about it? Adeline and Elizabeth are already waiting for us."

Jacob only frowned deeper as Simon swung his arm around his shoulders and began steering him in the direction of the drawing room. "What is going on, Simon?"

"Don't worry about it, my good friend. Soon, all your troubles will go away."

"I don't know what you're talking about."

"Cassie, is what I'm talking about. We know, Jacob. All of us."

Jacob didn't know whether to deny or to admit it. His face felt hot, his throat thickening.

Simon clapped him heartily on the back. "As I said, don't worry about it. Now that I know what is going on, I'm going to help you win your lady."

"It's useless, Simon. She's already made up her mind. I have not been able to convince her so neither will you."

Simon came to a stop in front of the drawing room and grasped Jacob by both shoulders. "You're looking at one of three people who knows Cassandra the best. If there's anyone who will be able to help you two, it's us. She's more stubborn than a mule but even she can be convinced."

Jacob took in the genuine eagerness in his friend's eyes and felt a smidgen of hope bloom in his chest. He didn't want to grab ahold of it. He didn't think he would be able to handle another bout of heartrending rejection.

But Simon was right. And for the first time in days, he was willing to try again.

## Chapter Thirty-Three

Cassandra couldn't take it anymore. This wasn't like her. She wasn't the type to wallow and pity herself for too long. It had almost been seven days since she'd left her chambers and it was about time she stopped worrying everyone around her and did something with her day.

She accepted the help of her lady's maid, getting dressed in a light blue morning gown and allowing her to lightly curl the front of her hair while the rest was twisted into a chignon. Only then did Cassandra feel proper enough to face her family for breakfast, after so much time hiding away from them.

She left her bedchamber, able to walk better now that her ankle had healed, and ran right into Elizabeth. Elizabeth's mouth parted in surprise, eyes going wide at the sight of her.

"Cassie! What are you doing out of your room?"

"What do you mean, what am I doing?" Cassandra continued walking, knowing that her sister would fall in step next to her. Elizabeth did so without hesitation. "I am going downstairs for breakfast."

"But you haven't been out of your room in days! I was just coming to try and drag you out. By force, if I had to!"

"You wouldn't have dared," Cassandra answered lightly.

"That isn't the point right now." Elizabeth grasped her elbow, forcing Cassandra to stop walking. "Are you feeling better now? Are you all right?"

Cassandra pursed her lips. Her first instinct was to deny that anything had been wrong in the first place, but that wouldn't be fair to Elizabeth. She'd been by her side the entire time, even when Cassandra had been standoffish and a little rude, telling her constantly that she wished to be alone. Elizabeth worried for her and pretending that nothing had been amiss was insincere.

Cassandra took her hand, squeezing it. She managed a smile that slipped off her face a second later. "I am feeling much better now," she answered, unable to stop herself from speaking vaguely.

Opening up to Elizabeth about what had brought her down was not something Cassandra ever intended to do.

Elizabeth's lips thinned, clearly not convinced. But Cassandra didn't want her pressing her on the manner, so she kept walking, quickly trying to change the topic.

"Is Mother and Father already at breakfast?" Cassandra asked.

"Father had an early meeting with a few of his partners and Mother has gone to have breakfast with Lady Hansel."

"So it will only be you and I then. It's a good thing I decided to come down today. You would have been terribly lonely."

Cassandra's attempt at humor fell flatly, but was quickly covered up when Elizabeth said, "Since it will only be you and I, why don't we have breakfast in the garden? It's such a lovely day out and I'm sure the fresh air will do you some good."

"Very well. That sounds like a wonderful idea."

"Lovely! I'll run ahead and inform the maids!"

Elizabeth hurried off before Cassandra could say anything. She watched her little sister go, then released a long sigh. She thought it would have been easier pretending that she was fine now, but every time she looked at Elizabeth, all she could think about was Jacob.

And when she thought of him, the pain in her heart was too much to bear.

Cassandra sighed, shaking her head to banish him from her mind, even though it did no good. Distraction was what she needed to forget him. To take away the agonizing image of him, his heartbroken expression when she'd told him to stay away from her. It followed her into her dreams, was the first thing that she thought of when she opened her eyes in the morning. Every time Elizabeth came to visit her, all she could think about was the fact that her dear sister would have the one thing she'd ever wanted for her own.

It was one thing to be fated to be a spinster, a recluse from the ton for her embarrassing image. It was another thing entirely for happiness to be so close, yet unattainable.

*Enough! I don't want to think about this anymore. I've done quite well being an outcast all this time so this shouldn't be much different. There's no need to continue dwelling on it.*

With renewed vigor, she continued on her way downstairs and out to the garden. She spotted Elizabeth already there, with footmen setting up breakfast around the tiny iron-wrought table. When Elizabeth spotted her, she excitedly waved her over.

"It's a lovely morning, isn't it?" Elizabeth said excitedly.

"Quite so," Cassandra agreed, the smile she managed slipping off her face an instant later.

Elizabeth sat, brushing her skirt out as the footmen began to take their leave. "Oh, Cassie, you don't know how happy I am to have breakfast with you this morning. You haven't been eating much lately and I was afraid that you would continue to waste away in your chambers."

"I doubt anyone would have allowed that to happen," Cassandra murmured. Since she hadn't yet found her appetite, she decided to pour herself a cup of hot chocolate for now. "Simon came bursting into my room a couple of days ago and I'm certain he would not hesitate to do it again, if I did not leave first."

"Yes, he is rather worried about you. Adeline as well." Elizabeth hesitated, anxiously scraping jam onto her toast. Cassandra watched her curiously. Elizabeth had never been very good at hiding her thoughts.

"Is something wrong, Lizzie?" Cassandra asked her.

"Oh, nothing at all. I was just wondering...well, are you truly all right now?"

Cassandra tried not to sigh. "It is nothing you need to worry about."

Elizabeth did not hesitate to hold back her own sigh. "I had wondered if perhaps your stumble was what had gotten you so down. I know quite well how cruel the ton can be. But you have never been the type to let the words of others get you down for long."

"A lady can only handle so much," Cassandra stated with a shrug. She paid keen attention to her hot chocolate, avoiding her sister's intent gaze.

"Yes, I agree. Especially when she finds herself in love with a gentleman she doesn't believe she deserves."

Cassandra's heart thudded in her chest, but she didn't react outwardly. Slowly, she raised her eyes to meet Elizabeth's. "I'm not sure what you mean."

"The Marquess of Charlington. You are in love with him, aren't you?"

"Elizabeth—"

"There isn't any use denying it, Cassandra. No matter how much you try, your eyes give you away."

Cassandra opened her mouth to respond but no words came out, her mind utterly empty. Panic swelled in her, the fear that had remained hidden deep within in her consuming her at once. Here it was. Elizabeth had found her out and now she was going to hate her forever. Jacob was hers, after all. Cassandra had no right to harbor these feelings. She should never have allowed her heart to—

"Cassie." Elizabeth reached out to grasp her hand, squeezing her gently. "I could not be happier for you."

"Happy?"

"I know what you are thinking. And goodness, I would be so angry with you right now if it weren't for the fact that you have the most genuine and selfless heart of anyone I've ever known. How could you really think to put me above your own feelings?"

"Lizzie…"

Tears shown in Elizabeth's eye, even as a smile stretched across her face. "You have been fighting your affection for the marquess because of me, haven't you? Do you think you would be getting in the way of my future?"

"You are the only hope of our family," Cassandra murmured. It pained her to be so honest, to reveal the things she'd only ever kept to herself, but only the truth mattered right now. "I will be a spinster for the rest of my life and I have come to terms with that. But you…you are beautiful and kind and you deserve a husband who will take care of you for the rest of your life."

"As do you, Cassie." Elizabeth reached out to caress Cassandra's cheeks. Tears burned the back of Cassandra's throat, a knot bobbing within. "Don't worry about me. I will be fine. I have no romantic affection for Lord Charlington and I would never want to get in the way of your feelings." She paused, searching Cassandra's face. "Do you love him, Cassie?"

Cassandra couldn't hide it any longer, couldn't keep the tears at bay. As they streamed down her face, she nodded slowly. "With all my heart."

Elizabeth's answering smile was bright despite the tears on her face. She quickly wiped it away. "That was all I needed to hear."

## Chapter Thirty-Four

"What do you mean?"

Elizabeth got to her feet, pulling Cassandra up with her. "Just promise me that you won't be upset with me, Cassie."

"I'll make no such promise," Cassandra stated, frowning in confusion as her sister began to steer her away from the gazebo, heading deeper into the garden. "Where are you taking me?"

"It is a surprise."

"I don't like surprises."

"Oh, come now, you and I both know that isn't true." Elizabeth threw a grin over her shoulder. Her steps were hurried and excited, and Cassandra was barely able to keep up.

She swallowed her questions, knowing that she wasn't going to get anything else out of Elizabeth no matter how much she pressed her. Her curiosity only continued to grow as Elizabeth pulled her down to the rose bushes, which used to be Cassandra's favorite place to be. It had a small clearing where she would often have picnics on warm days, but she hadn't thought much about it since the start of the Season.

Elizabeth slowed to a saunter but her grin did not fade in the slightest. Cassandra's heart began to speed up but she bit on her tongue, looking around for whatever it was Elizabeth was trying to show her.

And then, she saw it.

Or rather, *him*. He stood in the center of the clearing, a large bouquet of peonies in one hand with his other hand tucked behind him. Cassandra felt her knees grow weak at the sight of him, his handsome features softening with an anxious smile. Elizabeth drifted away, disappearing behind her with a hand on Cassandra's back, steering her further into the clearing. Cassandra hadn't even realized that she'd been frozen to the spot and she quickly closed her gaping mouth.

Jacob said nothing. He only studied her as she took him in. He seemed so beautiful at that moment, so perfect that, as she approached, Cassandra was struck with the urge to reach out and touch his cheek—if only to make sure that she wasn't dreaming. She didn't take note of the beautiful picnic spread behind him until she was upon it. Cakes, tea, and even fruits, were on display across a wide, soft-looking blanket. More peony petals were scattered all over the blanket and a couple bound books were sitting to the side. It was perfect, so much like the picnics she would have during the summer when she was younger and had nothing to stress about.

Only this time, the love of her life was standing right before her.

"Jacob," she breathed. "What are you doing here?"

"Isn't it obvious?" he asked with a twinkle in his eyes. Cassandra was still too surprised to respond properly, simply staring at him. He sheepishly scratched the back of his head. "I wanted to do something special for you."

Cassandra swallowed. She glanced behind her, but Elizabeth had disappeared. "Did Elizabeth ask you to do this?"

"She didn't have to ask me, but she helped. Simon and Adeline as well. They wanted to help *us*."

Her heart sank. "So, they know."

"Apparently, I was not as discreet as I thought I was," Jacob chuckled but Cassandra couldn't bring herself to laugh. She was so happy yet so afraid. Only one of those emotions felt familiar, felt proper, in a situation such as this.

"Jacob, this doesn't change anything. You know that—"

"It changes everything," he cut in. His smile fell, his eyes growing serious. He stepped closer, sending her heart skittering across her chest, and gently offered her the bouquet. Cassandra couldn't stop herself from accepting it. "I am willing to spend every single waking hour of the rest of my life trying to show you just how much I love you. I want nothing more than to wake up with you by my side, to share a life and a family with you. With you, Cassandra—"

"Jacob, please—"

He seized her hand, keeping her from turning away. "With you, Cassandra, everything makes sense. Without you, it feels as if I am missing a vital piece of who I am. I am nothing without you. Your smile, your laugh, the way you challenge me, your stubbornness. Every part of you makes me who I am today and I will not stop until I have shown that to you in any way that I can. I want—no, *need*—you to know how loved you are, Cassandra."

Tears filled her eyes, burned her throat. Cassandra tried to muster up the strength to turn him away but all she wanted to do was throw her arms around him.

"Lady Elizabeth has no feelings for me. I regret ever attempting this courtship when I knew deep down that this was not what I wanted. You are the lady for me but I know how much you value her support. Every time you turn me away, I know that you are doing so because you think it is what's best for your sister."

"It is," she insisted.

But Jacob only patiently shook his head. "There is no use forcing a marriage between two people who do not want it. And neither does your father. Lord Wiswall called off the marriage before I could and I will be eternally grateful to him for it. I have a feeling that even he understands where my heart lies."

Cassandra didn't want to hear those words. She didn't like the hope spreading throughout her, soothing the pain that had claimed her for the past few days. If both her sister and her father were fine with calling off the union, then perhaps she truly could...

Suddenly, all she could see was the ground rising to meet her before everything went black. All she could hear were the snide, cruel comments about her the moment she was out in public. Nothing could stop the shame that came with being an outcast to society. And, no matter what Jacob said, even he would not be able to handle such embarrassment by being next to her.

"I cannot," she murmured, bowing her head in the hopes that he wouldn't see her tears. "You do not want to be with a lady like me. I only bring shame and scandal everywhere I go. When I am noticed, I am gossiped about until there is nothing left of my reputation. I know more than anyone else what that will do to your own reputation if you are seen with me."

He cupped her chin, tilting her head up to meet her eyes. Cassandra was shocked to see his own tears shining back at her. "It pains me to hear you speak about yourself in that way. And it pains me even more to know that you do not see yourself the way I do. You are utterly beautiful, Cassandra. Anyone who says otherwise has not truly seen you and are content to make assumptions based on the veil that you wear. But from the moment I laid eyes on you, I was taken by your wit. Your beauty only serves to accentuate how perfect you are within."

"You are only just saying that…"

He brought her closer, his fingers moving from her chin to brush her hot cheek. "Believe me when I say that I am willing to spend the rest of my life convincing you of how beautiful you are if that is what I must do to make you understand."

She couldn't look away from him. The tears in his eyes, the conviction in his voice…she was scared. But she was so deliriously happy too.

If she'd ever doubted him before, she did not now. He loved her. There was no denying it, no hiding what was so plainly before her. And she could not fight her own feelings any longer. Cassandra wanted to love him out loud. She wanted nothing more than to share her life with him, not caring what anyone else thought about her. But the tears burning her throat made it difficult for her to say the words.

"I love you, Cassandra," Jacob murmured. "And, if you will have me, I would love the honour of making you my wife."

She closed her eyes, a sob escaping her throat. "Yes," she breathed, opening her eyes to show him how much she meant her words. "Yes, I would like nothing more."

A look of relief washed over his face before he smiled brightly. Without warning, Jacob pulled her into a tight embrace, forcing a laugh of surprise from her lips.

"You've just made me the happiest man in all of England, Cassie," he whispered as he pulled slightly away to look at her.

"No happier than I," she told him with a warm smile.

And then he leaned in, pressing a tender kiss on her lips. Cassandra froze, her heart thundering so loudly that she was certain he could hear it. After a second, she began to relax, pressing into the perfect curve of his lips. How odd, she thought. Even his lips seemed to be made to fit hers.

Jacob pulled away, brushing tenderly at the curls against her temple. "I suppose we should begin eating now before our food grows cold."

"Yes, though I should warn you. If Lizzie truly did help you set this up then she will come sneaking around soon to see how things are going. Quite nosy, she can be."

Jacob chuckled, gently helping her sit on the blanket. "I would not mind at all. Had it not been for her, I would not have had the courage to make this grand gesture. I'd lost hope of you ever accepting my love for you."

"I'd always accepted it, Jacob. It was my own love that I refused to acknowledge. I felt afraid and selfish."

Jacob still held on to her hand as if he never wanted to let go. "And now I get to spend the rest of my life making sure that you never regret choosing me."

"I never will." And simply because she wanted to, Cassandra leaned in to kiss him again. Her betrothed, her love. Simply hers.

# Epilogue

*One Month Later*

"If you don't stop, you're going to sweat right out of your clothes."

Jacob rolled his eyes at Simon's droll tone, not taking his eyes off the door of the chapel. Chatter droned within the wide space, guests conversing with one another while they wait for the procession to begin. And Jacob was already regretting asking Simon to be his best man.

"Don't you have something better to do?" Jacob asked, waving a dismissive hand at Simon. "There's no need to bother me at a time like this."

"What should I do then? Mingle with your guests? I cannot think of anything more boring."

"But poking fun at me is far more interesting to you," Jacob noted sarcastically and he didn't miss the way Simon flashed him a grin.

"You know me too well, my friend," Simon said. He clapped a heavy hand on Jacob's shoulder. "Lizzie is doing a fine enough job entertaining our friends. Meanwhile, I have already grown quite bored with their presence and so I thought trying to make you less anxious would be better."

"I'm not anxious," Jacob told him. "I'm excited."

Simon hummed, mumbling something under his breath that Jacob did not quite hear. He didn't bother to ask him to repeat. Cassandra would be arriving any second now. All his attention was focused on the door, waiting for the moment his bride would walk through.

For every day he'd been betrothed to Cassandra, Jacob had longed for this moment to finally arrive. And now that it was here, he hardly knew what to do with himself. The chapel was full, friends and families crowding the space and mingling with each other until it was time for the procession to begin. He knew that it might be more proper to speak with a few of them, but he found himself incapable of conversation when the only thing he could focus on was the fact that today, he was going to be married.

"Don't let my teasing get to you," Simon's voice floated back in. "During my own wedding, I could hardly keep my excitement in either."

Jacob looked curiously at his friend, but Simon's attention was now focused on Elizabeth, standing with a couple of her friends. She laughed at something one of them said but, as if she sensed Simon's eyes, her gaze fell on him. The mirth in her eyes morphed into tender affection, her smile growing a little softer, before she returned her attention back to the conversation.

Jacob still couldn't believe that they were now married.

Cassandra had explained how Simon would pine after Elizabeth when she wasn't looking and how frustrating Cassandra had found it watching her sister deny her feelings for him as well. But after Jacob's confession, it seemed Simon decided there was no reason to keep his own feelings hidden as well. He had confessed his love to Elizabeth the very next day and, as it turned out, Elizabeth was far less stubborn in accepting it than Cassandra was. Simon had asked for her hand in marriage right then and there and, after receiving Lord Wiswall's blessing, quickly began the preparation for their wedding, which happened last week.

Cassandra had wanted to take things a little slower. She said that she didn't care about what the ton thought of having a younger daughter marry before the eldest. She'd only wanted to take back the time she'd missed turning Jacob away. The wedding would come eventually, she would tell him, so there was no reason to rush.

Now that today was the day, Jacob thought it had not come soon enough.

Suddenly, heads began to turn towards the door. The chatter grew louder and everyone hurried to take their seats. Simon patted Jacob on the shoulder once more before stepping off to the side. Jacob was vaguely aware of the vicar coming to stand behind him.

His heart thundered in his ears, his eyes trained so hard on the door that they began to strain. When the doors opened, Lady

Wiswall came through first and then Cassandra's lady's maid. Jacob's eyes glazed over them as if they did not exist.

Cassandra ascended the steps like a goddess, grasping a vibrant bouquet of peonies and lavender in her hands. Their eyes met almost instantly and the world around them disappeared. She was breathtaking. Her hair was coiled atop her head, only a few tendrils framing the sides of her face. Cassandra's gown was a pale blue, ornate stitching lining the sleeves and the hem, with a silk overlay around the skirt. She moved slowly, as if she were walking on air, and it took Jacob another moment to realize that she was walking to the slow pianoforte being played in the corner of the room.

A hush went over the chapel. Jacob knew what they must be thinking. Cassandra had gone so long wearing her veil that everyone had begun to assume what she must look like underneath. It pained him to know that she had also begun to think of herself as unappealing because of it.

But now, no one would be able to deny her beauty.

The scar on her left jaw only accentuated her charm. Her eyes were alive with warmth and glee and when she licked her lips, Jacob could only think about how perfectly they molded against his.

He felt a bite of pride at the confidence in her stride, knowing that it must have taken her quite a lot to come out in public without her veil. But that was yet another reason he loved her so much.

"You're drooling," she teased when she was upon him.

Jacob grinned, reaching out to take her hands. Cassandra stretched her bouquet behind her without looking and Elizabeth quickly rushed up to take it. "I cannot help it," he told her. "I have been thinking about this moment for so long and now that it is finally here, it feels like a dream."

"You took the words right out of my mouth." She squeezed his hands, glancing at the crowd of guests. "They're all staring at me."

"They're struck by your alluring beauty, Cassie," he told her tenderly, pleased with the way her cheeks colored at that.

The vicar cleared his throat before she could respond, reminding Jacob what they were here for in the first place. The vicar began reading from the Book of Common Prayer but Jacob was hardly listening. When it came time for them to repeat their vows, he stumbled over his words, lost in Cassandra's eyes. But he didn't care, simply because it made her laugh.

Yet when the time came for Jacob to present Cassandra's ring, he did not hesitate. He pulled the small box from his pocket, opening it to reveal his grandmother's ring. Cassandra gasped at the sight of it.

"You don't know how long I have been waiting for this moment," he murmured to her as he grasped her hand and slowly slid the ring onto her finger. It fit perfectly, as if it had been made for her hand.

"Jacob, it's beautiful," she breathed, admiring it.

"You are even more so," he responded and the grin she gave him made everything they'd been through worth this moment.

He pulled her into his arms, closing his eyes as he pressed his lips gently against hers. She leaned into it, touching him tenderly on the arm as the world around them disappeared once more. Had the vicar not cleared his throat once more, Jacob wasn't certain he would have ever pulled away.

"How does it feel?" she whispered to him. "Now that I am your wife?"

"As if I have been waiting for this my whole life." No words had ever felt truer.

Congratulatory guests swarmed them once they were finished signing the marriage certificate, more so Cassandra than Jacob. He could tell that she was unaccustomed to the attention, and the moment she began to grow a little flustered, he swept in, claiming that they had a wedding breakfast they needed to get to. Cassandra gave him a grateful smile, courteously thanking everyone for coming as they made their way to the carriage.

The wedding breakfast was being held at Edingdale Manor, though hosted by Jacob's grandmother. Cassandra had met his grandparents a few weeks prior and they had loved her. Angela herself would not stop talking about her every chance she got and the moment they arrived at the manor, she was the first to sidle up to Cassandra's side, whisking her away.

Jacob watched them with a smile, warmed by the sight.

"She has taken quite a liking to her."

Jacob's good mood plunged at his father's voice. He didn't bother to look at him. "She has a wonderful personality, though I suppose you must find that hard to believe."

He noticed the way Henry flinched at Jacob's targeted words. "I did not give her much of a chance. I admit that." Jacob didn't bother to respond. Henry heaved a sigh. "I see the error of my ways now, Jacob. I should not have spoken about her the way that I did, nor should I have forced a decision upon you without considering how you felt about it."

"What brought this change of heart?" Jacob asked, a little incredulous. He hadn't spoken to his father since he informed him of his betrothal, assuming that Henry no longer wanted anything to do with him for defying his wishes. And Jacob had thought the same. It pained him to know that his father did not accept Cassandra, but he wouldn't allow it to eclipse the happy future he had with his wife.

"I gave it a lot of thought," Henry explained. A rueful smile touched his lips. "And your mother gave me a piece of her mind on the matter."

Jacob huffed a laugh. It felt a weight had been taken off his chest now that he'd received his father's acceptance. His spirits lifted instantly as he said, "Thank you, Father. That truly means a lot."

A tender moment of silence passed between them before Henry awkwardly cleared his throat. At that moment, Cassandra appeared, a small smile on her face. "Good day, Your Grace," she greeted Henry.

"Please," Henry said, scratching his stubble. "There is no need for the formalities now that we are family."

"I'm happy to hear that. I hope you're enjoying the feast?"

"Quite so." Henry cleared his throat again and Jacob bit his tongue to keep from laughing. It wasn't often he got to see his father so...stiff. "I shall leave you be then."

Cassandra giggled softly as she watched Henry walk off. She turned mirthful eyes to Jacob. "I think it will take a bit of time for him to grow accustomed to me."

"He is only feeling contrite, but he will relax in due time." Jacob grasped her hand. "Come with me. I want to show you something."'

Cassandra said nothing, raising her brow in question. Jacob tugged her out of the room into an adjoining parlor. He marched right over to the small desk sitting under the window and picked up the wrapped package on top.

"Here." He extended the package to her. "This is for you."

"A wedding gift?" Cassandra's voice was full of surprise and delight. "I didn't think to get you anything."

"You don't have to. I have been thinking about getting you this for a while now."

Jacob felt a flutter of nervousness as Cassandra gently unraveled the wrapping. A gasp escaped her lips as she raised the book in her hand. "Jacob," she breathed. "Is this the first edition of Romeo and Juliet?"

"Do you like it?" he asked gingerly.

"Like it?" Without warning, she threw herself at him, wrapping her arms around his neck. "This is the best gift I have ever received! I will treasure this for the rest of my life! I promise I will!

Jacob laughed, hugging her tightly. He pulled away just enough to press a tender kiss on her lips. "You don't have to get me anything. I am only happy to see you happy.

"Dear God, I love you." She hugged him tighter.

Jacob felt like his heart was about to swell right out of his chest. He kissed her on the top of her head, because he simply couldn't help himself. "I love you too, Cassie. Forever and always."

# Extended Epilogue

*Three Years Later*

"Do you think they've already arrived?"

Cassandra's question went unanswered for a few seconds as Jacob frowned at nothing, pondering. A smile touched her lips at the sight. He was so handsome, she thought for what felt like the tenth time that morning. His hair was styled closely to his head, a slight shadow crowding his jaw. Ever since they'd begun residing in Bath, Jacob spent nearly all his free time outdoors with his horses, and she could already see the result of his constant exercise in the cut of his shoulders. She could hardly believe that this handsome gentleman was hers, could hardly fathom how he'd only grown more endearing as time went by.

"Cassie?" Jacob's voice floated in, bringing her mind back to the present. "Are you listening?"

"Yes," she answered instantly but the look he gave her told her that he didn't believe her at all.

Jacob shook his head. "What were you thinking about?"

Cassandra bit her lip, wondering if she should say the words aloud. They were not alone, after all. Next to her was a small infant who was so focused on the toy in his hand that Cassandra doubted that he noticed the fact that they were currently en route to Hyde Park.

"I was thinking about you," she admitted after a moment, absently reaching out to rustle her son's, Edward's, hair. His strawberry blond hair was already beginning to curl much like hers. He leaned into her touch but his attention was still wholly on his toy.

"Oh?" Jacob stretched out a little, tilting his head to the side with a smile. "What about exactly?"

Cassandra huffed a laugh, rolling her eyes. "I may only be inflating your ego by saying this but I was just thinking about how much more handsome you have gotten over the years, which feels quite impossible. Can you believe that it has already been three years?"

"I can't," Jacob admitted. "Time flies so quickly when you're happy. Before we know it, Edward will be running through the hallways as a child and then pining after girls as a teenager."

"Running through the halls will be nothing to him in no time," Cassandra laughed. She tugged Edward closer to her side, only because she felt a sudden surge of love. He was already two and yet she couldn't believe she'd given birth to such a beautiful child.

And soon...

"You're telling me," Jacob agreed. "I can hardly keep up. And to answer your question, I think we might be the last to arrive actually."

"Oh, I'd hate to keep them all waiting."

"They'll be fine. They know that we've only just arrived in London for the Season yesterday, so they will assume that we need a bit more time to settle in."

Cassandra nodded and fell silent as the carriage came to a slow stop. A few seconds later, the door was opened by Edward's governess, who had been riding next to the coachman. She helped Edward out first while Jacob helped Cassandra. They held hands as they set down the path that would lead them to the large willow tree they had picnicked under all those years ago. As they approached, Cassandra could hear Simon's voice far before she saw him.

"If we don't get ahold of them now, they will disappear on us!"

"That's fine! They're children, leave them be."

Cassandra came to a halt, gaping at the sight before her. Simon was on his feet, chasing identical little girls around as they raced away from him, squealing in delight. Elizabeth was already seated on the picnic blanket, laughing hysterically at the sight while Adeline shook her head at the tall gentleman stretching next to her. That man was her husband, Ethan, who hurried forward a second later to help Simon capture the escaping, giggling twins. Cassandra and Jacob's parents were also in attendance but they were content to sit next to each other and watch all that was happening with stark amusement.

"What is going on here?" Jacob asked but before he could get anything else out, Edward let out a hysterical screech and rushed forward to join his twin cousins.

"Dear God, there's more of them," Simon wailed, while Ethan laughed loudly, missing the chance to scoop one of the twin girls into his arms. Cassandra giggled at the sight. She had to admit that Elizabeth's little girls were quite fast. Almost the next second, tears pricked her eyes as her emotions grew overwhelming.

"Cassie!" Elizabeth squealed when she spotted her. "I'm so happy to see you! Come over here, join us."

"One moment, Lizzie. I need to speak privately with Jacob first."

Jacob frowned at her, taken aback by the tears he saw in her eyes. Before he could ask her, Cassandra seized her hand, leaving Edward in the care of their large, ever-growing family, and pulled him behind the willow tree so that no one would hear them.

"What's going on, Cassie?" he asked, brushing the tear from her cheek. "Why are you crying? Are you hurt somewhere?"

"No, I...just the sight of Edward playing with Lizzie's twins made me a little emotional." She offered a watery smile. "And so I thought this might be the best time to tell you."

"To tell me what?"

She bit her bottom lip, pulling his hand towards her stomach. It was still rather flat, seeing that she'd only confirmed with her physician right before leaving Bath, but she was sure Jacob would understand.

His eyes went wide. "You mean..."

She nodded, a bright smile stretching across her face. "I am with child, Jacob. I'm going to have another baby—"

Jacob swept in for a kiss, cutting into her words. Cassandra laughed against his lips, more tears streaming down her face. "I'm so happy that I can't stop crying," she murmured when he pulled away.

"I'm so happy I could cry too." He kissed her tenderly on the top of her head. Three years later and he was still capable of making her heart skip a beat and melt right out of her chest at the same time. "Should we tell them?"

"Not yet," Cassandra said. "I want to enjoy it a little longer before I share the news. I just want this moment to be between us."

"Your wish is my command, my love." He kissed her again, as if he couldn't help himself. "What shall we name her?"

"Her? How do you know I will have a girl?"

"I just know. Trust me." Jacob pulled slightly away from the embrace, raising a brow at her. "We should go back. It sounds as if Simon's twins are besting him once more. He might need my help."

Cassandra simply nodded, squeezing his hand as they made their way back to their family. And she could already picture another child joining the fray, to receive all the love and care in the world so that they may never suffer the way she had.

The End

Printed by Amazon Italia Logistica S.r.l.
Torrazza Piemonte (TO), Italy